AF427610

Waking Dorothy Bradford

From the Author of *Out with the Tide*

Paul Ehrenreich

For Raelle, Sydney and Elias

CHAPTER ONE

Einstein and Inner Tubes

Rob Crosley had a habit of reaching over to the opposite side of the bed to make sure his wife was still there. Nearly two years had passed since Katie came back to live in the house and sleep in their bed, but he still worried her demons might return and drive her into seclusion again. She had suffered for many years from a social anxiety known as anthropophobia, a cumbersome word defined as a fear of other people. As was often the case with those affected by the condition, Katie's fear first manifested itself in large crowds. This wasn't so much of a concern, since it was easy to avoid large crowds. But then smaller gatherings began to be uncomfortable, and Katie found herself making excuses for not going to dinner parties or meeting up with friends. She started seeing therapists and taking medications, but her condition didn't improve. Eventually, it only took the presence of one person to trigger a flight response. Rob and her son, Danny, seemed to be the exceptions, until one night Rob lay down next to her and the room began to spin, sending Katie into a panic and straight out of the house.

She moved across the street, into the cottage she and Rob had built with the intention of renting out one day. There she stayed, growing vegetables in her garden, making improvements to the cottage, and taking her rowboat out in the bay. Rob visited her every day for as long as she could bear, which was generally not more than fifteen minutes at a time. He hoped the frequent visits would build some sort of tolerance and familiarity, but they always ended with Katie hiding in the bedroom and asking him to leave. She avoided everyone else, except for Danny. He was the only person who didn't provoke panic. She could be with him for much longer than fifteen minutes. This made Rob jealous.

Her road to recovery began when she was rowing her boat in the bay one day and a man with a waterproof camera swam up and took several pictures of her as she furiously paddled away. One of the pictures found its way to the Dorothy Bradford

Society, a local group of women who believed Dorothy was still alive. Dorothy Bradford was the Pilgrim wife of William Bradford, who drowned in the bay after the Mayflower anchored off Cape Cod in the winter of 1620. But the Dorothy Bradford Society didn't believe Dorothy had drowned. They believed she had survived her plunge into the icy waters and was living an immortal life on the Outer Cape, four hundred years later. One of their missions was to find Dorothy Bradford and prove her immortality. Many of the members scouted the beaches and woods, taking photographs of noble, sturdy-looking women performing physically challenging activities. The photos were presented at society meetings, but none of them sparked any interest until the picture of Katie turned up. When they saw the picture of her in her boat, fiercely pulling the oars against a rising tide, the members were sure they had finally found the immortal Pilgrim, and they sought her out. Since Katie was terrified of any attention, Rob tried to shield her from the society's fervent efforts to enlist her as their figurehead. After a chance encounter on her own with two Bradford devotees, Katie discovered that if she assumed the role of Dorothy Bradford, like an actor in a play, her fear of other people subsided. Apparently, Dorothy Bradford didn't have anthropophobia. By becoming Dorothy Bradford, Katie was able to function normally again. And she was able to move back into the house.

Rob's hand found nothing but linen, the covers thrown aside. At the time, which happened to be 2 a.m., he was the only person in the bed. He debated whether to get up or fall back asleep, but his bladder needed emptying, or as much of it as his prostate allowed him to empty. He stood over the toilet with both hands firmly planted on the tank cover, a similar position to the one he had assumed when his doctor worked a couple of fingers up his ass and announced that his prostate was only slightly enlarged, not out of the ordinary for a man in his fifties. "How many times a night do you get up to pee, Mr. Crosley? More than three?" Rob didn't keep track.

He found Katie in the kitchen, standing at the sink, washing dishes. The light over the sink was the only one on, casting a sinister glow in the darkness around her, as though she were carving up human remains.

"What are you doing, Dorothy?" he said. He called her Dorothy sometimes when she was behaving oddly, as she was now, a characteristic of the Bradford persona. Other times he called her Kay, but mostly he called her Katie. She looked like a Katie. She was ten years younger than Rob but could have been twenty based on her youthful appearance. People sometimes mistook her for Rob's daughter.

"I couldn't sleep," she said, sighing heavily.

"More of the dreams?"

"Yes. And a new one this time, too."

The light above the sink flickered, and for a moment, Rob thought the power would go out. Did the power company curb the supply of electricity during off-peak hours like his prostate stemmed the flow of urine? Katie looked up at the fixture. The current evened out, and the light steadied.

"Have you noticed that before?" she said. "The lights flickering?"

"No."

She placed the last pot in the dish drain and shut off the water, shaking her hands and drying them on the towel lying on the counter.

"Go back to bed, Rob. I'm okay. I'll be there in a minute." She pulled out a bottle of cleaning solution from the cabinet under the sink and began spraying down the counters.

"I want to hear about the new dream. Tell me."

She hadn't bothered to tie back her hair and had to keep flipping her head to the side to keep the long strands from dragging in the beads of spray on the granite countertops. Rob smoothed out his own hair, mindful that his appearance could be unsettling when he got out of bed. He had stopped cutting his hair a year ago, in large part due to his dislike of being strapped into a barber chair for half an hour. Barbers were poor conversationalists for the most part, and Rob wished they would keep their focus on their shears rather than talking about the weather. Katie offered to cut it but he decided he liked having long hair. People thought he looked like an athletic Albert Einstein.

"I had the usual ones first. The guy being buried in the woods, the two girls drowning in a pond, and an uprooted tree."

"Just as vivid?"

"Yeah, but I still have no idea who the people are."

"And who's in the new one?"

"No one. I only see a stone marker on a dune somewhere."

"A tombstone?"

"I don't think so, but there are words on it. Corn Hill, 1620."

"Corn Hill in Truro?"

"I guess so."

"The year 1620? When the Pilgrims landed?"

"That would seem to make sense."

When Katie was first introduced to the idea that she was Dorothy Bradford, she began having flashbacks to unfamiliar times and places. According to the past president of the Dorothy Bradford Society, a woman named Maggie Mason, these flashbacks were suppressed memories of her forgotten past. Maggie Mason, who was trained in psychotherapy, told Katie that the suppression of these memories was what caused her panic attacks. By accepting the memories as her own, Katie would be able to find inner peace, and her panic attacks would gradually disappear. This is what happened, more or less, but Katie later learned that the flashbacks may have been artificially induced. Maggie Mason was a proponent of psychedelics, and since many of the society's members suffered from various forms of anxiety and depression, she served special refreshments at the society meetings in the form of beer laced with small doses of LSD. Nobody knew about the LSD until Maggie was arrested and thrown in jail.

"You think these dreams are connected somehow?" The dreams were something new. Katie had never had Dorothy Bradford dreams before, if that's what these were—just the waking flashbacks, which continued after the LSD was confiscated by the police.

"I don't know, but I get the feeling someone's trying to tell me something. That I need to do something."

"You should drive over there and take a look."

"Somebody told me there's some kind of Pilgrim plaque on Corn Hill. Maybe I'll go tomorrow morning."

"You want me to go with you?"

"No. You have your bike ride tomorrow."

Rob had planned a long ride to Provincetown the next morning. The weather, which had been rainy for the past several days, was finally due to cooperate, and with only three weeks left until the start of the summer season, there wouldn't be many more chances to bike to Provincetown before the roads became thick with cars.

"Maybe Rachel can go with you," Rob said. Rachel was the manager of the Dorothy Bradford House, which is what the cottage across the street was converted to after Katie moved back in with Rob. The Dorothy Bradford House was a halfway house for troubled women. This had always been the primary mission of the Dorothy Bradford Society—to help troubled women pull themselves together so they wouldn't end up at the bottom of the bay like Dorothy Bradford. Pulling themselves together no longer included any help from LSD. The Dorothy Bradford House didn't allow drugs. Many of the residents were recovering drug addicts.

"I'll be fine. I like being alone, remember?"

"Take your phone."

"Corn Hill is only three miles away."

He still worried when she went out on her own. She had a history of disappearing, sometimes for days at a time, hiking into the dunes or woods, out of cell phone range. He knew these excursions were important for her continued well-being, and she was entirely capable of taking care of herself. Like Dorothy Bradford, at least the one who survived for four hundred years, Katie was a true survivalist. Perhaps he worried that one day she wouldn't come back at all and that Dorothy Bradford would so completely consume her, she'd lose touch with her real identity.

Katie finished her chores and announced she was going back to bed, hopefully to dream of things other than burials and drownings. Rob followed, trying to decide whether to visit the bathroom again. He stopped outside Katie's closet and peeked in, imagining he might see Sidney lying in his familiar spot on the floor among Katie's shoes. Sidney was their Australian Shepherd, who had finally been put to sleep at the ripe old age of sixteen. In his last few days, Sidney spent all of his time sleeping in Katie's closet, only getting up when Rob carried him out to the yard to let him pee. Sidney had stopped eating and could barely stand up anymore. "It's time," Katie said, though she had been saying that for a couple of weeks. Rob couldn't bear the thought of losing his dog, but he had come to realize that he had already lost him and that Sidney was getting no joy from living anymore. The vet came to the house and administered the injections right there on the floor of Katie's closet. Sidney passed quietly, with Rob lying next to him, holding the dog's head in his hands.

"Everything okay?" Katie said, watching her husband stare into the closet.

"Just missing Sidney," he said, and climbed back into bed.

◆ ◆

As predicted, the sky was clear the next morning, and the temperature hovered in the sixties. Rob pulled on his bike pants and road jersey, covered with colors so bright that no driver could ever miss seeing him. He tied a kerchief over his head, both to rein in his wild hair and to keep the sweat out of his eyes. He also wore a gaiter around his neck. It was useful not only for keeping things from flying into his nose and mouth but also for wiping away the stuff that came out. Finally, he coated himself with bug repellent. Mosquitoes had recently become thick and belligerent in South Truro thanks to an overflow of a nearby dike in Wellfleet. The brackish wash-over from Cape Cod Bay into the Herring River became an ideal breeding ground, producing tens of thousands of mosquitoes with flying ranges of up to ten miles.

As he was pumping air into his tires, a fox emerged from the trees and peered directly at him. Rob instinctively looked around for Sidney, who was just small enough that a fox might not back down from a confrontation, then remembered the dog was gone. Rob emitted a loud "Yip!" and the fox ran back into the woods.

"Have you developed Tourette's, or are your shorts too tight?" Danny Crosley was coming down the steps from the apartment above the garage. Danny was Rob and Katie's twenty-three-year-old son, who had recently moved back to the Cape to live full-time. Danny was a distance runner, and a good one. In fact, he was the best in the world at ten thousand meters, having won the gold medal at the last Olympic Games and broken the world record in the process. His father was there to see it, as was his mother, in the guise of Dorothy Bradford. Katie Crosley would have had great difficulty going inside an Olympic stadium filled to capacity. When Danny returned home, he wasn't sure about moving back into the house, so Katie and Rob built an apartment above the garage where he could live.

"What are you talking about?" Rob said, swatting at a mosquito while disengaging the pump valve from the rear tire.

"Uncontrolled monosyllabic shouting is a symptom of Tourette's syndrome," Danny said.

"You're an expert in neurological disorders now?"

Danny was dressed for a run. He continued to participate in international meets and planned to defend his gold medal at the next Olympics. His coaches had wanted him to stay in Boston, but he refused. When the Olympics were over and his brief international fame waned, he got a job with the Cape Cod National Seashore, protecting the wildlife and clearing debris from the many beaches, fire roads, and hiking trails that ran up and down the Outer Cape. He wanted to keep doing that. It kept him outside most of the day, which was where he was happiest.

"Where are you running today?" Rob said.

"Wellfleet. Ten miles."

"Race pace?"

"We'll see how I feel."

Race pace for Danny meant running ten miles in forty-five minutes, though that was on a track. Dodging cars and turkeys, which had also pervaded the Outer Cape, though not as severely as the mosquitoes, might slow him down by a few seconds.

"Are you heading that way? I could run alongside for a while," Danny said.

"I'm going up to Provincetown."

"I could run that way."

"You know I don't like it when you run with me. It makes me feel like an invalid."

"Well, people with neurological disorders shouldn't be riding bikes alone."

"I was yelling at a fox."

◆ ◆

There was little wind, and Rob made good time riding up Route Six to where it intersected with 6A. Even though the traffic was light, Rob avoided making left turns on Route Six if he could help it, so he turned right onto South Highland Road and pedaled to South Hollow, which took him under Route Six and onto 6A. From there, it was another ten miles along the bay to Provincetown, the last town on the Cape, the place where, in 1602, the English explorer Bartholomew Gosnold caught so much cod that he named the hook of land after the fish. One hundred and twenty-five years later, the tip of the Cape was formally incorporated as a township and named Provincetown. The town was home to a year-round population of three thousand, a number that increased twentyfold during the summer.

Since it was not quite summer yet and still relatively early in the day, Rob rode through town on Commercial Street, the three-mile-long main drag notable for its galleries, restaurants, bars, shops, hotels, drag queens, and the latest addition, marijuana dispensaries. The dispensaries had innocuous outdoorsy names that only hinted at what was inside, though they were given away by the uniformed security guards posted out front, making it seem like there were jewels inside instead of weed.

Rob made a quick detour back to 6A, called Bradford Street here, to ride past the former home of the Dorothy Bradford Society. The white-shingled house, sitting just below the Pilgrim Monument, had been owned by Maggie Mason, the society's founder and past president. After the society determined that Katie was the woman they had been looking for, Rob came to a meeting at the house to try and convince the members that Katie was not Dorothy Bradford and that they should stop chasing after her. Unfortunately, he drank too much beer and became too drunk to make any type of cogent argument, not that it would have helped. Beer-drinking was an important pastime of the Dorothy Bradford Society, owing to the fact that the Pilgrims themselves were big beer-drinkers. The water supply on sailing ships in the seventeenth century wasn't always safe to drink, particularly on long voyages, so the passengers and crew drank beer instead, sometimes as much as a gallon a day. Beer drinking also helped to take the edge off of being stuck on a small, leaky ship for two months in stormy seas. The Pilgrims landed on Cape Cod and then Plymouth, not because they intended to, but because they were tired of sailing and had run out of beer. Maggie Mason served her homemade beer at all of the society's gatherings and eventually started microdosing the stuff with LSD. Rob had drunk so much of it that while he was making his vain argument for the society to lay off his wife, he saw one of the gargoyles at the top of the Pilgrim Monument come to life and fly off into the center of town. That the gargoyle had stirred to life did not strike him as odd, and he wondered if anyone in Provincetown would even notice a gargoyle bounding up and down Commercial Street.

Rob didn't see anything different about the house now, or the monument, for that matter. He wasn't sure whether Maggie

Mason had retained ownership or if the government had seized the property. The house appeared to be vacant. After Maggie was hauled off to jail, the members looked to Katie and Rachel, who had been Maggie's assistant, to rehabilitate the society. That's when Katie asked Rachel to move into the cottage across the street and help her convert it to the Dorothy Bradford House. There, they would continue the society's mission of helping troubled women, without the use of illegal drugs.

Safe from the gargoyles, Rob turned back onto Commercial Street and headed toward Provincetown's sleepier West End. At the end of the street, he took a victory lap around the rotary that marked the end of town and the end of the Cape. The Provincetown Causeway, a mile-long stone breakwater, stretched across the water to Woods End Lighthouse, squatting in the distance on a small spit of land that dangled from the end of the Cape like a worm from a fishhook. Rob had never walked across the breakwater. A mile of damp, jagged boulders covered in bird shit seemed like the perfect place to break an ankle.

Deciding to take a short rest before heading home, Rob pulled into the mostly empty parking lot of the Provincetown Inn and promptly blew out the front tire of his bike. There was a loud pop and then the sound of escaping air. He had barely been pedaling and hadn't hit any potholes. There was no evidence of glass or other sharp objects lying on the blacktop. The inner tube had apparently just given up.

Rob dismounted, grateful that the tire had failed here rather than on the road. He walked the bike to a grassy area alongside the inn, then pulled off the tire and set about removing the inner tube and replacing it with one of the two spare tubes he carried with him. As he was threading the new tube into the tire, the door to one of the first-floor guest rooms opened, and a man walked out. He looked at Rob and waved, as though he had been expecting him. Rob had the urge to look behind him and see if there was someone else the man was waving to. He nodded his head instead. The man walked over.

"Looks like you've got everything you need there," the man said, pointing to the tools Rob had spread on the grass. He was short and compact, dressed a little more formally than someone on vacation would be, wearing slacks and a button-down shirt. He had short hair and was cleanly shaven, unlike Rob.

"I do, thanks," Rob said, wondering if the man had come outside just to talk to him.

"I do a lot of cycling myself," the man said. "Wish I had time to do it now."

Rob levered the tire back onto the rim, hoping the man, who was apparently not very busy, would leave. He didn't like being watched when he was working on something he had only done a handful of times before.

"You from around here?" the man said.

"Truro," Rob said. "Fifteen miles down the road."

"I had a meeting there yesterday."

"So I guess you're not on vacation, then," Rob said, now resigned to having a conversation. He attached the CO2 inflator to the tube stem and nudged open the valve. The tire inflated quickly.

"Nope. Business. My name's Mike Van Winkle, by the way. Here, take one of my cards." Mike Van Winkle held out a card. Rob had gotten up off the ground to reassemble his bike. He took the card. It said that Van Winkle was a private investigator.

"What are you investigating?" Rob said. "Or can I ask that?"

"I'm looking for someone," Van Winkle said.

"Well, the towns are pretty small out here. Shouldn't take long." Rob thought he was making a joke, but Van Winkle didn't seem amused.

"He's from Truro. Maybe you know him? Guy by the name of Sam Boland."

"Sammy Boland?"

"That's him. You know him?"

Rob did know him. Sammy Boland had been a caretaker in the area who was found to have been dealing drugs on the side, running heroin and other narcotics out of the basement of one of his clients' homes. The client's name was Tim Desmond, a neighbor of Rob's who lived a few hundred yards down the beach. Desmond had initially been arrested but was later found innocent of any involvement in the operation. The drugs, which came to the house by boat, were stuffed inside fish and stored by Boland in a refrigerator in Desmond's basement. Desmond never saw anything other than the fish. Sammy Boland disappeared after Desmond's arrest and was never found by the police.

Another of Sammy Boland's clients had been Maggie Mason, and it was presumed, though never proved, that he was the one who was selling her the LSD. Boland, a real jack of all trades, was also a photographer, and ironically, Maggie Mason hired him to take pictures of some of the recovering heroin addicts who passed through her home in Provincetown, hanging the photos on her walls. A short time later, Maggie asked him to photograph a certain woman in a rowboat—the woman she believed was Dorothy Bradford.

"He was all over the news two years ago," Rob said. "People say he was killed by the drug cartel."

"How do you know he worked for a cartel?"

"I don't," Rob said, unsettled by the change in Van Winkle's tone, as if Rob had somehow been involved. "That's what people were saying. The rumor mill's pretty thick out here."

"I get that," Van Winkle said.

"Hey, are you related to Pappy Van Winkle? The bourbon guy?"

"Sorry. Not much of a drinker."

Rob wasn't sure this was an answer. He collected his tools and stuffed them back into the pouch that fit into one of the water bottle brackets on his bike. He was reminded of the quote by Winston Churchill, who said, "Never trust a man who doesn't drink."

"Did Sammy's folks hire you? Or I guess it's just his dad, Jerry, now. I heard his mother died recently."

"*Can't answer that one,*" Van Winkle said. He hadn't really answered the last question either. "I'm sorry, I didn't get your name."

Rob almost said, Can't answer that one, but he had no reason to be an asshole. "Rob Crosley," he said. "How does a private eye not drink?"

Van Winkle smiled. Perhaps he did have a sense of humor. "Crosley?" he said. "The one married to Katie Crosley?"

"I guess you must know all about us if you're looking for Boland."

"It's quite a story. I saw the picture Boland took of her. Does your wife really think she's Dorothy Bradford?" Van Winkle sounded more curious than condescending.

"She is Dorothy Bradford," Rob said, preparing to mount his bike.

"Hey, before you go, can you tell me if you ever met him?"

"Boland? Once or twice at Tim Desmond's house. I saw him on the beach a few times, too, when he was chasing after my wife with a camera, though I didn't know it at the time."

"You're a friend of Tim Desmond?"

"Not really. I run into him on the beach once in a while."

"Did Boland ever do any work for you at your house?"

"No. We do that ourselves." Actually, it was Katie who did all the repair and maintenance work, but Van Winkle didn't need to know that. "Listen, I'm heading out. You should go see Don Hill at the Truro Police Department if you haven't already."

"That's where I was yesterday."

"Well, I hope you have better luck than he did." The police spent a year trying to find Boland, then gave up.

Van Winkle bent down and picked something up off the pavement. He tossed it into the bushes. Rob wondered if it was a nail.

"Your son's the runner, right?" he said.

"He is," Rob said.

"Gold medal?"

"He lets me wear it sometimes."

"So your wife is Dorothy Bradford, and your son's an Olympic athlete. What do you do?"

Rob clipped into his pedals and said, "This!" Then he headed back to the rotary, keeping watch for any nails on the pavement in front of him.

CHAPTER TWO

Corn and Weed

Katie drove through Truro Center and turned onto Castle Road, heading west back toward the bay. Corn Hill Beach was only a mile from the house along the water, but because of the inlet to Pamet Harbor, it wasn't possible to walk there along the beach. She had thought about taking her rowboat but didn't want to leave it unattended while she was poking around in the dunes. The boat was more of a scull than a rowboat, and because it was custom-made, it drew a lot of attention. The boat had been an important part of her life when she was suffering from her panic disorder; it was one of the few things she would leave the house for. It was also the thing that first caught the attention of the Dorothy Bradford Society. The boat had become an integral part of the Bradford mystique.

As it was still off-season, the beach parking lot was empty. No stickers were required until July. Katie drove to the north end of the lot at the foot of Corn Hill. There, she found a shell pathway that led to a small area bounded by a split-rail fence. Inside the fence were a couple of benches and a flag pole with two boulders on either side. She had been to Corn Hill Beach a few times but had never noticed the monument before. She walked into the fenced area and read the plaque on the boulder to the left of the flag pole.

SIXTEEN PILGRIMS

LED BY

MYLES STANDISH WILLIAM BRADFORD

STEPHEN HOPKINS EDWARD TILLEY

FOUND THE PRECIOUS INDIAN CORN

ON THIS SPOT WHICH THEY CALLED

CORN HILL

NOVEMBER 16 1620

AND SURE IT WAS GODS GOOD PROVIDENCE

THAT WE FOUND THIS CORN FOR ELSE WE

KNOW NOT HOW WE SHOULD HAVE DONE

There were no markers that said "Corn Hill 1620" like the one she'd seen in her dream. The plaque on the other boulder had nothing to do with Pilgrims, though it did contain punctuation. In 1929, someone named Ralph S. Barnaby broke the American soaring record held by the Wright Brothers. He had flown from Corn Hill in a motorless aircraft for fifteen minutes and six seconds. He was given an International Soaring Certificate. And a plaque.

Katie looked back toward the entrance, thinking she might have missed the marker, and found a man and a young boy sitting on one of the benches. They had not been there when she came in. The man was large and muscular, with a beard and long blond hair that hung down to his shoulders. The boy's hair was nearly as long but dark in color. He looked nothing like the man, and Katie wasn't immediately sure how they were related, if at all. The man looked at her and raised a hand in greeting. The boy kicked his legs like he was sitting at the edge of a pool. Katie said hello, and the man stood up and walked over. The boy followed.

"This isn't actually where they found the corn," he said. He stood a full foot taller than Katie and had a weathered face, typical of the locals on the Outer Cape—people who spent most of their time outdoors. He looked more like a Scandinavian than a New Englander, though.

"I was wondering," Katie said.

"The spot is further up the hill."

"Is there a small marker somewhere that says Corn Hill 1620 on it?" The boy had come alongside her and taken her hand. She almost hadn't noticed at first. He had a very light touch. He couldn't have been more than five years old, she thought. There was a time when Katie would have cringed if someone approached her. It used to be that she'd only venture from the cottage to places where she wasn't likely to see anyone else, and if she did, she would keep her distance or find a place to hide.

"Sorry," the man said. "Dak is very friendly, but only to people who are also friendly. Like you."

"It's nice to meet you, Dak," Katie said, not sure how the boy would know she was friendly. Perhaps it was her expression. People always said she had a kind face. Dak smiled.

"He's quiet, though," the man said.

"My name's Katie," she said to the boy.

"I'm Dak," the boy said, keeping his gaze on her.

"We can take you to it," the man said. "The marker you're thinking of."

"Are you from around here?"

"We are. Up the hill. Dak wanted to come see the flag."

Dak let go of Katie's hand and ran over to the pole. He grabbed it with both hands and craned his neck to look up at the flag fluttering in the westerly winds blowing off the bay.

"I'm Erik," the man said. "Come, I'll show you." Erik headed toward the street and waved for Katie to follow.

"What about Dak?" she said. Dak was now spinning around the pole, still looking up at the flag.

"He'll catch up," Erik said, pressing on.

Not comfortable leaving the boy alone, Katie extended her hand and said, "Dak, do you want to come with me?" Dak let go of the pole and raced over to take her hand, and they headed off together, following Erik up Corn Hill.

◆ ◆

Corn Hill was by no means a gentle incline, and Erik set a brisk pace up the narrow, two-lane road. Katie was breathing heavily when they got to the top and turned onto what looked to be a private drive. Dak, still full of energy, let go of her hand and raced ahead.

"Is this where you live?" Katie asked Erik, who was now waiting for her to catch up. Ahead of them was a row of cottages.

"Not far. This is where the marker is." He led her off the drive and down a sandy path. There beneath a small pine was the stone marker Katie had seen in her dream, the one that read *Corn Hill 1620*. Dak had sat down next to the marker. He was digging in the sand.

"No digging, Dak," Erik said. The boy stopped and lay down on his back.

"This is it, then?" Katie said. "Where they found the corn?"

"Found is putting it politely," Erik said. "The people who lived here buried their corn in this spot. The Pilgrims dug it up and took it for themselves."

"They stole it?"

"That's probably more accurate." Erik went over to the marker and pulled Dak up from the sand. The boy latched onto Erik's leg. The two of them stood in front of the marker as though visiting a grave.

Katie closed her eyes, thinking she might find something in the inner recesses of her "Dorothy" brain that would explain why the marker cropped up in her dreams. She tried to conjure an image of her long-dead husband, William, pulling the corn out of the ground along with his Pilgrim cohorts and rushing back to the Mayflower before the natives caught them in the act. Katie, or Dorothy in this case, had always believed that the natives were the ones who rescued her from the bay and saved her life. She owed more to them than to the Pilgrims. The plaque at the base of the hill made the discovery of the corn seem like an act of divine providence, when it was more an act of vandalism.

Katie opened her eyes and found herself alone. Erik and Dak were gone. There was no sign of them. She walked up the driveway, thinking they might be outside one of the cottages, but there was no one there either. She walked around to the back. Each cottage had a small deck that looked out over the bay. A dog barked, but Katie still didn't see anyone.

A path led down to the water. Katie took it and walked back to the parking lot along the beach, still as confused about her troubling dreams as before. And now there was the mystery of the large, blond-haired man and the small boy. They had left without saying goodbye. Or perhaps they had never been there at all.

♦ ♦

Back home after an incident-free return trip from Provincetown, Rob showered, wolfed down a collection of leftovers from the refrigerator, and then headed for the beach, taking a beach chair with him.

The beach was deserted, except for a couple walking their dog. They were far enough away that Rob couldn't be sure in which direction they were heading or what type of dog it was. He stopped to talk to any dog owner he saw, asking them how they liked the dog, where they had gotten it, whether it was a rescue—that sort of thing. He was collecting information on what his next dog should be. He had already decided it wouldn't be another Australian Shepherd. There was no replacing Sidney.

The sun was warm, and he took off his shirt and put his chair down near the water. Though pale from the long Cape winter, he had grown leaner from all the bike riding he'd been doing. There had been little snow, and so long as the temperature was above forty and the wind wasn't howling, he got out on his bike and rode at least four times a week. And if the weather was bad, he'd cycle indoors on his stationary bike under the direction of some scantily clad gym girl spinning her pedals in a far-away studio while barking out encouragement and pithy aphorisms. "You guys are awesome! Reach over and high-five your neighbor!" There was no one next to Rob, and he wouldn't high-five them if there were.

Rob fell asleep by the water. When he woke up, he was no longer by the water, he was in it. The tide had come in, and the waves, if you could call them that, were lapping at his feet. There was also a smell, but it wasn't anything the bay could have served up. It was a fragrant, herbal smell. Someone was smoking pot, and he knew who it was.

"Hello, Helen," Rob said, getting up from his chair. He had had enough sun. His skin was turning red.

Helen Schantz was sitting in the sand behind him, a lit joint in her hand. She had on the pale-colored beach robe she was fond of wearing and a large floppy hat. Helen was Rob's pesky neighbor, with whom he shared the wooden stairs that led down the dune to the beach. Though they had been neighbors for several years, Rob was never quite sure Helen knew who he was. She never referred to him by name. She was extremely fond of Katie, though, as most people were. Katie helped her out whenever something in her house needed fixing. And two years ago, Katie had shown her how to build a rack for her firewood. More precisely, Katie had built the rack for her.

Helen Schantz lived in isolation for the most part, much like Katie had, but for different reasons. Helen wasn't scared of other people; she was suspicious of their motives. A widow, she lived alone in her large beach house, only venturing out to sit on the beach or go to the store. Rob sometimes spied her through the trees while he was working in the yard. He believed she was always watching him, sure he was up to no good, waiting to catch him out in some lecherous act. Sometimes he would hear Helen Schantz yell at him from her deck, "You there, who are you? Do you live here?"

Then, one cold autumn day, Rob found Helen sitting at the top of the stairs to the beach, staring out at the bay. This was totally out of character for Helen Schantz. She was not the type of person given to introspection or to sitting in a place that was not meant for sitting. He asked her if she was okay, and she said that she was, with a hint of a smile on her face. Smiling was also out of character for Helen Schantz. It was then that Rob saw the joint in her hand. Helen Schantz was the last person Rob would have expected to see smoking marijuana. She had very strong opinions about drugs, none of them good.

"You know, it's legal now," she said.

"Yes."

"Do you smoke?"

"I can't have any," Rob said, making it sound like he was prone to some hideous side effect. What he wanted to say was that he didn't want to share a joint with Helen Schantz.

"That's a shame. Do you need to get by? You can go ahead." She waved her arm like she was directing traffic.

"When did you start smoking?"

"Yesterday."

Rob wanted to ask how she had gotten the pot. She would have had to drive to one of the dispensaries in Wellfleet or Provincetown. Or perhaps they delivered. Everyone delivered now.

"You know what I think?" Helen said, looking down at the stairs. "We need to do something about all this poison ivy."

There was a thick carpet of poison ivy on the hillside under the stairs. Rob was allergic to poison ivy and wanted to kill all of it, but Helen Schantz was violently opposed to killing any vegetation. She yelled at him anytime she saw him wandering around with anything that had a nozzle on it.

"I'm sorry, what did you say?" Rob said. He was stunned. He wanted to hear her say it again.

"We need to get rid of the poison ivy," Helen said. "I'm going to get rid of it for you." And she did, spending the next two weeks uprooting all of the poison ivy under the stairs, stoned out of her mind.

In a few short months, Helen Schantz became an accomplished stoner and an advocate for marijuana use. She was stoned throughout the day, and when she wasn't killing poison ivy, she was fond of staring out at the water, as she was now, sitting in the sand, watching Rob come out of the water with his chair.

"Why were you sitting in the water?" she said.

"The tide came in. I fell asleep."

Helen Schantz nodded in a way that made it clear that she knew about the tides. "Do you remember that guy?" she said, gesturing toward the water with her joint hand. "The one who went out in the water to take Katie's picture?"

Rob itched his sunburned skin. It had always been a challenge talking to Helen Schantz, and it was no easier now that she was stoned all the time. "Yes, Helen. I remember him."

"They never found him, did they? Everyone thought he drowned or was eaten by a shark. Just to take a picture of Katie in her rowboat."

"No, they never did find him," he said. The guy, of course, was Sammy Boland, the man Mike Van Winkle was looking for.

Rob imagined Van Winkle interviewing Helen Schantz. That would be some conversation.

"They thought she was Dorothy Bradford," Helen said. "From the Mayflower."

"She is Dorothy Bradford, Helen."

Helen took a drag off her joint and nodded. "What about your son? Is he here, too?" She always seemed to be interested in the comings and goings of the Crosleys. Except for Rob.

"He lives here now, yes."

"In the garage?"

"Above the garage, Helen."

"And what about your dog?"

"Sidney died last year."

"He was a good dog. I miss him." Helen Schantz had once pulled the geriatric dog out of the poison ivy while Rob watched helplessly. She had carried the dog back to her house and hosed off the poisonous oils with a garden hose. "Is Katie home?"

"She's across the street."

"Where?"

"In the Bradford House, Helen." The woman was positively out of her mind. Rob needed to find a way to break off the conversation.

"Who lives there now?"

"Besides Rachel, there are three residents now."

"What are their names? Are they heroin addicts?"

"They might have been. I'm not sure. You should ask Katie." He watched Helen Schantz remove a seed from her mouth and saw this as an opportunity to leave. "Well, enjoy the beach, Helen," he said, starting for the stairs.

"It feels like summer to me. Does it feel like summer to you?"

Rob quickened his pace.

CHAPTER THREE

Gravesites and Chainsaws

When Katie got back from Corn Hill, she stopped at the Bradford House to visit with Rachel and the residents. Rachel was the live-in director of the house. The residents were the women who stayed there, sometimes for a few days, sometimes a few weeks. Many of them were recovering from drug addiction, some dealing with anxiety and depression. Nominally, the Bradford House was considered a place to transition from the hospital or rehab, but some of the residents came here from their homes, needing a place to escape. A social worker came by once a week to meet with the residents and help them sort through whatever obstacles they were facing. Katie liked to attend these group sessions, too, both to observe and to deal with her own obstacles. But her primary role was to provide the women with outlets to help them cope. She took them on long hikes through the woods and on the beaches and taught them survival skills like building shelters and living off the land—all things she had been doing for the last forty to four hundred years, depending on who you were talking to.

Elaine Snow was also there when Katie arrived. Rachel and Elaine were long-time members of the Dorothy Bradford Society, both of whom had quickly shifted their allegiances to Katie after the departure of Maggie Mason. Rachel was a large woman, strong and physically imposing, but with a soft and caring demeanor that was popular with the residents. She had lived in the original Dorothy Bradford House in Provincetown and performed various administrative tasks for Maggie Mason, but was not so much involved with the residents there. She was not at all involved in making the beer.

Elaine, on the other hand, was a demure wisp of a woman who harbored something of an inferiority complex. She had dreamed of being the one to find and photograph Dorothy Bradford, knowing the achievement would bring her great acclaim. Elaine was something of a photographer, too, and always had her camera with her, but she had missed out on capturing the iconic photograph—that honor going to an anonymous man with a waterproof camera, the man who turned out to be Sammy Boland.

Katie found Rachel and Elaine in the living room. The residents were in the back yard, lying in the sun. When Katie was in the house, everyone addressed her as Dorothy, her Pilgrim name. Some of the residents adopted Pilgrim names, too. Susanna, Priscilla, and Elinor were popular with the residents. No one else ever took the name Dorothy.

"Hello, ladies," Katie said, coming through the door.

Elaine stood up.

"Elaine, you don't always have to stand up when I come in," Katie said. "I'm not royalty."

"Yes, you are," Elaine said. "And you can call me Alice."

"You have a Pilgrim name now, too?"

"Yes," she said proudly. She sat back down on the couch. Her feet barely touched the floor.

"Where have you been?" Rachel said. Like Rob, she was always mindful of Katie's comings and goings. "I saw you leaving in the car."

"I've had an interesting morning," she said, and she told them about her chance encounter with the man and the boy on Corn Hill.

"What did the man look like?" Elaine said, her eyes wide.

"Tall, muscular, blond hair down to his shoulders. Do you know him?"

"Did the boy look like an Indian?"

"Native American, Elaine," Rachel said.

"Call me Alice."

"He could have been, I guess," Katie said. He had much darker skin than his father. If it was his father. They didn't look alike.

"Didn't you realize who they were?" Elaine said. She was up off the couch again and had her arms in the air, like she was signaling a successful field goal.

Katie looked over at Rachel. Rachel shrugged her broad shoulders. "Should I have?"

"That was the Blonde Norseman!"

"Who?"

"If anyone had seen him before, I thought you would have, Dorothy."

"Stop being so cryptic, Elaine," Rachel said. "Who is the Blonde Norseman?"

"When the Pilgrims dug up the corn, they also dug up the gravesite of an Indian boy and a blond-haired man. The blond-haired man is known as the Blonde Norseman. He and the boy have haunted Corn Hill ever since."

"What are you saying, Elaine?" Katie said. "That they're ghosts?"

"Yes!"

"I don't know about that."

But Elaine was adamant. She was an ardent believer in ghosts and was always quick to point out how many there were on Cape Cod, like in the haunted house in Barnstable, known befittingly as The Barnstable House, where eleven known spirits were in residence. Elaine had visited The Barnstable House a number of times, and on one of her visits, she saw the ghost of a little brown-haired girl named Lucy. The tour guide told her that Lucy had been playing hide and seek with her mother and climbed into a trunk, closed the lid, and suffocated. "Either that or she drowned in a well," the guide said. "People are drowning all the time on the Cape. There's a lot of water here."

Elaine sat back down on the couch, and her expression grew stern. "You need to be careful of the Norseman," she warned Katie. "He might want to take revenge on you. Your husband, William Bradford, was the guy who dug him up."

"I'll be fine, Elaine. I haven't seen this guy or the boy in any of my dreams. Just the marker."

"Who have you seen in your dreams?" Elaine said.

"A man being buried in the woods and two girls drowning in a pond."

"Wow," Elaine said, then closed her eyes, as though getting in touch with the afterlife. "I'll bet the man was Thomas Ridley," she said, opening her eyes again. "He died in 1776 and was buried in the woods. He had smallpox, and they didn't want his body nearby, so they hauled him off to some remote spot and buried him there. I don't know anything about two girls in a pond. How about Goodie Hallett? Have you seen her in any of your dreams?"

Katie shook her head. "Who's that?"

"She's a witch," Rachel said, rolling her eyes. "Elaine's looking for her now. She's her new quest."

"The Witch of Wellfleet," Elaine said. "People have seen her wandering the dunes searching for Sam Bellamy, and I'm going to find her. Call me Alice."

"Sam Bellamy was a pirate," Katie said. "I've heard of him."

"Have you seen him in your dreams?"

"I probably will now," Katie said. "Where do you get all this stuff, Elaine?"

"On the internet. They were engaged, you know, Bellamy and Goodie Hallett. While he was off pirating in the Caribbean, Goodie discovered that she was pregnant with his child. She had the baby, but it died suddenly. Goodie cried out, and a nearby constable heard her. He arrested her for murder, even though the baby had just choked on a piece of straw, and for childbirth out of wedlock. She was thrown in jail but escaped somehow. The townspeople decided she was a witch and stoned her on the town pier while she was waiting for Bellamy to return. She fell into the ocean and was thought to have drowned. When Bellamy came back, his ship, the Whydah, was caught in a fierce storm and came apart. Like Goodie, his body was never found. She's been searching for him ever since."

"Some people think she found him and that he took her back to the Caribbean," Rachel said.

"She would never leave the Cape," Elaine said. "She's here."

Katie sighed. She had never placed much stock in ghost stories. Then again, she had never placed much stock in immortality, and here she was nearing her four hundred and twenty-fifth birthday.

"I'll bet you knew them all, Dorothy," Elaine said. "That's why they're in your dreams."

"The Blonde Norseman wasn't in my dreams. And he was dead before the Mayflower got here, so I couldn't have known him."

"You knew his ghost, then. And the boy's ghost. You know what you should do? You should go back to Corn Hill and leave some corn by the stone marker to ask their forgiveness."

"Do we have any beer?" Katie said, growing weary of Elaine's paranormal expositions.

"We always have beer," Rachel said.

Katie got up and went into the kitchen. Rachel followed. The Dorothy Bradford Society no longer brewed their own beer, but they still drank it.

"We should go see Tom Ridley's grave," Elaine called from the living room. "Maybe you'll see him, like you saw the Norseman."

"You know how to get there?" Katie said.

"I have a rough idea. People have gotten lost, though."

Katie was always up for a walk in the woods. And there was something intriguing about a man who spent eternity hidden in a forest. She wondered if he had led his life that way, too—living off the colonial grid, isolated and alone, only to be felled by a contagious disease.

"You won't get lost, Elaine," Rachel said. "You'll have Dorothy Bradford with you." She popped open the beers and then lowered her voice and said to Katie, "She can get a little crazy with this paranormal stuff."

◆ ◆

Like his mother, Danny Crosley liked being outside, especially in remote areas where there was no pavement or traffic noise. Thanks to the creation of the Cape Cod National

Seashore in 1961, the vast majority of the Outer Cape was protected from new development. Much of it had never been developed at all. Save for the beach erosion, the land west of Route Six, all the way from Eastham to Provincetown, looked much the same as it did sixty years ago. The National Park Service was responsible for maintaining and monitoring the National Seashore, and Danny became a ranger to do just that. The Park Service was, of course, thrilled to have an Olympic gold medal winner in their employ, but soon found that they also had gained a capable ranger who worked hard and was committed to protecting the sanctity of the seashore.

Currently, Danny was working in a part of the Truro woods, north of the kettle ponds that straddled the Wellfleet-Truro line. There were several hiking trails that ran through these woods between Collins Road and the Atlantic. The winter storms brought down a tangle of branches and trees, and those that landed on the paths had to be cleared away. Danny and another park ranger were tending to a trail in a section of the woods, a half mile from the Atlantic. The other ranger, whose name was Nardo—Danny wasn't sure of his first name—was a hard worker, too, but he talked too much.

"Hey, Gold," Nardo said. Gold was what Nardo called Danny after his Olympic medal. "Did you run today?"

"You know I ran today."

"How far did you run?"

"Ten miles."

"What was your time?"

Danny rolled his eyes. Nardo asked the same questions every time they worked together. "It wasn't a race, Nardo," he said.

"Do you ever just run for fun? You know, just go out for a run, no GPS watch?"

"Every run is fun. Unless I get hit by a bus."

"Have you been hit by a bus?"

This went on until the path debris lightened enough so that he and Nardo could split up and work separate sections of the trail on their own.

"Call me if you run into any downed trees," Nardo said, swatting a mosquito on his neck. Nardo was in charge of the chainsaw. He loved the chainsaw, particularly the sound it made. Whenever he was cutting something, he would mimic the sound—a loud nasal whine. Sometimes he started his vocal accompaniment a second or two before pulling the trigger, as though this was a necessary part of getting the saw to function properly.

Danny headed east along the trail, flinging downed branches into the woods. Nardo set off in the opposite direction and vanished into the trees. Danny came to the edge of the woods, where the trees gave way to beach vegetation and sunlight. He took a deep breath, as though drawing in the silence around him. The path turned to sand and rose to the top of the dunes overlooking the beach. This particular dune was called Great Dune. Over one hundred feet in elevation, it was thought to be the tallest sand cliff on the Cape. Danny walked to the ridgeline and looked down. At one time, this stretch of beach was popular with nudists. He wasn't sure if it still was, but there was nobody down there now, clothed or otherwise, just a couple of seals bobbing in the waves.

On the walk back to Collins Road, he turned onto another trail and found many more downed tree limbs. Some of them were large, and he knew he'd need Nardo and the chainsaw to clear them away. As he pulled his walkie-talkie from his belt, he saw a man further down the trail, heading toward him. He was young, probably not much older than Danny. He wore work boots, jeans, and a vest with lots of stuffed pockets. Danny thought he looked familiar. Danny waved and said, "Hello." The man turned around without responding and headed back the other way. There was a camera hanging from his neck. That's when Danny thought he knew who he was.

"Hey! Hang on for a minute!" Danny said, and he started after the man. The man moved quickly, though, and easily vaulted over the large branches that blocked the path. In what seemed like only a second or two, he was gone. Danny didn't give chase; the risk of catching a foot in one of the branches and tearing a ligament was too great. Besides, it wasn't his job to chase after suspected fugitives.

He got out his cell phone, but there was no reception in this part of the woods. He called Nardo on the walkie-talkie instead.

"Roger!" Nardo said.

"You say that at the end of the conversation, Nardo."

"Roger that! What's up? Need me to help?"

"I think I just saw Sammy Boland."

◆ ◆

By the time Danny emerged onto the small dirt lot alongside Collins Road, three police cars had arrived. Nardo had taken it upon himself to call the police, even though Danny wasn't sure it was Sammy Boland he'd seen. Nardo was talking to one of the officers earnestly, as though he'd been the one who saw Boland. Don Hill, the Truro police inspector who had uncovered Boland's drug operation two years ago, was there, too. Though he had found the sizable drug cache, he had never been able to find Boland, despite assistance from the DEA. Most people assumed Boland had been knocked off and dumped in a landfill somewhere, his suppliers worried Boland might rat them out in exchange for a reduced sentence.

"Hello, Danny," Don Hill said. The other officers gathered around. Nardo was left alone. Danny was a local hero, of course, and was used to drawing crowds. Danny knew Don Hill from the initial Boland investigation.

He described the man he saw in the woods, the vest, the work boots, and the camera. Danny had never actually met Sammy Boland, but there had been so many pictures and descriptions of him in the papers and on TV that he knew what he looked like. So did most of the people on the Outer Cape, many of whom called the police to say they had spotted him somewhere—the grocery store, the lumber yard, a bar. Nardo's call created a greater sense of urgency. It was the first call in nine months. And it was also on behalf of Danny Crosley, the Olympic gold medalist.

"Can you show us on the map where you saw him?" Don Hill said.

"I'm not exactly sure it was him," Danny said, pointing to the spot and indicating the direction in which Boland was running when he lost sight of him. "I didn't mean for Nardo to call."

"You guys did the right thing," Don Hill said.

"You could have chased him down, Danny," one of the officers said, eliciting laughter from the other officers.

"How about you guys go do your jobs?" Don Hill said, and gave the team instructions, whereupon the six officers headed off into the woods in teams of two. Don Hill stayed behind.

"Did you guys see anybody else out there?" Don Hill said.

"No one," Nardo said. "Just Boland."

"You saw him, too?"

"No. I mean, Danny saw him. I didn't see him. Danny didn't have bars where he was."

"Bars?"

"Cell phone reception. You know?"

"Any idea what he was doing out there?" Don Hill said.

"Probably taking pictures, right?" Nardo said.

"I'm asking Danny."

"Of course. Yes, sorry." Nardo stepped back and leaned against one of the police cars.

"Off the car, Nardo," Don Hill said.

"Right. Sorry."

"He did have a camera," Danny said.

"Boland never struck me as the type of guy to go hiking in the woods," Don Hill said.

A few minutes later, Rob pulled up in his car. Danny had texted to let him know about the excitement on Collins Road, and as it was only a five-minute drive from the house, Rob came to see. He parked on the road since the small lot was filled with police cars. He got out of the car and immediately drew stares. Expecting he would be going into the woods, Rob had put on a pair of pants, a long-sleeved flannel shirt, gloves, and a baseball cap. He also wore the gaiter he'd had on that morning for his bike ride to Provincetown, still damp from having been rinsed. The gaiter was up over his nose. The only visible skin was around his eyes.

"Dad?" Danny said.

"Hey, guys. Hello, Inspector."

Don Hill and Nardo looked worried. Danny looked embarrassed.

"What the hell are you wearing?" Danny said.

"I didn't know if I'd be going into the woods," Rob said. "There's poison ivy in there. And mosquitoes."

"Did Mom see you leave the house like that?"

"I think we've got it covered, Rob," Don Hill said. "No need for you to risk a skin rash."

"I have to be careful," Rob said. He pulled the gaiter down below his chin. He was getting warm. An hour ago, he was sunning himself on the beach; now he was dressed for the Arctic. He peered into the woods as if Boland might pop out from behind a tree. "How many guys do you have in there, Inspector?"

"Six."

"You think he's been living in there?"

Don Hill didn't answer. He preferred not to speculate. Two more police cars from Wellfleet arrived, and another four officers joined the search. There were now five police cars around the trailhead. There was never very much traffic on Collins Road, but the cars that passed by slowed to see what was going on. A woman on a bike stopped and asked if it was safe to continue.

One car pulled over and parked on the opposite side of the road. A man got out and jogged over to where Rob, Danny, Nardo, and Don Hill were huddled.

"I thought we might see you over here," Don Hill said to the man. The man was Mike Van Winkle, the private detective. He introduced himself around. He seemed very pleased to meet Danny and congratulated him on his gold medal.

"You've got a lot more clothes on than the last time I saw you, Mr. Crosley," Van Winkle said. The last time they'd seen each other, of course, had been that morning at the Province-town Inn.

"I thought I might be going into the woods," Rob said.

Van Winkle asked Danny all the same questions Don Hill had—the where, what, and when business. Don Hill bristled, and Rob figured he didn't care for Van Winkle's interference. But then, private investigators only got involved when the police failed, so why wouldn't Don Hill be defensive?

"Have you searched these woods before?" Van Winkle asked Hill. "In the last two years?"

"No reason to," Don Hill said. "This is the first time we've gotten a report of Boland being seen in the woods."

Van Winkle nodded. He looked at Nardo. "Who are you?"

"Name's Nardo," Nardo said. He pointed to the National Seashore patch on his shirt.

"Did you see Boland, too?"

"No. I was in a different part of the woods. Hey, can I ask you a question? Are you related to Pappy Van Winkle?"

"I don't drink," Van Winkle said, giving Nardo the same evasive response he'd given Rob. "Listen," he said, turning back to Don Hill. "Is it okay if I take a look in there, too?"

"As long as you notify me if you find anything," Hill said. "Don't get lost in there. Cell phone service is patchy."

"I grew up in the woods, Inspector. Kentucky." And with that, he headed onto the trail, disappearing into the woods.

"Kentucky?" Nardo said. "He's got to be related to Pappy, then. Son of a bitch."

"Who is Pappy?" Don Hill said.

"Pappy Van Winkle," Rob said. "Best bourbon in the world."

"Most expensive, too," Nardo said.

"Guess he didn't go into the family business," Don Hill said.

The search continued for the rest of the day, until the light bled out of the trees. Danny and Nardo left to go clear trails in North Truro. Rob kicked around with Don Hill a while longer, then went home when it became clear the police weren't going to find anything. Sammy Boland had slipped away again, if it was Sammy Boland, and there was no sign of any campsite.

♦ ♦

Rob and Katie had much to share that evening, what with the stories of Corn Hill and Sammy Boland. Rob, who had been thinking about bourbon all day, stopped at the liquor store on his way home and bought a bottle. He made an Old Fashioned for himself and a weaker one for Katie.

"Why does bourbon taste so different from scotch?" Katie said.

"It's made from corn," Rob said.

"Corn seems to be something of a theme today." She told Rob about the man and the boy she'd met on Corn Hill—Erik and Dak—and Elaine's theory that they were ghosts sprung from their graves when William Bradford helped himself to the natives' buried corn and dug them up in the process.

"What's a Norwegian doing on Cape Cod in the seventeenth century?" Rob said.

"Elaine says he was a Viking. Supposedly, they started coming here in the eleventh century."

"Elaine is an expert on Vikings?"

"And ghosts." She plucked the cherry out of the remnants of

her Old Fashioned and then told Rob about the planned trip to North Truro the next day to find the grave of Thomas Ridley.

"You're not going to dig that one up, too, are you?"

"Very funny. Elaine thinks that Ridley is the guy I see being buried in the woods."

"So you're becoming a ghost hunter now?"

"Elaine seems to think my dreams are all about ghosts. She says I shouldn't ignore them. Ghosts are apparently a big deal on the Cape."

"I've never seen one."

The lights in the house started to flicker again. Rob banged his hand against the wall, as if that would clear the clot that was impeding the flow of electricity. The power finally went out altogether, and the somber light from the moon hovering over Pamet Harbor was left as the only check against total darkness. The night grew cold, and Rob and Katie closed the windows, climbed into bed, and buried themselves under the covers.

CHAPTER FOUR

Plastic Owls and ORV Permits

The sun had just started to filter through the curtains when Rob and Katie were rudely awakened by a hyperactive woodpecker. The bird had landed on a gutter just outside the bedroom window and was having at it. The sound was deafening, like someone jackhammering a trashcan. Rob opened the window and yelled at the bird, emitting a "yip" very similar to the one he used with foxes.

"Fuck you, bird!" Rob said when the hammering didn't stop. "Go find a tree."

"I think it's a mating call," Katie said.

"I thought birds looked for worms in the morning. This asshole wants to get laid."

"I'll put some decoys up there this afternoon."

"What kind of decoys?"

"Plastic owls."

"Where do you find plastic owls?"

"Hardware store."

Katie fell back asleep, the woodpecker having finally moved on to other business. Rob lay in bed for a while, but when sleep didn't come, he got up and wandered around the house, deciding how to start the day. Rob no longer worked for a living. After Katie's condition worsened, he took a leave of absence from his consulting practice in Boston. Katie wanted to leave the city and move to the Cape, where there would be fewer people to avoid. They did so, and Katie's condition seemed to improve. Rob began working remotely and commuted to Boston three days a week. Life seemed to be returning to normal, but then one night, lying in bed with Rob, Katie suffered a major panic attack. She ran from the house in her bare feet and spent the night in the cottage they owned across the street. Rob hoped the fear would subside after a few days and she'd move back in, but that didn't happen. Katie was too terrified to go inside the house when Rob was there. He decided to leave his job at that point and devote himself full-time to protecting his wife's privacy and nursing her back to health. Money wasn't a problem. Rob could afford to be out of a job. What he couldn't afford was to be out of a wife.

It was at times like these, early in the morning in particular, that he missed his dog, Sidney. Before he got old and infirm, Sidney woke up at six-thirty every morning and leaned against Rob's side of the bed. Sidney never slept on the bed; his spot was among the shoes in Katie's closet. He sat quietly at first, panting a bit and staring at the bedroom door, the one that led to where the food was. Eventually he started to whimper, his cries growing in intensity, much like a cascading cell phone alarm, until Rob awoke and let him out for a pee. After the two of them ate breakfast, they went for a walk on the beach, where Sidney chased seagulls and found an inviting patch of sand where he could take a dump.

Rob took his laptop and a cup of coffee onto the deck and looked at websites dedicated to helping him choose the perfect dog. Large or small? Puppy or rescue? Long hair or short hair? Purebred or mixed? Shedder or non-shedder? Male or female? He answered a litany of questions, and the site decided that the perfect dog for him was a Labrador Retriever. Labradors were the most popular dog breed, and they were different enough from Australian Shepherds that Rob wouldn't be reminded of

Sidney. He took the test a second time, changing some of his answers. More Labradors. The site was rigged.

Katie got up and left for the Bradford House. She was taking some of the girls with her on the second leg of her Truro ghost tour. After the woodpecker gutter attack, she had dreamt again about the drowning girls and the man in the woods. The dream about the Corn Hill marker didn't replay. Rob wished her luck, though he had no idea what he meant by that. Good luck finding your ghost?

He pulled up a couple of sites about Cape Cod ghosts, including Thomas Ridley and the Blonde Norseman, all of which substantiated Elaine's accounts. There were any number of sightings of the ghosts through the years, and even a few blurry photos. He read a story about a woman in North Truro whose house was enveloped by fog one morning when a rocking chair in the corner started rocking itself. This was thought to be the work of Thomas Ridley, whose gravesite was not far from the woman's house.

His favorite ghost story was about Hannah, a "lady of the night" who was murdered in the front entrance of the Orleans Inn during the Roaring Twenties. At the time, the inn was a popular area brothel. Hannah's ghost had haunted the inn ever since, and she was sometimes seen dancing naked in the room directly above the entrance where she was done in. Hannah was not one of the ghosts in Katie's dreams. Not yet, anyway.

When he grew tired of paranormal research, Rob inspected the gutters along the roofline, looking for dents and trying to figure out how Katie would mount a plastic owl up there. A car pulled into the driveway and stopped by the garage. Rob knew the car and its driver, Steve Ridgeback.

Steve Ridgeback was a reporter with the *Cape Cod Gazette*. He had first inserted himself into the Crosleys' lives when he wrote an article about Danny's running exploits. This was before the Olympics, when Danny had first come out to the Cape to train. A large part of the reason he trained on the Cape was to be close to his mother. At the time, he was the only person whose company she could abide. But Rob and Danny kept this information from Ridgeback. He didn't need to know that Katie lived by herself in the cottage across the street and was terrified of other people. Ridgeback knew who Katie was, but he never met her until the Dorothy Bradford affair.

The article about Danny was the first of many that featured the Crosleys in one fashion or another. Ridgeback wrote about the missing photographer, the one who turned out to be Sammy Boland, and the pictures he took of Katie in her rowboat. Next came a story about the Dorothy Bradford Society and their belief that Katie was, in fact, Dorothy Bradford herself. Then came the stories about Sammy Boland and his drug dealing. The only thing Ridgeback hadn't been able to write about was what became of Boland. That opportunity had now presented itself.

"Hello, Rob," Ridgeback said, popping out of his car, a beat-up Subaru Outback.

"Where've you been, Steve?" Rob said. He had expected a visit. Ridgeback seldom called in advance; he just showed up. But this was typical of most year-round residents on the Outer Cape. During the off-season, Truro was like any other small town. Everyone knew everyone else. They just showed up.

"I called last night. Danny told me to come by this morning."

"You don't want to talk to me?"

"Did you see Boland?"

"No."

Rob walked down the driveway. Danny came outside. Ridgeback had traveled to the Olympics and seen Danny's triumph in the ten-thousand-meter race, which he then wrote about. Danny was not a big Ridgeback fan, though. Ridgeback tended to sensationalize events, larding up his stories with superlatives. In his articles about Danny, he made him out to be some kind of superhero, and always included his photo. As a result, Danny was recognized everywhere he went. There weren't many heroes on Cape Cod, and even fewer Olympic medalists.

They exchanged nods. People on the Cape had never been keen on handshakes anyway. Most of them worked with their hands and had all manner of grit lining the fissures of their palms. It was out of courtesy that they didn't shake hands.

"You knew it was him right away?" Ridgeback said to Danny.

"I didn't know it was him. I thought it was him. He had on that vest, the one with all the pockets. He looked familiar."

"Did you ever actually meet Boland?"

"No. I just saw the pictures."

"How far away were you when you saw him?"

"Ten yards."

"Did you call out his name?"

"No. I waved."

"And he ran in the opposite direction?"

"Right."

"You didn't run after him?"

"Nope."

Rob worried Ridgeback was looking for someone to blame for letting Boland get away. *Olympic hero lets drug dealer slip through his hands!*

"Don't you write anything that says Danny should have chased after him," Rob said.

"Well, he's not a cop. And besides, we can't have our gold medal winner tripping over a root and breaking his ankle."

"Don't write that either," Danny said.

"You think he's been living in the woods this whole time?" Rob said.

"I spoke to Don Hill last night. He doesn't think so. They didn't find any campsites. It's really hard for someone to remain invisible out here for two years. My guess is that he was hiding out somewhere off-Cape and came back sometime after the police stopped looking for him." Ridgeback jotted down a few notes and then closed his notepad. "How's Dorothy?" he said. Ridgeback always referred to Katie as Dorothy, someone else he loved to write about. "Still running the society?" He nodded in the direction of the Bradford House across the street.

"She's fine," Rob said.

"I need to do a follow-up on her sometime, see how things are going. Drink some beer with the Bradford women."

"Well, I've got to get ready for work," Danny said.

"More trail work?" Ridgeback said. "Hey, next time you see Boland in the woods, take his picture, okay?"

"You bet," Danny said sarcastically. "I'll get him to smile, too." He bounded back up the stairs to his apartment, leaving Rob and Ridgeback in the driveway.

"You ever get woodpeckers hammering on your gutters?" Rob asked.

"No. Why would a woodpecker peck a gutter?"

"No idea."

"Hey, I'm writing a story about the Race Point Lighthouse. Driving up there tomorrow. Going to let some air out of the tires and take the Subaru into the dunes. You want to go?"

Steve Ridgeback was a notoriously bad driver who wasn't afraid to use his horn and swore profusely anytime another driver did something he didn't like. Rob once had the misfortune of being in Ridgeback's car for a trip down Route Six, and he had kept his head down most of the way, sure that someone would start shooting at them.

"Don't you need a permit to drive on the dunes?" Rob said.

"Of course!" Ridgeback said, a phrase he was fond of. "I already got one." He jogged over to his car and proudly pointed to the ORV permit. ORV stood for off-road recreational vehicle.

Rob had never been to the lighthouse on Race Point. The only way to get there, if you didn't have an all-wheel-drive vehicle or a boat, was to walk two or three miles from the nearest parking area. Katie had been to the lighthouse several times on her hiking adventures. She once hiked there from Ballston Beach, a fifteen-mile trek in the sand, and spent the night in the dunes, hiking back the next day.

"Where do you drive onto the sand?" Rob said.

"Race Point Beach. It's about three miles to the lighthouse from there."

"Is the weather going to be okay tomorrow?"

"Why are you looking for excuses? You don't have to go. I just thought you might like an outing."

Rob thought this made him sound like a geriatric. "Can I meet you at the beach parking lot?" he said.

"Why? I'll pick you up. It's on the way."

Rob tried to think of other reasons for driving separately other than self-preservation. Maybe he needed to stop at the hardware store to pick something up, like a plastic owl. "Fine," Rob said, surrendering. It wasn't a long trip to Provincetown, and the off-season traffic would likely keep the number of road rage incidents to a minimum. Ridgeback was generally set off by out-of-staters anyway.

"I'll come by at one o'clock."

Rob watched Ridgeback hop back into his ORV and head off. Then he pulled out his phone and entered the appointment in the calendar for the following day. He stared at the entry—the lone entry for the day. The lone entry for the week. He needed more things to do.

CHAPTER FIVE

Kettle Holes
and Dune Buggies

After Katie opened the Bradford House, she bought an SUV—a big one with three rows of seats—so she could take the residents on outings. Keeping the residents active was an important part of the recovery process, so she took them on long treks through the natural sanctuaries of the Outer Cape. There were any number of trails winding through the woods, some leading to the ocean, some to the bay. Katie knew most of them and the things to watch for along the way, like wild blueberry bushes or beach plum trees, and some lonely gravesites, too.

The search for Tom Ridley's grave was another opportunity for an outing, and Katie asked the girls if they wanted to come along. They were a tight-knit group, having grown close during their time at the house, and agreed. Like many residents before them, each had taken aliases based on the names of Mayflower passengers. One woman took the name Martha, and the other two both named themselves Agnes. Rachel tried to convince one of them to take a different name. "There was nothing special about Agnes," she said. "Agnes didn't even make it through the first winter." But the two Agnes's both liked the idea of having an awkward name, and there were no names less flattering than Agnes. They added descriptors to distinguish themselves. One of them became "Fat Agnes," and the other was "Lady Agnes."

Fat Agnes, who was recovering from heroin addiction and bulimia, was anything but fat. Lady Agnes was coming out of a relationship with a man who had kept her locked in the house and forbidden her to wear clothes. She had developed a fear of men as a result and became upset whenever she saw one.

Rachel stayed behind—she had administrative work to catch up on—so Elaine hopped in the front seat next to Katie. The two Agnes's sat in the middle row of seats. Martha was in the back. Elaine instructed Katie to drive to Montano's, an Italian restaurant on Route Six. She had been told that if they walked into the woods behind the restaurant and headed northeast, they would eventually find the grave.

"How far north?" Katie said.

"I don't know. First we find a pile of brush, then a sand pit, and then two big kettle holes."

"What's a kettle hole?" Lady Agnes said.

"Holes left by the glaciers from the Ice Age," Elaine said.

"You're a kettle hole," Fat Agnes told Lady Agnes. Fat Agnes enjoyed teasing Lady Agnes, who was quieter and more reserved. Lady Agnes never shrank from Fat Agnes's taunts, though. She was more than capable of holding her own, as long as men weren't involved.

"Maybe, but I'm not a remnant of the Ice Age, like you," Lady Agnes said. "You know what remnant means, don't you?"

"Be nice, girls," Katie said.

"Make her get out and walk," Fat Agnes said. "Bitch."

"We'll be walking soon enough. And no name-calling."

Katie pulled into the restaurant's parking lot. Montano's was one of only a handful of commercial establishments on the east side of Route Six between North Truro and Provincetown. Katie and Rob sometimes came here for dinner during the off-season.

"Is the food any good here?" Martha said. The large parking lot reminded her of the lots where she would meet her dealer and buy drugs. She had never bought drugs here, though. The lot was too visible.

"Very good," Katie said. "Huge portions."

"You hear that, Agnes?" Lady Agnes said to her bulimic friend. "Huge portions."

"No jokes about our conditions," Katie said. "Right? Maybe it's time we find a new nickname for Kristin other than *Fat Agnes*."

"Sorry, Dorothy," Lady Agnes said. While they were encouraged to talk about their problems, they weren't allowed to make fun of them. This was one of the rules of the Dorothy Bradford House.

Elaine pulled out a piece of paper from her pants pocket. She looked at it for a moment, then peered into the woods.

"What's that?" Katie said.

"A map," Elaine said.

"I thought you didn't know where we were going." Katie looked at the map, but it only showed Route Six, the restaurant, and a red line giving the approximate route to the gravestone.

"We go that way," Elaine said, pointing to an opening in the fence along the edge of the parking lot.

They plunged into the woods on a narrow, sandy trail, which gave way to an old fire road. The traffic noise from Route Six stayed with them for a time. The fire road ended, and they came to a fork.

"We should take the one on the left if we're going to keep heading north," Katie said. She was charting their course on the hiking app on her phone.

"I'm sorry about the large portion comment," Lady Agnes said to Fat Agnes. "That wasn't cool."

"You wouldn't believe the amount of food I used to eat," Fat Agnes said. With all the walking she was doing now, the muscles in her legs were starting to come back to life. She felt stronger as they hiked deeper into the woods. "It all ended up in the toilet."

Lady Agnes took Fat Agnes's hand, and they walked together like that for a while.

Elaine stayed out front, keeping her eyes close to the ground and staying alert for landmarks. They came to a large pile of brush, and Elaine shrieked.

"We're on the right track!" she said. "This is the brush pile!" The pile was more of a wall, really, twenty yards long and five feet high. It looked like a fortification, a place for soldiers to take cover.

"What do we look for next?" Katie said.

"A sand pit."

"Left or right?"

"Left."

The sand pit appeared fairly soon after. Elaine hurried her pace, then stopped at the base of a sandy incline at the far end of the pit.

"This way, I think," Elaine said, heading off to the left. After a few hundred yards, she started going in circles, scouting the brush for the headstone. After fifteen minutes of mistaking tree stumps for gravestones, they decided to go back to the sand pit and try another route. They found a set of footsteps leading up the sand hill and followed them. At the top, they found a trail that led into the woods. The trail didn't last long, and very soon they were picking their way through brush and low branches, trying to maintain a northward course. After another ten minutes, the pine-filled terrain dropped off into a deep, bowl-shaped valley.

"I think this is one of the kettle holes," Elaine said, and she charged ahead, tracing the rim of the valley.

"Are we lost?" Martha said. In addition to being a recovering heroin addict, Martha suffered from social anxieties and was the quietest of the group. She also became easily rattled in stressful situations.

"We're exploring," Katie said. "We're not lost because we know the way back, right?" She showed Martha the route they'd taken on her phone. Martha looked behind her, scanning the trees for landmarks.

"It feels like we're lost," she said.

Katie stayed with Martha, leaving Elaine to pick their route through the trees and around the kettle holes. A few minutes later, with two deep valleys on either side of them, Elaine screamed.

"I see it!" she said, scrambling off the path. They came to a small clearing, and there it was—a solitary gravestone in the middle of the woods. She dropped to her knees to get a closer look. The marker was no more than two feet high. The etching had faded over time, but the letters were legible. It read:

M. THOMAS RIDEEY, Jun.

1776

"I thought you said his name was Ridley," Lady Agnes said, crowding in behind Elaine with the other girls.

"They spelled it wrong," Elaine said.

"Poor bastard," Fat Agnes said. "They bury him all alone in the middle of nowhere and can't even spell his name right."

"I knew we'd find it," Elaine said, sounding extremely proud of herself. She took a few photos of the stone and then had Katie and the girls stand behind it for a group shot. Martha and the two Agnes's then sat down in the pine needles and drank from their water bottles.

"This doesn't look at all familiar," Katie said to Elaine. "I've never seen this in any of my dreams."

"Ridley's ghost could be watching you right now, just like the Blonde Norseman was watching you on Corn Hill," Elaine said.

Katie glanced around. The depths of the kettle holes were dim and lifeless. They were well away from the traffic noise of Route Six now, and the forest had fallen into an eerie, woody silence.

There was only one body in the ground, but the site was a grave-yard nonetheless, the second one she had visited in as many days.

"I don't feel anything, Elaine," Katie said. "And I don't see anything, either." This wasn't entirely true, though. Katie was starting to feel a little anxious—a stirring of nerves in her stom-ach. She took a breath and closed her eyes.

"I'd feel better if you called me Alice."

Katie opened her eyes and fixated on the "E" that should have been an "L" on the headstone. The flutter of nerves sub-sided. "Thomas Ridley doesn't have anything to do with the Pilgrims," she said. "He lived a hundred years later."

"Maybe you knew him. You can't say for sure. Your dreams might have nothing to do with the Pilgrims."

"Do we have to worry about ticks out here, or is it still too early?" Lady Agnes said. She had pulled up her shirt and was examining something on her stomach.

"Everybody should take showers when we get home and do a thorough check," Katie said.

"I can check your kettle hole if you like," Fat Agnes said to Lady Agnes.

"You guys are disgusting," Martha said.

"If I were a tick, that's where I'd go," Fat Agnes said.

"I think it's time we head back," Katie said, feeling the need for some time alone.

"Yes!" Martha said. "This place gives me the creeps."

"We haven't seen Ridley yet," Elaine said.

"What?!" Martha screamed, looking at the space in front of the headstone as if Thomas Ridley's pocked hand had popped out of the ground. She jumped up off the forest floor, pine needles stuck to her backside, and ran off in the direction from which they'd come.

"Wipe off your butt, Martha!" Fat Agnes said.

♦ ♦

While Katie was off looking for ghosts, Rob was walking south along the bay beach. He typically walked this way since there was only so far he could go in the opposite direction before coming to the jetty at the harbor inlet and having to turn around. To the south, he could walk all the way to Great Island in Wellfleet if he wanted to, though he never did. That kind of walk, almost five miles, was what Katie did, not Rob. And Wellfleet was where all the mosquitoes were.

Rob usually turned at or before Ryder Beach, a mile away. Walking in the sand was nice, but the beach was sloped toward the water, which meant that one foot was always landing at a lower point than the other. This made his hips, already stiff from all the bike riding he did, feel uncomfortable. He had begun a regimen of daily stretching exercises, once again led by exuberant online trainers, and this helped relieve the stiffness. He missed the days when all that was required to recover from a strenuous workout was a couple of beers and a shower.

The morning was overcast but warm. The breeze blowing from the south carried hints of summer. The beach was deserted and, owing to the relatively calm weather of the past few days, free of any tidal debris. The only thing of note that Rob came across was a sea bird of some sort, sitting alone on the shore while a flock of similar birds dove in and out of the water, catching fish. The bird did not move as Rob walked by, and he expected there was something wrong with it. He wondered whether there was a bird rescue league he should call, but then a bird wasn't a beached whale or even a seal, for that matter. If it was a baby bird in distress, he felt sure he would have intervened, but this bird looked old and worn down, ready for a peaceful end. He convinced himself there was nothing to be done, though he turned to look back every so often, hopeful the bird would rally and fly off.

Presently, Rob came to the low-slung, modernistic beach-front home of Tim Desmond. The home had been the clandes-tine storage site of Sammy Boland's drug operation. Desmond had employed Boland to take care of the house and had allowed him to set up a workshop in the basement where he could keep his tools. There was also a large freezer in which Sammy stored bait fish. The fish were delivered directly to the house by boat. Tim Desmond was an avid fisherman, and Sammy had convinced him to keep a supply of bait in the freezer. Desmond never knew that the fish were stuffed with illegal narcotics.

Rob sometimes found Desmond fly-fishing on the beach. He would stop, and the two of them would discuss rods and reels, even though Rob knew nothing about either of these things. Desmond was not fishing today, but Rob spotted him on the deck of his house. Desmond was leaning over the railing, looking down into the beach grass like he had dropped something.

"Everything okay?" Rob called out. Desmond's head snapped up in surprise, as though a bird had crashed into one of the sliding glass doors.

"Oh, it's you, Rob," Desmond said, sounding oddly relieved.

"Did you lose something?" Rob said, sensing something was not right with Tim Desmond. But then something was always not right with Tim Desmond. He was plagued by misfortune. Prior to the Sammy Boland drug debacle, he had come under fire for the "decadent design," as the papers called it, of his newly-built house. During final inspections, it was discovered that the house encroached on property setbacks, and the town zoning commission and board of selectmen prohibited Desmond from occupying the house until the matter was resolved.

For a time, it looked like he might have to demolish the home, or at least that portion of it that crossed the line, but in the end Desmond made a large settlement to the town, and he was allowed to move in.

Desmond waved to Rob, beckoning him to come up to the house. Then he went back to peering into the beach grass.

"Did you see anyone else?" Desmond said when Rob arrived on the deck.

"Where?" Rob said.

"Around the house."

"Just you. Why?"

"He's back."

"Who?"

"Boland."

Now Rob looked down into the grass. "He's here?" he said, expecting to see Sammy Boland crouched under a bush.

"I've seen him," Desmond said. "And I've heard him in the basement."

"How did he get into the house? Didn't you change the locks?"

"I think he goes in through the basement window. Right down there." He pointed to the side of the house. "See how the grass is matted down there?"

"Danny saw him in the woods yesterday," Rob said.

"Really? Where?"

"Off Collins Road. The police came. They didn't find him."

"But he's here. He's come back," Desmond said.

"If he ever left." Rob watched a biplane putter its way north over the water, heading for Provincetown Airport. It was the type of plane that hauled advertising banners up and down the coast during the summer—hawking beer and insurance. Perhaps this one was reporting for duty early, gearing up for the Fourth of July and the beginning of the summer season.

"I'll get him," Desmond said. "That son of a bitch."

"Why would he come back here, though?" Rob said.

"I have no fucking idea," Desmond said. "But he gets into the basement and starts hammering the pipes."

Rob wondered if Tim Desmond was right in the head. There were plenty of paranoid people on the Outer Cape, and he now thought Desmond might be one of them.

"That doesn't make sense either," Rob said, thinking of the woodpeckers hammering his gutters. "Why would he hammer your pipes?"

"He's tormenting me. He thinks I was the one who called the cops on him."

"Well, have you called them now?"

"What are they going to do? They've had two years to find the guy. Cops only make things worse."

Rob told Desmond about Mike Van Winkle, wondering if the private detective might have already paid Desmond a visit.

"I haven't seen him," Desmond said. "Who hired him, Boland's dad?"

"He wouldn't say."

"Who else would it be?"

"I thought it might have been you. Especially now that Boland's back."

"I don't have any use for investigators, public or private," Desmond said. "I'll tell you, though, if I see Boland on my property, I'm going to pop him."

Rob wasn't sure what Desmond meant by "pop." Was he going to shoot him with a gun or just punch him in the face? He knew that Desmond owned a couple of guns; he had mentioned them in passing one day when the fish talk had run dry.

"You should call the police, Tim. There were officers from Wellfleet and Eastham up here yesterday, too."

"They're no better."

It was this type of anti-authoritarianism that had put Desmond in disfavor with town officials and resulted in the delay of an occupancy permit for his house for nearly three years. No one was surprised when the drugs were discovered in the house, and even though Desmond had had nothing to do with them, there were still plenty of folks who felt he must have been involved.

"You should get some security cameras," Rob said.

"They're on the way. Spotlights, too, with motion sensors." Desmond cocked his head and looked up. "Did you hear that?" he said.

"What?" Rob looked up, too.

"There's someone on the roof."

With that, Tim Desmond ran into the house, leaving Rob alone on the deck. Rob wasn't sure if he was meant to follow, but he didn't want to. He expected Desmond was going for his guns, and Rob wanted no part of that. He walked quickly back to the beach, then looked back to see Tim Desmond standing on his flat roof, gun in hand.

Tim Desmond has lost his mind, Rob thought. Perhaps he needed to start smoking pot, too, like Helen Schantz, something to quell the paranoia and give him back his sanity.

Rob headed toward home and found the sea bird lying on its side, its eyes closed. He knelt down for a closer look. There were no signs of life. The bird was dead. Rob figured that burying the bird or tossing it in the water was probably the wrong thing to do. He made a few calls to the town and was finally connected to someone who told him to put the carcass in a plastic bag, tie it up, and dump it in the trash. Rob explained that he was out for a walk and wasn't close to home.

"You could bury it," the official said.

"I don't have a shovel."

"Leave it then. Scavengers will take care of it."

Rob ended the call. The thought of leaving the bird to the vultures was not sitting well with him. "Shit," he said. Where was this sorrow coming from? For a bird? He scouted along the base of the dunes and found a broken piece of fencing that he used to dig a hole. He flipped the bird into the grave and dumped in some seaweed and a few rocks. "Rest in peace, bird," he said. Then he filled the hole with sand and went home.

◆ ◆

In true Cape fashion, Steve Ridgeback arrived to pick up Rob at 1:30, a half hour later than planned. Time was just a suggestion on the Cape, regardless of the season. An appointment for 1:00 meant that this was the earliest time you could expect to meet.

"Does this make you late for your appointment at Race Point, too?" Rob said, nervous that Ridgeback might need to drive faster than usual.

"We're fine," Ridgeback said.

We're fine so long as the car is in park, Rob thought as he settled into the passenger seat, making sure his seatbelt was securely fastened. He wondered if it was too late to back out.

In any event, he'd brought along a flask full of whiskey that he planned to use liberally on the trip to Provincetown.

"What is it you're doing there?" Rob said as Ridgeback turned the car around.

"Three-point turn."

"I mean at Race Point."

"It's a fluff piece on the lighthouse and the accommodations up there."

"They have accommodations?"

Ridgeback behaved himself for the first part of the trip, but when Route Six opened up to four lanes he hit the gas and pushed the speedometer up to seventy. The speed limit was fifty. When he came up behind a car in the passing lane, he tailgated and honked the horn until the car moved over. It was at these times that Rob scrunched down in his seat and took long slugs from his flask.

"Are you drinking?" Ridgeback said, only noticing the flask now. "What have you got in there?"

"It helps me tolerate your driving," Rob said.

"What's wrong with my driving?"

Ridgeback brought the car to a stop at the light at Race Point Road. There were two cars in front of them and three behind. Rob checked each of them to make sure no one was jumping out in a fit of rage.

"I'm glad you came along, Rob," Ridgeback said. "I want to get your opinion on something." The light changed, and he made the turn toward Race Point. Rob noticed that Ridgeback drove slower when he was talking.

"On what?" Rob said.

"I want to write a book about Danny. The whole thing. From childhood to the Olympics. Is that something you think he'd be okay with?"

There was a car just ahead, but Ridgeback kept a reasonable distance behind. Rob knew it wasn't okay. Even if Danny was interested in a book, Steve Ridgeback wouldn't be the guy to write it. Still, Rob didn't want to anger Ridgeback while he was behind the wheel.

"You'll need to ask him, Steve."

"Well, he's going to say no, isn't he?"

"He's never been much for attention. You want me to talk to him about it?"

"Please. And tell him you think it's a great idea."

"Will I be in it, too?"

"Of course! And Katie."

"What about Dorothy Bradford?"

"I'll leave that for another book. This one's about Danny."

They drove past the Provincetown Airport and arrived at the Race Point Oversand Station a short time later. Ridgeback got out of the car and let some air out of the tires for the ride to the lighthouse.

"That's an awkward name," Rob said. "Oversand Station." He said it twice, accenting different syllables, trying to make it sound more natural. The alcohol was having the desired effect. He stumbled on the s's.

"They made up a new word, didn't they?"

There were two other vehicles in the lot, also having their tire pressures adjusted. These were jeeps, though, and Rob wondered if Ridgeback was sure his Subaru would make it through the sand without getting stuck.

"You don't need a jeep to do this?" Rob said.

"Hell, people take RVs out there. I wouldn't want to drive one of those in the sand, though. Not sure I'd want to drive one on pavement either."

"Certain death," Rob said.

Once Ridgeback was satisfied his tires were sufficiently flattened, he clapped his hands and pointed to the passenger door, signaling Rob that it was time to move out, as if they were on some military maneuver. Ridgeback pulled out of the lot, shifted into a lower gear, and headed into the dunes. The engine roared. Realizing that Ridgeback wasn't able to go more than twenty or thirty miles an hour, and feeling pleasantly drunk, Rob relaxed and enjoyed the gentle rocking motion of the car as it bounced its way across the rutted sand road on its mushy tires. A small commuter plane appeared in the distance, looking for a time as though it might land on top of the Subaru, until it nudged to the right and touched down on the single runway at the airport.

"Now we're a dune buggy!" Ridgeback shouted. He didn't need to shout, but he was clearly experiencing some sort of Oversand adrenaline rush. He banged his hand on the steering wheel, and Rob was reminded of the way his online cycling instructors would bang their hands on the handlebars to make everyone pedal faster.

Ridgeback was, in fact, going faster now, and even though there weren't any cars in front of him, Rob thought it might be a good idea to keep Ridgeback's mind, and his foot, off the accelerator.

"I ran into your old buddy, Tim Desmond, this morning," Rob said.

"I haven't heard much about him lately. Used to be, a day didn't go by that his name wasn't in the paper. Thanks to me, of course." Ridgeback had covered Desmond's battle with the town over the construction of his house and the subsequent drug bust. Ridgeback and Desmond did not like each other in the least. Desmond, incensed about the *Cape Cod Gazette*'s relentlessly negative coverage, once hauled off and punched Ridgeback in the nose. "What's he up to? Anything I can write about?"

"He told me he's seen Sammy Boland around the house. I think he's lost his mind."

"Wouldn't surprise me a bit," Ridgeback said. "Him losing his mind, I mean. Why would Boland come back to the house?"

"Desmond thinks he's looking for revenge."

"For what?"

"Calling the police, I guess."

"Desmond didn't call the police. He didn't know anything about the drugs until they raided his house."

"Like I said, he's losing his mind."

"Maybe I'll pay him a visit. See what's going on."

"Call first. He's got a gun."

Before long, the lighthouse was visible in the distance, perched atop a hill. Ridgeback told Rob what he knew about the history of the place. The original lighthouse was built in 1808 and was replaced in 1876 with the current cast iron structure. Two keeper's houses sat on either side of the lighthouse. Each of the homes was available for rent during the summer season. One building was a white clapboard A-frame that looked very much like a residence. The other building was a squat, one-story brick structure that looked more like a rural post office than anyplace someone might live.

A very congenial woman from the Cape Cod Chapter of the American Lighthouse Foundation greeted Ridgeback. Rob went along for the tour of the lighthouse but decided to skip the keeper's houses after nearly stumbling down the lighthouse steps.

"You want to take the car onto the beach?" Ridgeback said.

"You don't want me driving your car right now," Rob said. He didn't want to be responsible for getting it stuck in the sand or driving it into the sea. "I'll walk."

The beach was rutted with vehicle tracks. There were no homes on this part of the Cape, and unless you were prepared to hike three or more miles, the only way to get here on land was by four-wheel-drive vehicle. Rob walked south onto the sandy spit that ran between the bay and Hatches Harbor. Two kite surfers were in the harbor, racing along the shoreline, their brightly-colored kites swollen with wind. He plopped down in the sand and watched them for a while, wondering how they kept from being plucked out of the water and launched into the dunes. Two women sat on the hood of a jeep and watched, too—kite-surfing groupies.

The water was a bit rougher in the bay. This was the point where the Atlantic swept around the tip of the Cape and collided with the warmer water in the bay, dragging along seaweed, buoys, and seal remains and depositing them on the bay beaches.

Rob finished the last of the whiskey in his flask and took off his shoes. He considered stripping down to his underwear and going for a swim, but the kite-surfing groupies looked a lot closer now—had they moved?—and one of them had a pair of binoculars pointed in his direction. Rob waved. The woman lowered her binoculars and said something to the other woman. Rob noticed there were now three kite surfers on the water. Or was it four?

He decided to take off his shirt, then got up slowly and walked down to the water. Before he got there, he noticed a man further up the beach lying on his stomach, right at the shoreline. He thought it was a body at first, swept onto the beach along with the seal remains and seaweed, but then noticed that the man, who wore only a bathing suit, was pointing a camera toward a group of birds bobbing in the waves.

Rob squinted, wishing he had his own binoculars. Besides taking pictures of women in rowboats, Sammy Boland also photographed shore birds. Was this him? Rob thought it improbable that he would stumble on the fugitive two days after Danny had, particularly here in such a remote section of the Outer Cape. He took a few more steps and nearly tripped over a piece of driftwood.

"Son of a bitch!" Rob yelled, kicking at the driftwood with his other foot.

The man looked in Rob's direction and then stood up. Rob collapsed in the sand and grabbed at his foot like he'd stepped on a landmine. There was no blood, though, and the pain was tolerable, thanks in part to the whiskey. Rob crab-walked to the water and stuck his foot in, along with most of his leg. He looked up and saw the man hurrying off toward the dunes.

Rob fumbled for his cell phone, thankfully still dry, and called Steve Ridgeback. "I saw a guy on the beach who was taking pictures of birds," Rob said. "I thought he could have been Sammy Boland, but I'm not sure."

A few minutes later, the Subaru roared onto the beach. Ridgeback drove the car right up to where Rob was sitting.

"Where is he?" Ridgeback said, jumping out of the car. "Why are you sitting in the water?"

"He ran off. That way."

"How far could he have gotten? You didn't follow him?"

"I hurt my ankle."

"Why aren't you wearing a shirt? Are you sure it was Boland? You've had a lot to drink, you know."

Ridgeback went back to the car and fetched a pair of binoculars. He scanned the beach. "I don't see anybody," he said. "There's no chair or blanket. No vehicle. Where did he come from?"

"Maybe he's staying at the lighthouse?" Rob said.

Rob and Ridgeback drove back to the keeper's house to ask about the guest list. There were no single white males staying in either of the houses. In fact, there were no males at all. A group of women had rented both houses for a reunion of some kind.

They had all driven out to the beach for the day, according to the property manager. Rob and Ridgeback drove around the property and along the access road, but found no one. Then they went back to the beach to look for the women. They weren't hard to find. There were twelve of them, sitting in beach chairs and drinking beer. Most of them were topless.

"That's not something you see every day," Ridgeback said.

Rob didn't want anything to do with a group of half-naked women, but Ridgeback had no problem walking right up to them. The women scrambled to hide their breasts and their beers as Ridgeback approached, thinking he might be a park ranger. Technically, alcohol wasn't allowed on the National Seashore beaches. Neither was nudity.

"They didn't see anyone," Ridgeback said after a quick exchange with the women. "But I don't think they were in the mood to talk to me."

"Let's go," Rob said. "It's too hot out here anyway."

"I'm going to walk along the dunes first. Look for footprints," Ridgeback said.

Rob grimaced, feeling trapped. Nothing good ever came from getting in a car with Steve Ridgeback. He thought about walking back to the Oversand parking lot and calling a cab, but that would take an hour of trudging through hot sand with no water and a bad foot.

Rob sat down at the base of the dune and watched a group of seals bobbing in the waves, scanning the shore as though looking for a place to sunbathe. Out of the corner of his eye, he noticed something moving further down the beach, in the opposite direction from where Ridgeback had gone. He turned his head and saw what looked like a dog emerging from the dunes. The animal, gaunt and gray, its nose close to the sand, trotted across the beach toward the water. There, rolling in the surf, were the remains of a seal carcass. Rob realized that what he was looking at was not a dog, but a coyote. He had seen a few coyotes before, some in his own back yard, but none as menacing-looking as this one. The animal sniffed at what remained of the seal carcass and then looked up and stared directly at Rob. "Oh shit," he mumbled, and thought about leaving the beach quickly. He chose to remain still, though, and averted his eyes so as not to be appear threatening. The animal looked in the opposite direction, literally making sure the coast was clear, and then bit into one end of the carcass and yanked hard, pulling the seal clear of the surf and onto the beach. After another quick glance in Rob's direction, the coyote went about ripping a large chunk of flesh from the carcass, emitting a low growl in the process. Once the flesh came free, the coyote turned back toward Rob as if to show him the spoils and then scampered back into the dunes. Rob got up and walked quickly to the

Subaru. He got inside, both for the shade and the protection, and waited for Ridgeback to return. He did not have to wait long. Ridgeback broke off his search half an hour later.

CHAPTER SIX

Sluiceways and Wolfhounds

That night, Katie was startled from sleep by yet another dream of the drowned girls. She shot up from her pillow and screamed, "No!" Rob shot up, too, thinking she was having a panic attack. He had been having his own dark dream about a gilled coyote crawling out of the sea and snatching people off the beach. Katie jumped out of bed and said, "I think I know where it is," then raced out of the bedroom. Rob followed her, relieved she was okay, thinking she meant to hop in the car and drive to wherever "it" was that minute. But instead, she went to the wall map of Wellfleet and Truro that hung in the living room and turned on a lamp.

"What are you doing?" Rob said.

"Here," Katie said, pointing to a spot on the map. Rob looked closer. Her finger was on a thin strip of land that separated two Wellfleet ponds. "This is where they were."

"Who?"

"The girls in my dream. They must have drowned in one of these ponds."

"How do you know that?"

"I saw the sluiceway in my dream."

Rob looked closer. "There's a sluiceway?"

"Between Gull Pond and Higgins Pond. A small channel of water." Katie stepped back from the map; her eyes were still glassy from sleep. "The trees weren't there. It was all open. I was standing on a hillside and could see the two ponds and a third smaller one in the distance."

Rob looked at the map. The third pond was Williams. The three of them were laid out in order of size, like a flattened snowman.

"Then I saw the girls in the water struggling to get to shore. They were screaming." She shivered.

"Which pond were they in?"

"I'm not sure. I wasn't on the hillside anymore. I was on the shore. It was awful. They couldn't swim. What were they doing out there?"

"I guess Dorothy is going to drive over there?" he said. "You want me to come along?"

Katie nodded and nuzzled her face into Rob's chest.

"Can we wait until it's light out?"

They went back to bed, but Rob started hearing odd noises from the basement, which perhaps weren't odd at all. After his visit with Tim Desmond and the possible sighting of Sammy Boland at Race Point, Rob was experiencing a little paranoia of his own. He went to the basement and made a thorough inspection, checking to see that the exterior door was locked.

The basement was generally cooler than the rest of the house, but Rob felt a chill that made him wish he had put on some clothes. He stood barefoot on the concrete floor and listened to the boiler belch exhaust gas into the outside vent, trying to decide if that was the noise he had been hearing. He turned to go back upstairs and then saw two dead mice lying on the floor. They were side by side, facing in the same direction, neatly laid out, like they were on sale at some Chinese meat market. It seemed odd that two mice would literally drop dead in their tracks at the same time.

"Are those mice?" Katie had come downstairs to see what was going on.

"They were," Rob said. "Must have gotten into the rat poison. I don't know why they're in the middle of the floor, though. It's like someone put them there."

Katie took a closer look. Then she went to the exterior door to make sure it was locked.

"I already checked," Rob said. "No one was down here."

"Do we need to worry about Sammy Boland?" she said. "I mean, it seems like he's stalking our family, doesn't it? First Danny, then you."

"I don't think the guy I saw was Boland. Danny's not sure either. But even if it was Boland, why would he stalk us? We had nothing to do with his drug business."

"Tim Desmond didn't either."

"Tim Desmond is nuts. Boland may be back in Truro, but he's not breaking into people's homes and leaving dead mice on the floor."

"What is he doing, then?"

"Taking pictures of birds, living in the woods? I don't know." Rob put on a pair of work gloves and scooped the mice into a plastic bag. "They'll find him soon enough, Kay. He doesn't seem to care about staying out of sight anymore. And now the Van Winkle bourbon guy is looking for him, too. They'll get him."

◆ ◆

The next morning, Helen Schantz wandered into the Crosleys' yard and stared up at the roof. Rob saw her from the kitchen window. There was a time when Helen Schantz would never have come into their yard, but now that she was a pothead, boundaries no longer seemed to concern her. Rob went outside and said hello, but Helen Schantz wouldn't take her eyes off of whatever it was she was focused on. She looked puzzled, and stoned, too, of course.

"You've got an owl on your roof," she said.

"Two of them," Rob said. "There's one on the other side."

Helen looked at the bird even harder. "It doesn't move," she said. "Is it sleeping?"

"It's plastic."

"Don't be ridiculous."

"It's a decoy, Helen. Scares the woodpeckers away."

"What's wrong with the woodpeckers?"

Rob explained about the gutters, then realized there hadn't been any jackhammering that morning. The owls had done their job!

"How did it get up there?"

"Katie put it there."

"How long will it be staying?"

"You know, I'm not sure. Katie will know."

"Do you have to feed it?"

"It's plastic."

"I can see it from my house. I wasn't sure what it was at first. Maybe a hawk."

"How about some coffee, Helen?"

Helen Schantz didn't answer, which was just as well since Rob didn't want to bring her coffee anyway. She turned to walk back to her house but kept her eyes on the owl the whole way, as if worried the thing might swoop down and pluck her eyes out.

"Was that Helen?" Katie said, coming outside.

"She thought our owl was real. She might still think it's real."

"Did you notice? No woodpeckers this morning."

"I know," Rob said, smacking his arm, his hand coming away with blood. "Can we find something to scare away the mosquitoes, too?"

◆ ◆

There were a few cars in the Gull Pond parking lot when Rob and Katie arrived. The air temperature was fine for swimming, but Rob expected the pond water to be pretty cold, not yet fully released from winter's frigid grasp. The people who were here today, though, weren't the types to splash around in plastic inner tubes. These were serious swimmers, people who tied buoys to their waists and did full laps around the pond.

Gull Pond was the largest of the Wellfleet kettle ponds, nearly a mile and a half in circumference. During the summer months, all forms of sailboats, windsurfers, paddle boards, and kayaks carved up the water. Rob and Katie were never there to see them, though. Permits were required to park in the lot during the summer. Rob wasn't much of a swimmer, anyway. And if he ever needed to swim, he'd swim in the bay.

They walked north along School House Hill Road and quickly lost sight of the pond. The map showed a road a half mile away that branched off to the right and led to the sluiceway between Gull and Higgins ponds. Katie figured this spot might trigger something in her memories since she had seen it so clearly in her dream.

Katie maintained a brisk pace, as she typically did when hiking, and Rob kept up. He had put on his jeans, boots, and long-sleeved flannel shirt again, both for the mosquitoes and the poison ivy. Katie wouldn't let him wear the balaclava. "People lock their doors and call the police when you wear that thing," she said. "You're not going to get poison ivy on your face."

"If I get poison ivy on my hands and then touch my face, I will," he said.

"Don't touch your face."

They came to the right-hand turn, and in a matter of minutes, they could see water on either side of them.

"None of these trees were here," Katie said. "And there was a house back there somewhere." She pointed in the direction from which they had come.

Soon they came to the sluiceway. Rob had expected something more substantial, something you could drive a boat through, but there was barely six inches of water running between the two ponds. Even if someone was in a kayak, they'd have to get out and drag the thing from one pond to the next.

"Not much of a sluice," he said, stepping across the floodgate. "What do you call this thing, an isthmus?"

Katie ignored her husband and stood on the shore facing Gull Pond, trying to imagine two girls struggling to keep their heads above water. A gentle breeze rustled through the scrub pines—the ones that weren't there in her dream.

"You getting anything?" Rob said.

"It's so peaceful here. I can't imagine anything bad happening."

Rob turned and walked through the tree-lined sluiceway to Higgins Pond. Higgins was maybe half the size of Gull Pond. And like Gull there were barely any houses to be seen along the shoreline, thanks again to the National Seashore.

It was then that Rob noticed the man standing in the water lilies off to the right. At the man's side was a giant dog that looked like something out of a post-apocalyptic fantasy night-mare, the kind where all living things have been genetically altered by the nuclear fallout. The dog stood three feet tall at the shoulders and probably weighed as much as Rob did. It looked perfectly capable of taking him down and ripping out a jugular vein.

"Katie!" Rob called, sure he was looking at one of her apparitions. Perhaps the dog had chased those poor girls into the water and dragged them to the bottom. The man said hello and waved. He remained at ease as his enormous dog began lumbering through the water toward the sluice. Rob froze and then had the urge to run.

"She's very friendly!" the man said, emphasizing the word 'friendly' in the way dog owners do when their pets are preparing to mount dinner guests.

Rob drew his arms in tightly and tried to look like a tree or a pole, something the dog would rather pee on than dismember. The dog arrived and shoved his snout into Rob's stomach. The dog's head was the size of a watermelon, its hair matted down by a mix of pond water and drool.

"Molly!" the man called. The dog turned and galloped back to its owner, kicking up vast amounts of pond water.

"That's some dog," Katie said, hopping over the sluiceway.

"Are you sure it's a dog?" Rob said.

"Sorry about that," the man said. He waded over with the dog, whose name was apparently Molly. This didn't strike Rob as being the right name for this type of animal. She needed to be called Brunhilda or Irmgard. Possibly both.

"What kind of dog is that?" Rob said.

"Irish Wolfhound," the man said. "Dog of war. Originally bred to drag men off horses and chariots. It's a good thing you weren't on a horse."

"I've never seen a dog that big," Katie said.

"Sorry she's not on a leash," the man said. Molly was nuzzling up against Katie now. "They don't do any good anyway. The last time I had Molly on a leash, she dislocated my shoulder. It wasn't her fault. She saw a squirrel. I hope you guys like dogs."

Rob told the man about Sidney and that they were in the market for a new dog.

"Don't get one of these," the man said. "Unless you live on a moor. You don't live on a moor, do you?"

"We live in Truro."

"Well, they'll keep the coyotes and turkeys out of your yard. Molly once took down a turkey and brought it into the house. She was very proud of herself."

"I think we'll go for something smaller," Rob said.

"Do you live around here?" Katie said.

"I do. Been here my whole life," the man said. "Except for when I have to work. Then I'm in New York. I'm not sure about New York anymore. Or work for that matter."

Rob thought the man might be a kindred spirit. But then, he used to think Tim Desmond was a kindred spirit, too. Certainly, there were people who could be interesting at first, only later to have their tediousness bubble to the surface like methane gas from a landfill. The man wore a bright red bathing suit and a wetsuit jacket. His giant dog, Molly, who was now sitting quietly next to Katie, had a bright red collar that matched the man's bathing suit. Rob decided the man had potential. If he invited them back to the house for a drink, Rob would say yes, so long as Molly remained outside.

"I wonder if you could help us out," Katie said, petting Molly, who had decided to lie down in the sluice, effectively creating a dam between the two ponds. Rob thought Katie was going to tell the stranger about her nightmares, but she reframed the story into a more accessible form. "I remember coming here to the sluiceway when I was a kid," she said. "The pines weren't so tall, and I remember a cottage somewhere close by. I'm wondering if it's still here."

"That's Gull Cottage you're thinking of," the man said. "Back that way, a few hundred yards."

"Do you know when it was built?"

"Eighteenth century, by a man named Josiah Higgins."

"They named the pond after him?" Rob said.

"Two of his children, actually. It used to be called Newcomb Pond."

"What happened to the children?" Katie said. All at once, she saw the scene play out in front of her: the two girls thrashing in the middle of the pond, struggling to get to the shore, their screams echoing across the pond.

"They drowned," the man said. "Are you all right? You look like you've seen a ghost."

Molly got up, and the dammed water gushed through the sluiceway into Higgins Pond. The dog lifted her massive paw and placed it on Katie's arm as if to comfort her.

"Oh, how awful," Katie said.

"Were they girls?" Rob said.

"Don't know," the man said. "Sorry if I upset you."

"Don't be silly," Katie said, regaining her composure. "I was the one who asked."

Rob and Katie said goodbye to the man, who said he needed to get Molly out of the pond before she took her afternoon dump.

"You can't imagine the size of her shits," the man said. "And she'll happily take them in the pond if given the chance. Not a pleasant sight and not good for the water quality. Anyway... Nice meeting you both." Then he and Molly headed back into the water lilies.

Katie sat down in the sand next to the sluice and looked out across Higgins Pond. Twelve thousand years ago, there was a massive block of ice here, left behind by the receding glaciers, burrowing its way into the soil, then melting to create a vast water-filled kettle hole that would eventually take the lives of the two young girls. Rob sat down next to her, disappointed that the man had not invited them for drinks. He was thinking of a Bloody Mary just then—something with a celery stalk and lots of ice. Kettle ice.

"You saw them, didn't you?" Rob said. "The Higgins girls." There was a long strand of dog drool on his pants. He doused it with sand and brushed it off.

"It seemed so real. I heard them screaming for help."

"Maybe you were here when it happened, back in the eighteenth century. Maybe you saw them drowned."

"It doesn't tie in with the other dreams."

"Does it have to?"

"Maybe I was Josiah Higgins' wife. Maybe they were my kids who drowned."

"I'm the only man you ever married, Kay, besides that William Bradford SOB."

Katie sighed. "I sometimes wonder if I would have been better off without Dorothy Bradford," she said.

"No, you wouldn't. You'd be back in the cottage, hiding from me and the rest of the world. Dorothy Bradford gave me my wife back."

Katie put her hand on Rob's and squeezed it. "You're absolutely my favorite husband," she said.

CHAPTER SEVEN

Shaved Legs
and Flesh Wounds

Fat Agnes was taking an early morning walk. She had tried to get the other girls to come along, but they refused to get out of bed. This was the third day in a row she'd gone walking before breakfast. She found that exercise put her in a positive frame of mind for the rest of the day. And she liked the way the muscles in her legs ached when she got back to the house. She'd sit on the floor of the living room and stretch her legs while the other girls, having finally dragged themselves out of bed, drank coffee and waited for the grogginess of sleep to clear.

Unlike the previous mornings, when she had gone down to the beach, she decided to walk on the road today. She pumped her arms and experimented with her stride, sometimes taking long steps and sometimes shorter, quicker ones. She had her phone in her jacket pocket but wasn't listening to music. No earphones for Fat Agnes. She preferred to listen to her breathing instead. During her illness, she ignored the signals from her body—the alarms that went off from a lack of nutrition. Now she paid close attention to how her body responded to different activities and didn't want to be distracted from them.

She walked on the right side of the road, looking over her shoulder when cars came up behind her. They all gave her a wide berth. Occasionally, she would encounter other walkers on her side of the road, heading in the opposite direction. She thought this was curious. Why would they go against traffic? Then a runner went by, also against traffic. He moved gracefully and was by her so quickly that she almost didn't recognize him. She turned to see Danny Crosley slowing down and coming back to her.

"You're one of the Agnes's, right?" he said, now jogging alongside. Agnes quickened her pace for his benefit. She noticed his legs were shaved. The muscles in his calves stood out like carved marble.

"That's right," she said, now looking down at her own calves, which barely stood out at all. Her legs were so tiny that her sneakers looked like clown shoes. The bulimia had shrunk her entire body except for her head, her hands, and her clownish feet. She had retained her good looks, though. Even as her body wasted away, people, men and women alike, continued to be entranced by her wide-set eyes and high cheekbones.

"You're a walker?" he said.

"Only for three days."

"Most people don't even walk for one day. Good for you, Agnes."

"You can call me Kristin," she said self-consciously. "I only use Agnes in the house."

"My mom talks about you. She thinks you're doing really well."

"Ha!" she said. She had a cute guttural laugh that sounded like she intended to clear her throat but decided to toss off a chuckle instead. "Your mom's a very wise person."

"Well, she's been around a long time, right?"

Kristin smiled. The road tipped uphill, and she shortened her strides. "Four hundred years, is it?"

"What do you think of that stuff?" he said. "Does the Dorothy Bradford story work for you?"

"There's something about getting out of your body for a while," she said. "Some of the pressure comes off when I'm Agnes. Agnes doesn't think about her weight."

"I get that. My mom was terrified of other people until she became Dorothy."

"Some people think she really is Dorothy."

"Do you?"

"I don't not believe it," she said. "How's that?" She was breathing heavier now. She slowed a bit. "Why do some people walk on the right side of the road and others on the left? Which one is right? I mean correct?"

"Left," Danny said. "You always want to be facing traffic."

"Because?"

"Because of cell phones. You want to see the cars coming toward you so you can get out of the way if the driver isn't paying attention."

"I guess that makes sense." She checked behind her and moved to the left side of the road. Danny followed. She had met him once before, when she first arrived at the Dorothy Bradford House. He was helping his mother cut down a dead tree. They stopped what they were doing and came over to welcome her. She had no idea he was an Olympic star. Why would she? When he won his gold medal the previous summer, she was lying in a hospital bed recovering from a heroin overdose.

"You ever think about running?" he said. He was walking now, having abandoned the slow jog. He let her set the pace.

"I don't think my body could handle running," she said.

"You start slowly," he said. "You're already off to a good start, walking a few miles every day."

"And I'm already exhausted."

"Did you eat anything before?"

"No."

"You should. Half a bagel with peanut butter. Maybe some Gatorade."

"I've never been very good with eating."

They turned around, shifting to the other side of the road, and Danny accompanied Kristin on the walk back to the house. He stayed on her right, moving in front of her when a car approached. She asked him what it was like to compete in the Olympics. He said it was an incredible high, then caught himself and apologized for being insensitive. "Poor choice of words," he said. But she didn't mind. She needed to find highs like that.

They were not far from the house when they heard the scream. Danny wanted to sprint ahead, but he stayed with Kristin. He took her hand, and they ran as best they could. Rachel was outside when they arrived. She was a gentle soul, despite her size, but now she looked absolutely livid.

"Son of a bitch," she said, her eyes searching the trees.

"What happened?" Danny said. "Is everyone okay?"

"Who screamed?" Kristin said, huffing and puffing.

"Martha went into the bedroom to get dressed," Rachel said,

also breathing hard. "A man was at the window, staring at her. She screamed, and he ran away. Did you see him?"

"We didn't see anyone," Danny said.

"She knew who it was," Rachel said. "Sammy Boland."

They called the police. Rachel and the two Agnes's huddled around Martha on the back porch, consoling her. Rachel was motherly to all of the residents who came through the Bradford House, but she was particularly protective of Martha. Rachel was drawn to the most vulnerable of the women who stayed at the house, and Martha was certainly that. An only child whose parents both worked long hours, Martha became a loner at a young age. She developed physically much earlier than her classmates at school and was teased relentlessly because of it. She wore loose-fitting sweatshirts to hide her breasts and was always careful not to draw attention to herself. By the time she was in the eighth grade, she had fallen in with a group of out-liers—girls like her who found social interaction painful. She was introduced to marijuana and found that smoking the stuff made it easier to fit in. She became more popular at school and soon abandoned the sweatshirts for tight-fitting clothes that showed off her physical attributes. She fully blossomed in high school. No longer a loner, she fell in with older boys who intro-duced her to new forms of pleasure. One of them introduced her to heroin. She became an addict. By the time she reached her senior year, she had overdosed twice. The second time, it nearly killed her.

Rob and Katie arrived back at the house from their trip to Gull Pond. Don Hill and two officers arrived soon after. Mike Van Winkle was there, too, though nobody could figure out how he had gotten the news that Boland was at the Dorothy Bradford House. Not to be outdone, Steve Ridgeback joined the crowd a short time later. News on the Outer Cape traveled fast.

"Are you sure it was Boland?" Don Hill asked Martha, who had come outside with Rachel. "We've been getting a lot of calls lately from people who think they've seen him."

"I'm sure," Martha said.

"You know him?"

"He used to sell me dope," she said, emphasizing *used to*. "I think Fat Agnes bought from him, too."

"Fat Agnes?"

"Kristin," Rachel said. She gave Don Hill all the girls' real names, and he wrote them down. So did Mike Van Winkle. So did Steve Ridgeback.

"So Fat Agnes is Kristin Harris, and Martha, your real name is Haley Keyes?"

Haley, alias Martha, nodded.

"Do you have any idea why he was here? Was he looking to sell drugs?"

"I don't take them anymore," Martha said nervously, wary of the inspector's scrutiny.

"I'm not sure how he'd know the identity of any of the girls here," Katie said.

"But you do have recovering addicts here."

"Yes. We do."

Don Hill wrote down a few more notes. "Mind if I get a look inside the house?" he said. "Just need to see that bedroom window."

"Lady Agnes is on the porch," Rachel said. "She should be all right."

"What's wrong with Lady Agnes?" Ridgeback said.

"I'll take you inside, Inspector," Katie said, "but let's have everyone else stay out here, if that's all right." She led Don Hill into the house. Martha went with them. Mike Van Winkle seemed perturbed that he had not been allowed to go in, too.

"Seems like everyone here has seen Boland now except for me," Van Winkle said.

"I haven't seen him yet," Ridgeback said, giving Rob a sideways glance.

"I haven't either," Rob said. "Or at least I don't think I have."

"What does that mean?" Van Winkle said.

"I saw someone at Race Point yesterday who looked like Boland, but I don't think it was him."

"I'd like to hear more about that."

"What about his dad?" Ridgeback said, eyeing Van Winkle.

"What about him?" Van Winkle said.

"Well, if Sammy's really back on the Cape, you'd think he would have stopped by to see his dad at some point. Though if he did, I guess the old man wouldn't need you anymore."

Van Winkle smiled, knowing that Ridgeback was trying to get him to admit that he was working for Jerry Boland. "I assume you've already asked Jerry that question," he said.

"Of course!"

"And?"

"Hasn't seen him. Doesn't believe any of the stories, either."

"Tim Desmond says he's seen him at his house," Rob said.

"Really?" Van Winkle said. "Maybe I need to go over there again. He doesn't answer the door or his phone."

"Keep your head down," Rob said. "Tim's not a fan of investigators."

"Tell me about it," Ridgeback said, a victim of Tim Desmond's right hook. He finished scribbling in his notebook and then turned his attention to Danny, thinking this might be a good time to bring up his book idea. "How are you doing, Danny?" he said.

"I haven't talked to him yet," Rob said, sensing what Ridgeback had in mind.

"Talked to me about what?" Danny said.

"Steve wants to write a book about you. A biography."

"That's not going to happen," Danny said, glaring at Ridgeback.

"Well, I can write the book with or without your cooperation," Ridgeback said. "But I'd rather have your involvement. The book won't be anywhere near as good without it."

"He talked to you about this?" Danny said to Rob.

"He asked me how I thought you'd react. It wasn't hard to guess."

"If you like, we can co-author the book and turn it into an autobiography," Ridgeback said. "I'm pretty sure I can get a nice advance from a publisher." Ridgeback started throwing out six-figure numbers. He had no idea how much a publisher would pay.

"No thanks," Danny said.

"You should think about it for that kind of money," Rob said.

Don Hill came back outside with Katie and briefed Van Winkle and Ridgeback on what he had learned, which was very little. No one seemed to have any idea why Sammy Boland would have come to the Dorothy Bradford House.

"You think he might have been looking for Dorothy Bradford?" Van Winkle said.

"Why?" Rob said.

"He spent several days looking for her two years ago."

"You should go up to the house and make sure he didn't try to get in there," Katie said. "We've been out most of the morning."

Don Hill sent the officers off to look for Boland, then followed Rob, Ridgeback, and Van Winkle up to the house. Danny hung back with his mother, who wanted to stay at the Bradford House to help calm Rachel and the girls after their ordeal.

"Are you okay?" he asked his mother. "You look a little frazzled."

Katie told him about the trip to the sluiceway and her visions of the drowned girls in Higgins Pond. "I feel like I might have been there when it happened," she said.

This was the reason Danny didn't want Steve Ridgeback to write a book about him. The book would be about his mother's so-called four-hundred-year life as much as it would be about him and his running. People would think Katie Crosley was out of her mind.

"Do me a favor and don't repeat that in front of Ridgeback," he said. "He'll make it a front-page story."

"Rob told me he wants to write a book about you."

"It seems like everybody knew about this book except me."

"You should let him. He really admires you."

"He'd write about you, too, Mom. And Dorothy Bradford."

Katie waved her hand dismissively. "He's already written plenty about me and Dorothy," she said. "Listen, I'm going inside to be with the girls. You had a good run?"

Danny nodded. "Tell Kristin I enjoyed our walk."

"You walked with her?"

"For a while."

Katie smiled and squeezed her son's arm. "That was sweet of you."

"Don't make it sound like I was doing her a favor."

"Of course not. Do you want me to have her come back outside?"

Danny rolled his eyes and headed back to his apartment over the garage.

◆ ◆

Rob sat alone on the beach. Katie wouldn't come with him because she didn't want to leave the Bradford House. She wanted the girls to know they were safe there. She planned to spend the night as well.

There was no evidence that Boland had gone to Rob and Katie's house or that he had tried to get inside. It made no sense that he would have. As much as Don Hill hated to speculate, he could only think that Boland had come to the Bradford House looking for Maggie Mason, who had been one of his biggest clients. But Maggie Mason was still behind bars.

Rob was reading a copy of the *Cape Cod Gazette*. It carried an article by Steve Ridgeback about Sammy Boland's resurfacing on the Outer Cape. There was a picture of Boland with a phone number to call if anyone saw him. Rob was gratified to see that neither he nor Danny was mentioned by name in the article. This was surprising. Ridgeback was always quick to drop names. He supposed that Ridgeback was being careful not to piss off any of the Crosleys, Danny in particular, so as not to damage his chances of writing a book.

Rob had brought a towel with him, but he had no intention of going in the water. The bay was still freezing, even though the air temperature was pushing into the seventies. The sand was warm, though, and Rob had thoughts of spreading his towel and lying down on it. Before he could, his cell phone rang. It was Steve Ridgeback.

"Are you ready for this?" Ridgeback said.

"Ready for what?"

"You'll never guess."

"I don't want to guess."

"Tim Desmond shot Mike Van Winkle."

"What?"

"After he left the Bradford House this morning, Van Winkle went over to Desmond's house to talk to him about Boland. No sooner did he set foot on the property than Desmond winged him with a handgun."

"Jesus. Were you there?"

"Of course! I got there a few minutes later. I wanted to hear what Desmond had to say."

"Is he okay?"

"Just a flesh wound. When I got there, Desmond was wrapping up Van Winkle's arm."

"He thought Van Winkle was Boland."

"We heard all about it. I've never seen Desmond talk so much about anything. I guess he felt guilty about shooting the guy, so he told him everything."

"Nobody called the police or an ambulance?"

"Van Winkle said not to bother. The bullet just grazed his arm. Apparently, it wasn't the first time he's been shot."

"But you can't just shoot someone who comes onto your property, can you?"

"Only in self-defense. Doesn't matter. Van Winkle didn't want to press charges. He only wanted to hear about Boland."

"And what about you? Aren't you going to write about the shooting?"

"I wanted to hear about Boland, too. Desmond said he'd let me stay and listen if I swore not to write anything about the shooting. And Van Winkle said he'd deny it anyway."

A dog barked, and Rob saw a woman and her dog walking toward him. The dog was a female Labrador Retriever with a beautiful chocolate coat. The dog came right up to Rob and put one of her damp paws on his leg.

"What is it, girl?" Rob said.

"What girl?" Ridgeback said.

Rob told Ridgeback he'd call him back and ended the call. The dog sat up straighter and made a soft whimpering noise that reminded Rob of the noises Sidney would make when he wanted attention.

"Sorry," the woman said, catching up with her dog. "Brie wants you to be her friend." The woman had on a large t-shirt that fell down to her thighs. Her long legs were bare, and Rob assumed she had a bathing suit on under the shirt.

"Beautiful dog," Rob said, petting Brie between her ears. "How old?"

"She's fourteen months and happy to be out of the car."

"Where are you coming from?"

"New York."

"City?"

"Brooklyn."

"You like it there?"

"I do, but I'm moving to London next month." The woman produced a tennis ball from somewhere under her t-shirt and tossed it in the bay. Brie took off before the ball hit the water. "Unfortunately, I can't take Brie with me." The dog snapped at the water like she was trying to catch a fish. Eventually the ball settled in her mouth, and she turned and paddled back to shore.

"What are you going to do with her?"

"I'm visiting friends here who I'm hoping will take her."

"Well, if they don't want her, I'll take her. I need a dog." Rob was only half kidding, or maybe not kidding at all. He had a sudden urge to offer the woman money if she'd agree to sell him the dog on the spot, like Brie was the last living dog on the planet.

"Are you looking for a lab?"

Rob told the woman about Sidney, who was not a lab but had lived to be sixteen. He included this part to convince the woman of his exceptional dog-owning qualifications. He had no idea who the woman's friends were, but they couldn't possibly be as capable of caring for a dog as he was. He gave the woman his number and told her to call if she wanted to bring the dog by the house.

"Well, it's nice to have a back-up plan," she said. "I'm not sure my friends really want a dog. I think they like the idea of having a dog. But they didn't want to come walk her. That bothered me." Her voice trailed off, and Rob felt certain she was ready to make other arrangements for Brie. "I'll call you. Maybe tomorrow?"

The woman, whose name was Natalie, tossed the ball into the water again, and Brie gave chase. Sidney had not been a swimmer. Rob once threw a ball in the water, and the dog sat down and watched the ball drift off into the bay.

"Any time," Rob said. "I live at the top of the dune there. Brie can come down to the water every day."

"You'll have to keep her ears dry. Labs get ear infections."

"Not a problem."

"Will she be alone in the house during the day?"

"No. I don't work. I mean, I'm mostly retired. My wife works from the house. We're here all the time. Our son lives here, too. Brie will have plenty of company."

Natalie nodded and smiled, eyeing Rob carefully now, as if looking for any signs of character flaws. Rob was glad he was wearing a baseball cap. He hadn't combed his hair in a week.

"I'm going to call you," she said.

CHAPTER EIGHT

Strawberries and Ziploc Bags

After a quiet but restless night at the Bradford House, Katie came home. She and Rachel had had a good conversation with the residents about Sammy Boland. Lady Agnes didn't know Boland, since she was never a drug user. Fat Agnes and Martha, on the other hand, had both bought heroin from Boland on a regular basis. Both of them had overdosed on Boland-supplied narcotics, but in neither case was Boland around when the overdoses occurred. Boland never shot up with the girls. He wasn't a user. Both girls were quiet at first when Katie asked if either of them had had any type of relationship with Boland that went beyond drugs.

"Strictly business," Fat Agnes said eventually, her eyes cast downward. Katie could tell Sammy Boland was a painful subject for the woman, a part of her past she was trying to erase from her memory.

"Business," Martha said sheepishly. "Though sometimes I got the impression he wanted more from me than just the cash."

"Why?"

Martha shrugged. "The way he looked at me. The things he said."

"Like?"

"Once he said that we could be together if I ever cleaned myself up."

Rachel nodded. "So you think he came here to see how you were doing? To see if you had cleaned yourself up?"

"Maybe."

That night, Katie and Rachel slept in shifts. A Truro police cruiser drove by the house twice over the course of the night. At daybreak, Katie got up and went home. As she neared the front door, she began to feel an old and unexpected anxiety building inside of her, to the point where she didn't know if she'd be able to control it. She closed her eyes and said "Dorothy Bradford" out loud, and she kept saying it until the anxiety passed. It wasn't a full-on panic attack, but it was a panic attack nonetheless—something she hadn't experienced in two years. She worried that her dreams were the cause and that she'd need to gain a fuller understanding of what they meant if she was to keep the anxiety at bay. "Dorothy's home," she said as she opened the door and stepped inside.

She decided she needed the day to herself—a day of seclusion. It was a reliable tool she could always fall back on when the world started spinning too quickly. While Rob slept, she washed up, then put on shorts and a t-shirt. She packed her daypack with a towel, some food, and water. She left a note for Rob so he wouldn't worry that she'd run off, though that's exactly what she was doing. Only for the day, though. Long enough to get herself back in order and perhaps make some sense of the dreams.

To that end, there was one more thing she considered bringing along. She went downstairs to her workshop and opened the middle drawer in the tool cabinet. There were three hardware trays in the drawer, and she lifted the middle tray and pulled out a manila envelope. Inside the envelope was a sheet of blotter paper. The paper was perforated into half-inch squares. Each square contained an image of a bright red strawberry.

She'd been given the envelope by one of the Bradford Society members, a woman named Connie McPherson, one week after Maggie Mason was arrested. "What is it?" Katie had asked, but Connie McPherson didn't know. The envelope had been sealed, and Maggie's instructions were that Connie should give the envelope to Dorothy Bradford if anything happened to Maggie. At the time, Connie assumed that "anything" meant Maggie's death, but Connie didn't like holding onto the mysterious envelope, especially after learning why Maggie had been arrested, so she took the opportunity to unburden herself.

There was a letter in the envelope. Katie read it after Connie McPherson hurried off, relieved of her responsibility. The letter said,

Dear Dorothy,

If your fears return and you find it difficult to manage them, use these lysergic acid tabs to help calm your mind and find clarity. Place one tab on your tongue and let it dissolve. Or you can drop it in a mug of beer, if you like. I'm hoping you'll never need to use them, but they're here for you just in case. I've used the tabs in my therapy, and they've proved very effective, particularly in your case. They'll help you to reconnect with Dorothy Bradford. Each tab contains a microdose of acid. It's enough to get you where you need to be, but not so much that you'll have to worry about bad trips or paranoia. Don't take more than one tab at a time. Good luck, and be well.

Katie's first thought, after reading the letter, was to turn the envelope over to the police. She didn't need to end up like

Maggie Mason, sitting in a jail cell. But that would only happen if she shared the tabs with other people or slipped them into their beers. Besides Connie McPherson, no one else ever needed to know about the envelope, and that included Rob, who was the more likely of the two of them to use the tabs recreationally or say something he shouldn't. The tabs had "proved very effective, particularly in your case," Maggie had said in her note, and Katie knew this to be true. Though Katie hadn't been aware at the time, Maggie had started dosing her with LSD from the first time they met, and coupled with becoming Dorothy Bradford, her panic attacks had gradually subsided and then were gone. For this reason she decided to hold on to the tabs. She could always dispose of them later. She hid the envelope in her tool cabinet and promised herself she would only use the tabs if the panic attacks returned. They hadn't until now.

Using a small pair of scissors, Katie cut out one of the tabs, the first one on the sheet, and dropped it into a Ziploc bag. She put the bag in her backpack, then returned the blotter paper and hardware tray to the cabinet.

♦ ♦

Katie walked south on the beach, just beyond the Truro-Wellfleet border, about two miles to a remote stretch where there were no houses or public beaches. She often rowed her boat to this spot, but given her plans for the day, she didn't want the boat nearby. She spread her towel, sat down, and ate some of the food she'd packed. Then she took the strawberry tab out of the Ziploc bag and placed it on her tongue.

After a minute, wondering if she should have brought along a bottle of beer to drop the tab into or maybe just stuck it in her water bottle, she lay down on her towel and watched the large puffy clouds race across the sky. The clouds were a cottony color at first, but after a while, they took on different hues, some red, some blue. Some of them expanded and tumbled over neighboring clouds, like lava pouring out of the mouth of a volcano.

Eventually the clouds started dropping into the bay, one after another. Katie saw a large sailing vessel on the water, sails unfurled, navigating through the fallen clouds. It was the Mayflower heading toward Plymouth as it had the day after Dorothy Bradford had fallen into the bay and been lost to the depths. The ship disappeared and was replaced by a man on a hoverboard. The man had his arms in the air and was yelling at the top of his lungs as he shot across the water at high speeds. He went back and forth at different elevations above the water. Katie watched the hoverboarder in delight until a large seal crawled out of the water and came right up to where she was sitting.

"Hello," Katie said, and patted the seal on its head.

The seal looked at her, wiggled its whiskers, and said, "Hello, Dorothy. It's nice to see you again. Where have you been?"

"Right here," Dorothy said.

"As you should be," the seal said. "Have you seen any sharks?"

"No sharks."

"You'll let me know?"

"Of course."

With that, the seal headed back to the water and swam off.

At various times, though time had become meaningless now, beach walkers wandered past where Katie was sitting. Some of them said hello, and some ignored her. Some looked human, others not so much. A woman wandered by and stopped to look at the sky. She wore leggings but was naked from the waist up. Two antennas protruded from the top of her head. Katie looked up where the woman was looking and saw a circular ship hovering just below the red and blue clouds. The ship made a humming sound, like a blender set on low. Katie wanted the ship to land on the beach, but the sun came out and melted all of it away, hanging low over the bay, casting a runway of shimmering light on the surface of the water.

The sand took on an amber tone, giving up the heat it had collected during the day. The air was still, and the beach was quiet. Nothing floated in or above the water except for the setting sun.

Another group of beach walkers appeared, coming from the south. Two of them were men, and the other three were children. There didn't appear to be anything unusual about these people, no antennas anyway, and Katie wondered if she was coming to the end of her acid trip. As they came closer she smiled at the men, figuring they had arrived for a long weekend and taken their kids to the beach while their wives ran to the store for groceries.

"Hello, Dorothy," the taller man said. She hadn't noticed the long blond hair, now tied in a ponytail. The dark-haired boy was crouching in the sand, playing with a clump of dried seaweed. The other two children were girls, looking very much like sisters, maybe ten or eleven years old. The girls were stunning to look at. They had large, wide-set eyes and long brown hair, and the tips of their noses turned up slightly. They smiled at her, and she felt a shiver rush up her spine and settle in her chest.

"Do you remember us?" the man said. "We met at Corn Hill the other day."

Katie was having a hard time finding words. Earlier in the day, when she was struggling with her anxiety, five strangers might have driven her into a panic. But she wasn't panicking now. She was sealed inside the Ziploc bag with the strawberries.

"Marvelous," the second man said. "She hasn't changed a bit." He was small and skinny and looked unwell, like he had recently been sprung from captivity.

"Yes, I remember you," Katie finally answered the blond man. Had he called her Dorothy? She couldn't remember. "Erik and Dak. It's nice to see you again." She flashed a smile and then returned her attention to the girls.

"I'm Thomas," the skinny man said. "You came to visit me the other day, but I didn't show myself. I was worried about the others who were with you. I didn't want to frighten them."

Katie had no memory of this man. There was nothing remarkable about him, though she was sure she would have remembered him if they had met.

"It's time we formally introduce ourselves," Erik said. "And tell you why we've come to see you." Dak got up from the sand and stood next to Erik, giving the impression that he had rehearsed his part in the presentation. "You've met me and my son, Dak, of course."

"And I'm Thomas Ridley," the mousey man said. He bowed. "I saw you, but as I've said, you didn't see me."

Katie closed her eyes. She saw the tombstone. *M. Thomas Rideey, Jun. 1776*. Her eyelids felt heavy, and she wondered if the visitors would be gone when she opened them.

"And I'm Sarah Higgins, and this is my sister Amy," one of the girls said. The two girls stood close together. Sarah put her arm around her sister.

Katie managed to open her eyes and found that she was

looking directly into the sun. Much of the light had gone out of the sphere, though, and she was able to gauge the distance between its nadir and the horizon. The sun seemed to be dropping abnormally fast. The water beneath it began to sizzle.

"And I'm Dorothy Bradford," Katie said.

"You're known by many names," Erik said.

"Back in our day, you were called Elizabeth Hatch," Thomas Ridley said.

"Mrs. Hatch," Amy Higgins said.

"This can't be news to you," Erik said.

"Why can't it?" Katie said. Her mouth was dry. She would have loved some water, and then remembered she had some in her backpack.

"You were Dorothy Bradford. Then Leah Walker, then Elizabeth Hatch. We lost track of you after that."

"We thought you had finally died," Ridley said.

"But immortals never die," Erik said. "You left Cape Cod."

"For two hundred years," Sarah Higgins said.

"You came back as Katie Crosley," Ridley said.

"And we're glad you returned," Erik said.

"Perhaps your memory is spotty?" Ridley said.

Katie drank from her water bottle and looked at the sky, wondering if the hovercraft would return, along with the half-naked antenna people. "This stuff makes me see things," she said, pulling the empty Ziploc bag out of her backpack and waving it at Erik.

"Don't doubt what you see, Dorothy," Erik said.

"And don't be afraid," Tom Ridley said. "We're not in the business of haunting. We're benevolent spirits."

"There are some who are not," Erik said.

"Which is why we've come to you," Ridley said.

"You're ghosts, all of you?" Katie said. There was a broken clam shell in the sand close to her foot, and she thought about stepping on it to see whether she'd feel any pain. But she'd have to get up to do that and she didn't want to get up. "I have a friend who believes in ghosts. Her name is Elaine. She'd be losing her mind right now."

"We prefer to be called spirits. *Ghost* has such a negative connotation."

"And how is it that you all know me?" Katie said. "Am I a ghost, too?" She rubbed her foot against the jagged edge of the shell and tried to create some sensation.

The Higgins girls giggled. "You're not a ghost," Amy said. "You're a witch!"

"White witch," Ridley said, glaring at Amy.

"A white witch!" Amy said.

"We needed to be sure," Erik said. "It's been so long since any of us have seen you. The dreams were our way of signaling that we needed to meet with you. When you came to see me and Dak on Corn Hill and then went to visit Tom's grave and Newcomb Pond, we knew you were still someone we could count on."

"It's not Newcomb Pond anymore; it's Higgins Pond!" Amy said. "We were on the bottom for five days."

"Amy is so stupid," Sarah said. "She wanted to float out into the middle of the pond on a log."

"You came with me!" Amy said.

"Because I knew you'd fall off!"

"Girls, behave," Erik said.

Dak dropped the clump of seaweed he had been dissecting and walked directly into the water. Katie thought the boy would stop when the water reached his waist, but he kept going. The water came up over his t-shirt, and then his head, his long hair splayed on the surface like sea grass.

"He's not a seal," Katie said, suddenly worried the boy was in trouble. No one else paid him any attention.

"He can't die twice," Ridley said matter-of-factly.

Katie rushed into the water and then worried that she shouldn't be in the water when she was tripping. Things were beginning to seem real again.

"Where are you going, Dorothy?"

She turned to find Dak standing at the water's edge, clean and dry, with no sign of having just been submerged. He cocked his head, looking at her like she was the one behaving erratically. She stood in the water, unsure of what to do next.

"What is it you *can* remember?" Erik said.

◆ ◆

"There you are," Rob said as Katie walked through the door. "Did you fall in?"

She peeled off her wet shirt and shorts and left them in a pile by the door. "Can you get me a towel?" she said, now pulling the sports bra over her head.

Rob watched intently as his wife stripped, tempted to take his clothes off, too. A piece of seaweed clung to her upper thigh like an unruly strand of pubic hair. It was rare anymore that Rob saw his wife naked in the daylight, or any light for that matter. Sex happened in the dark. He marveled at the suppleness of her skin and the firmness of her breasts. Her body was remarkably unchanged from the time they first met. "I guess I really am immortal," she'd sometimes say, throwing on clothes she'd worn twenty-five years ago. His thoughts of making dinner were supplanted by thoughts of making love.

"Rob! Towel!"

Unable to shake his aroused state, Rob tossed his wife a hand towel from the kitchen.

"Seriously?" she said. She threw the hand towel back at him and headed for the shower. Rob followed, still harboring lascivious thoughts. She shooed him away and told him to make himself a drink. More bourbon concoctions.

"Do you want one?"

"No!"

♦ ♦

They sat on the porch. The sun was mostly below the horizon now, and the sky was streaked with currents of pink and orange. Katie was oddly quiet, so Rob told her about Brie, the Labrador Retriever he had met on the beach, and the prospect of adopting her. Katie nodded and asked why the owner was getting rid of her. Rob had already explained that the woman was moving to London.

"Right," she said. "You did say that."

He could tell something was bothering her. She had been acting strangely since coming back from the beach in her wet clothes. She had taken a long shower, something she never did, and then paraded around the house wearing only a Dorothy Bradford Society t-shirt. He was acutely aware of her state of mind and always on the lookout for signs of panic.

"What's going on with you?" he said. "Did something happen

on the beach? Did you run into one of the Dorothy stalkers?"

"Nothing like that. I'm fine. I needed a day off."

"Thanks for the note, by the way. Are you sure you don't want a drink?"

Katie's brain was still settling from the acid. She wasn't going to chase it with alcohol, even though that's what Maggie Mason used to do when she diluted her LSD with beer. "Better not."

"You didn't have a panic attack, did you?"

"I felt a little anxious this morning. All back to normal now."

"Did you have more bad dreams last night?"

"No. Not last night."

There was more to it. He had the sense that she was hiding something. She had left her hair loose, and part of her face was hidden by the dangling tresses. "Did you see Sammy Boland?" he said.

"When?"

"Today. On the beach."

"No." She'd seen plenty of things on the beach, but not Sammy Boland. "Has anyone else seen him today?"

"Rachel called this afternoon to ask if I knew when you'd be back. She didn't say anything about Boland snooping around."

"That's good. I'll go down to the house tomorrow."

Katie closed her eyes. She wanted to tell him about her panic attack. She wanted to tell him about the LSD tabs, too, and what she'd seen on the beach. But there was so much of it, and she didn't feel like talking right now. She would tell him eventually, but she needed to come to terms with what she'd seen and figure out if it was real or imagined.

The sun was down now. A thin cloud layer rolled in from the south, masking the stars but allowing a feeble light from the moon to leak through. A flying insect bounced off one of the screens and buzzed angrily. Katie jumped.

"It's just a bug, Kay."

She stared at the spot where the bug had hit the screen and said, "The toilet's leaking."

"What?"

"In our bathroom."

"You want me to change the flapper? Dorothy does that stuff."

"You can do it."

Katie lay down on the chaise and stared at the ceiling fan. The blades had started rotating, and she couldn't tell if the fan had come on somehow or if the breeze blowing through the porch had put it in motion.

"Can I ask you something, Rob?"

"Okay. But just this once."

"Do you think I'm a witch?"

Rob had finished his drink and was fishing for the cherry at the bottom of the glass. "What?" he said.

"Some people think Dorothy Bradford is a witch."

"Who called you a witch?"

"No one."

"That's it, isn't it? Someone called you a witch."

"Well, yes. But not in a bad way."

"Who?"

"Just someone on the beach who recognized me."

"Who was it, Kay?"

Katie followed the rotation of the fan blades with her eyes and found that the blades seemed to stop for a second when the movement of her eyes matched their spin.

"The ghosts," Katie said.

CHAPTER NINE

Vinyl Gloves and Indica

Rob decided to ride his bike to Wellfleet the next morning to pick up a flapper at the hardware store. After he pulled out of the driveway, a car passed by, and the driver honked the horn—never a good omen for a cyclist just starting out on a ride. Rob waved, careful not to extend any fingers that might be misinterpreted, and mumbled, "My wife's a witch, you know." A moment later, the bike's rear tire blew out. "Shit," he said, stopping the bike and unclipping his shoes from the pedals. He leaned over the handlebars and stared blankly at the road in front of him. This was the second flat tire in as many days. But this one was a rear tire, and rear tires were a pain to change because the greasy chain had to be removed from the gear cassette. Rob hoisted the bike onto his shoulder and carried it back to the garage, wondering what he had done to deserve so many flat tires and leaky toilets.

He turned the bike upside down and freed the tire, having put on a pair of disposable vinyl gloves to keep the grease off his hands. Danny came downstairs, dressed for his morning run, except for his feet, which were bare. He held a cup of coffee in his hand. Rob could never tell if Danny was getting ready to go running or if he had just returned. Danny hardly broke a sweat when he ran. He stood by the garage door and stared at his father for a while, quietly sipping his coffee.

"This may be a stupid question," he said, "but how do you get a flat tire before you even get on the bike?"

"How is it my only child turned out to be such an asshole?" Rob said.

"Bad parenting."

Rob ripped the inner tube from the tire and tossed it aside. "Here's another question: do you think Mom is a witch?"

Danny was standing on one foot now, something runners did when they weren't running. "A good witch or a bad witch?" he said.

"Did she tell you about the dreams she's been having?"

"A little. I really want to go see Tom Ridley's grave."

"She was at the secret beach yesterday, and I think she fell asleep and saw all five of the ghosts together. They called her a white witch."

"What's that?"

"A good witch, I think."

"Well, I saw her on the roof with an owl the other day." Danny picked up the discarded inner tube and looked for the puncture. "She doesn't think they're real, does she?"

"They have names, and they talk to her now."

"Uh oh. What do they say?"

"That they've known her since she arrived on the Mayflower."

"I guess I need to talk to her."

"Please. She usually tells you more than me."

"That's because she likes me. Hey, did I hear you might have seen Sammy Boland up at Race Point?"

"I'm not sure it was him. Just a guy taking pictures of birds. I don't know why Sammy Boland would go all the way out there to look for shore birds."

"Maybe he's watching us."

"Why would he be watching us?"

"I don't know. We keep running into him." Danny shifted his weight to the other foot. His father slid the tire into place and pulled the chain back onto the cassette.

"Why do you do that?" Rob said. "You look like an ostrich, standing on one foot."

"I think you mean a flamingo. Balance is everything." Danny raised his right foot and placed the sole against the inside of his left thigh, barely wobbling. "Hope you have better luck on your ride."

"I'm not going back out. Too much bad karma. Besides, I don't have any more inner tubes."

"Ghosts and karma," Danny said. "My parents are very spiritual."

♦ ♦

Katie was on her knees, pulling weeds out of the vegetable garden next to the Bradford House. Her mind kept replaying what she'd seen on the beach the day before. Much of it was muted now—the alien, the seal, the hoverboard, and the Mayflower—slowly fading like images in a hazy dream sequence. The meeting with the ghosts, however, and everything they'd told her remained clear and present, the details easily recalled. But if the ghosts were also induced by chemicals, why wouldn't her mind let go of them too? Why were they as clear now as the uprooted weeds lying on the ground in front of her? She tried to put them out of her mind, but each time she did, her heart beat faster. Something told her that if she tried to ignore them, the panic would return. She had to appease them, if only for her own well-being. They'd asked her to do them a favor, something that seemed ludicrous. She hadn't shared this part of the story with anyone yet. Not even Rob.

"Ludicrous," she said out loud.

"What's ludicrous, Dorothy?"

She looked up from the weeds to find Elaine Snow standing at the edge of the garden. She had her camera around her neck, as she always did, in case there was an opportunity to photograph something remarkable. Pulling weeds was apparently not remarkable.

"Are you okay?" Elaine said.

"I think so," Katie said, though she was probably not okay. "Why?"

"You look bothered."

Katie got up and stretched her legs, stiffened from the weed-pulling. "I suppose I am," she said.

"Rachel is inside with the social worker. Do you want to talk to the social worker?"

Katie smiled. Despite her naiveté, Elaine could be very intuitive. Talking to a mental health expert was probably not a bad thought, but Katie had another idea.

"What are you doing right now, Elaine? Do you have a few minutes?"

Elaine's mouth dropped open. She instinctively grabbed her camera. "Me?" she said.

"Or Alice, if you prefer."

"Okay, sure. Anything. Where are we going?"

Katie brought Elaine into the front yard, and they sat in lawn chairs facing so close that their knees almost touched. Elaine's heart was racing. All of Dorothy Bradford's attention was focused on her and no one else. She expected Dorothy was about to give her an important assignment, something only she could be entrusted with. Elaine leaned forward and listened carefully.

"I want to tell you some things, Alice, and ask you some questions."

"You can ask me anything, Dorothy!"

"We need to keep our voices down, okay?"

Alice winced and dropped her head. "I'm sorry," she whispered. "Are they listening?"

"Who?"

"The ghosts."

Dorothy smiled and patted Alice on the thigh. "You are very intuitive, you know."

"Thanks. Did you have another dream?"

"I'm not sure what this was."

Alice's eyes widened. She straightened up and opened her mouth to speak, then remembered to keep her voice down. She hunched over and leaned forward.

"Did you see them?" Alice dropped her voice another notch and said, "Tell me everything, Dorothy. You can trust me."

"I know I can, Alice. You won't tell this to anyone, right?"

"Never! Unless you say it's okay." Elaine hunched down in her chair. "Sorry, that was too loud."

"They came to me yesterday on the beach: Erik and Dak, Tom Ridley, Sarah and Amy Higgins."

"Holy shit," Alice said, and immediately covered her mouth. "Sorry, I don't usually swear."

"It's okay, Alice."

"They visited you? The ghosts?"

"They prefer to be called spirits."

"That's not as scary."

"They think so, too."

"Why did they visit you?"

"Because I'm a white witch."

"Well, everybody knows that."

"They do?"

"Sure. You're immortal, and you use your powers to help people."

"And spirits, too, apparently."

"Really?"

"Let's not get ahead of ourselves."

Alice nodded and got her notebook out of her backpack. "Is it okay if I write things down? I won't show it to anyone."

Dorothy nodded. "Did you ever hear the name Catori in any of the stories about the Blonde Norseman?"

"I don't think so. Why?"

"How about Leah Walker or Elizabeth Hatch?"

Alice screwed up her face, hoping to find an answer other than no, but the names were not familiar to her. She shook her head. "Are they spirits, too?" she said.

"They're me. Or they were me."

"You were an Indian?"

"No, Catori was Erik's wife," Dorothy said. "They met in 1605, just after Erik landed on Cape Cod. Erik wanted to take Catori home to Norway with him, but she wouldn't leave the Cape, so he stayed and became a member of the Pamet tribe. They married and had a son named Dakota, or Dak, for short. When Dak was eight, he and his father were killed in a lightning storm and were buried on Corn Hill. Five years later, the Pilgrims arrived and dug up the cache of corn that the tribe had buried. In the process, they also dug up the grave of Erik and Dak."

"And released their spirits."

"That's what Erik told me."

"What about Catori?"

"She survived. Catori was one of the women who looked

after me after I fell off the Mayflower. After she died, I went off on my own. Several years later, sometime in the late 1600s, I became Leah Walker."

"Why did you change your name?"

"I couldn't be Dorothy Bradford anymore. Dorothy would have been in her nineties by then. At the time, most people didn't live past fifty, and none of them didn't age."

"You didn't age?" Alice said.

Dorothy smiled and cocked her head.

"Of course you didn't age," Alice said. "That was stupid."

"Nothing you say is stupid, Alice."

"Okay. Thanks for saying that. I worry about sounding stupid all the time."

"Don't."

Dorothy told Alice about Leah Walker, who had little to do with any of the spirits. She had married a fisherman who spent all his time catching cod in the North Atlantic. She lived alone most of the time in a huge house in the center of Provincetown. When the fisherman died, Leah wandered off into the dunes and came back in the 1700s as Elizabeth Hatch.

"And nobody recognized you as the fisherman's wife?" Alice said.

"I waited until everyone I knew was dead."

"What about kids? Did you have kids? Are your descendants

out there somewhere?" Alice gasped. "Am I one of your descendants?

"No kids. And Elizabeth Hatch was a spinster."

Alice frowned. "Okay. How many more of you are there?"

"They're not sure. I left the Cape after I was Elizabeth Hatch, and the spirits lost track of me. Until now."

"So was Elizabeth the one who knew Tom Ridley and the Higgins girls?"

"That's right." Katie leaned in and raised her eyebrows. "Apparently Ridley had the hots for me."

"He did?"

"He said I was the most beautiful woman in Truro."

"You were? I mean, of course you were!"

"Elizabeth Hatch was a schoolteacher and didn't want to marry anyone, according to Ridley. Anyway, he was a fisherman, too, and I'd had enough of fishermen. He ended up marrying another woman named Elizabeth, and they had ten kids. He came down with smallpox in 1776 and died. His family buried him in the woods. The town wouldn't let him be buried in the graveyard because of the smallpox. He wasn't happy about that."

"Can you blame him? He's all alone out there. And they spelled his name wrong. Poor guy. Does he still have the hots for you?"

"Maybe. But he doesn't drift through the house, watching me get in and out of the shower. The spirits, or these spirits anyway, don't haunt people. They might visit you once in a while, but they're completely friendly. They're not going to spook you."

"It sounds like you like them."

"You know, I think I do, Alice," she said, and she realized this was true. Katie dropped her Dorothy persona for a second and saw that the conversation with Elaine was having the desired result. She was feeling relieved. Tears welled in her eyes.

"So, the Higgins girls were your students?"

"Yes," she said, wiping away the tears.

"You're sad?"

"I guess so."

"Because they drowned?"

Dorothy nodded.

"Can I ask some questions now?"

"Sure."

"When you left the Cape, where did you go?"

"I don't know."

"And why did the spirits come to you? Did they ask you to do something? Do they want you to resurrect them? Is that it?" Alice said.

"What do you mean?"

"You're a white witch. Do they want you to bring them back to life?"

"I'm not sure that's in my wheelhouse, Alice."

"So what is it then?"

"There's one more spirit. But I think we need to call this one a ghost."

◆ ◆

Rob ended up driving to the hardware store to pick up a flapper for the toilet. On the way home, he passed a cyclist and remembered that he had forgotten to stop at the bike shop. He'd gotten so caught up in assessing the various brands of flappers at the hardware store that the inner tubes had completely dropped out of his mind. Who knew flappers were so exotic? They ranged in price from six dollars to eighteen dollars. Who needed an eighteen-dollar flapper? He bought the cheapest one and drove home.

Other than having to adjust the length of the chain running from the tank lever to the flapper a couple of times, the replacement went smoothly and the toilet stopped leaking. Having fixed one leaky fixture he immediately found another one when he went to the refrigerator to get some water from the dispenser. A puddle had formed under the refrigerator.

"Shit," Rob said, tapping the puddle with his toe as if to make sure it was really there. "What now?" There were no visible signs of a leak inside the refrigerator, so he pulled it away from the wall and checked the rear. Sure enough, there was water leaking out of the ice maker's fill tube. Rob turned off the ice maker, then closed the valve on the water line. The leak stopped. He mopped up the water and shoved the refrigerator back in place. He suspected the fill valve needed to be replaced, but he wasn't going to do anything until Katie took a look at it. Katie would know what to do.

Still feeling the need for exercise and not wanting to run or cycle indoors, he went to the beach, set up his chair, and waded into the water, with thoughts of swimming along the shore for a while. But a while for Rob meant five minutes at most. Rob hated swimming. Swimming was nothing more than an exhausting effort not to drown. He stopped when the water came up to his waist. He waved his arms and took a few mighty breaths, steeling himself for the headlong plunge. Before he did, and looking for excuses anyway, he noticed a man walking at the edge of the water. He was tall and had long blond hair. He looked out of place on the beach, dressed in jeans and work boots, the kind with reinforced toes and thick treads. Rob stepped on a sharp rock and yanked up his foot, looking down in the water for someplace sandy to land.

"Fuck!" Rob said, checking his foot for blood. The blond-haired man stopped and looked to see what had happened.

"Are you okay?" he said.

Rob waded back to shore, satisfied that the skin on the bottom of his foot hadn't been broken. Rob didn't know the man, but he looked familiar in a way, and in a moment, Rob realized he fit the description of the man Katie had met on Corn Hill, the one who had shown her the 1620 marker.

"I'm okay," Rob said. "Just stepped on the wrong end of a shell."

"Should have been wearing these," the man said, pointing to his shit-kickers.

"Are they comfortable in the sand?"

"I'm used to them. I work in construction. We're renovating a couple of houses in Truro. One down the beach, and one up on Corn Hill. When we break for lunch, I sometimes take a walk."

"You know Corn Hill pretty well?"

"I live there during the off-season. Stay in the house of one of my former clients. Keep an eye on it for him during the winter."

"Sounds like a good deal. Do you know anything about a 1620 marker?"

"Sure. Literally a stone's throw from the house. People sometimes leave corn there. Repaying the Indians, I guess. You sure you're okay?"

Rob realized he was standing on one foot, much like Danny had in the garage that morning.

"Working on my balance," Rob said.

The man waved and continued down the beach. Rob checked his foot again, still balanced on one foot.

"Who was that man?" a voice called out from behind.

Rob spun on his one foot to see Helen Schantz coming towards him, carrying a bag and a beach chair.

"And why are you standing like that?"

Rob set both feet down in the sand. The muscle in his calf, the one that had been supporting all his weight, tightened up. He reached down to massage it. Helen Schantz dug through her beach bag and pulled out what looked like a box of playing cards. She opened the box and removed an elegant custom-rolled joint. "You look like you could use one of these," she said, offering him the joint.

He stared at the thing. It looked nothing like a joint. It had its own filter and was cone-shaped, fatter at the end, and tapered at the filter. It was as alien a thing as work boots on the beach. Rob accepted it, and Helen gave him a lighter. He lit the joint—"joint" seemed too harsh a name for such an elegant bit of packaging—and took a long, healthy drag. He prepared himself to cough, but the cough never came. The smoke was smooth and faintly sweet. His lungs felt warm. The tightness in his calf evaporated.

"It's a new Indica blend," Helen said. "Very mellow." She set up her chair right next to Rob's chair and sat down. Then she lit her own joint.

Rob sat down, too, and took another big hit. Helen Schantz, the woman who used to ask him how soon he would be leaving the Cape, was right there, practically in his lap, puffing her weed in a state of euphoric bliss.

"Have you ever heard of the Blonde Norseman, Helen?" Rob said, already feeling the first wave of the cannabis's influence.

"Is that a strain of weed?"

"My wife's first husband dug him up a while ago."

"Katie was married before?"

"Oh, yes. His name was William Bradford. He was a Pilgrim."

Helen took a hit and held in the smoke for what seemed like fifteen seconds. She was a champion stoner.

"We are all pilgrims," she said. "How is your owl, by the way?"

"You know the owl?" he said.

"You introduced me."

"It's not real."

"None of us are real," she said.

"Ghosts aren't real, either."

"Have you ever seen one?"

"How could I have? They're not real," he said.

"Are you sure?"

"I'm worried my wife is seeing them."

"Does that bother you?"

Rob shrugged. Nothing was bothering him right now. He

took another hit. "You don't mind if I take a nap, do you?"

"Indica can make you sleepy."

Rob stuck his joint in the sand, reclined his chair, and fell into a dreamless sleep.

CHAPTER TEN

Bathtubs and Sage

Rachel came outside, having left the social worker to meet with the residents in the Bradford House.

"Elaine, I didn't know you were here," she said. "Or should I call you Alice?"

It was all Elaine could do to keep from erupting with the news of Dorothy Bradford's latest adventures, but she stopped herself, aware of the promise she'd made. She had developed a bond of trust with Dorothy and didn't want to jeopardize losing it. She looked at Dorothy Bradford.

"It's okay, Elaine," Katie said. "You can tell her, if you want."

"So, we're not calling you Alice anymore?" Rachel said.

Elaine didn't care. She had too much else on her mind. "Guess what?" she said, looking down at her notes, trying to decide where to start.

"What did I miss?"

"Dorothy met the ghosts! I mean spirits. They like to be called spirits."

Elaine spoke rapidly as she unloaded the details of Dorothy Bradford's past. Katie could see Rachel becoming increasingly agitated as the story progressed. She had expected this from Rachel, who had come to believe that the Dorothy Bradford Society needed to move away from breeding fantasies. Katie believed this, too, which was all the more reason for Rachel to feel burdened by what Elaine was saying.

"There's more, though. Right, Dorothy? Another ghost?"

Rachel folded her arms and stared at the ground. Without looking up, she said, "Are you sure this wasn't another one of your dreams, Katie?"

Elaine gasped. She had never heard Rachel call Dorothy Bradford by her alias.

"It could have been," Katie said. "It was just so lucid; so many particulars."

"Could it be these people you saw were playing a hoax?"

Katie hadn't considered this. There were certainly a lot of people in the world who indulged in role-playing games. Some believed that Katie was one of them.

"Maybe. But three of them were kids. I'm not sure how you'd get them to play along, acting like they were dead. Besides, I've seen them in my dreams. And you're the only two people who know about my dreams, besides Rob and Danny."

"And you've met the Norseman and his son before!" Elaine said.

"Listen, I'm looking to you two to help me sort through this thing. For my own good. It has nothing to do with the Bradford Society, and we don't have to share it with anyone else. Right, Elaine?"

"I'm not telling anyone," she said.

Katie and Elaine looked to Rachel for her approval, and she nodded, though her arms were still folded in front of her.

"There is more, though, and here's where it gets a little dicey," Katie said.

"Maybe I should sit down," Rachel said, and she got a chair and formed a circle with Katie and Elaine.

"The reason the spirits came to me is that they need my help."

Elaine started scribbling notes again on her pad.

"What are you writing?" Rachel said.

"I'm taking notes. In case I forget something." She held up the pad and flipped through the pages she'd already filled.

"Let me get through this, okay?" Katie said.

"Sorry," Elaine said.

"The spirits told me that there are good ghosts, like themselves, and bad ghosts. The bad ghosts don't come along very often, but when they do, the spirits need to get rid of them."

"I bet I know why," Elaine said.

"I'll bet you do, too," Rachel said sarcastically.

"A bad ghost will go into a good ghost's house and scare the crap out of the people who live there, making them think that their house is no longer safe to live in. The next thing the good ghost knows, their house is being burned down."

"Who burns down their house?" Rachel said.

"I read about this guy back in 1730 named John Freeman who molested another man's wife. When the man found out, he split open Freeman's skull with an axe."

"Lovely," Rachel said.

"The man wasn't put in jail, but Freeman's ghost haunted his house and terrorized the man and his wife for months. The ghost would watch the wife while she undressed and sometimes hop right into the bathtub with her. She and her husband couldn't have..." Elaine cleared her throat, then looked at her feet.

"Sex?" Katie said.

"Right, because Freeman always came into the bedroom anytime they started kissing and stuff. Eventually, Freeman started haunting other women all up and down the Cape. It got so bad that the towns started burning down the houses that Freeman haunted and any others where ghosts lived. Then one day, he just disappeared. He was gone."

"That was three hundred years ago, Elaine," Rachel said. "Has anyone burned down a house lately?"

"There was a ghost in 1880 that spooked the Old Colony Railroad. He eventually disappeared, too."

"I'm not burning down the Bradford House," Rachel said.

"Nobody's burning anything down," Katie said.

Elaine scribbled a few more notes and then looked up from her pad. "Does this mean there's a new bad ghost?" she said.

Katie nodded.

"And the good ghosts need your help?"

"They want me to get rid of him."

"Who is it?"

"Sammy Boland."

◆ ◆

"Sammy Boland's dead?" Elaine said.

"That's what they told me," Katie said.

"And you believe that?" Rachel said. "Danny saw him in the woods. And Martha saw him right here at the Bradford House."

"Apparently they saw his ghost."

"Oh boy," Rachel said.

"But he didn't do anything bad, did he?" Elaine said.

"He scared the hell out of Martha."

"Right. So they want you to get rid of him. How do you do that?"

"I have no idea."

Rachel shifted uncomfortably in her chair. "There's no proof Sammy Boland is dead," she said. "They haven't found his body."

"They might never find it," Elaine said.

"Rachel makes a good point," Katie said. "Why do anything until we know for sure that Boland is dead?"

"Or until he's caught," Rachel said. "Then this all goes away."

"How did they get rid of the bad ghosts before?" Elaine said. "Who got rid of John Freeman?"

"It wasn't me," Katie said.

"Who then?"

Katie raised her eyebrows.

"Wait, don't tell me!" Elaine said.

"I'll bet I know," Rachel said.

"Goodie Hallett!" Elaine said. "She killed the bad ghosts!"

"Well, she didn't kill them."

"Right. Because they were already dead. What did she do

then? Did she exorcise them?"

"I don't know. And the spirits don't know either. Whenever they needed to get rid of a bad ghost, they went to see Goodie Hallett, and she took care of it."

"So where is she now?"

"They don't know. They don't think she's on the Cape anymore."

"I'll bet Sam Bellamy finally came back and took her away."

"I wish he hadn't. With her gone, the spirits need another white witch to take her place. That's why they came to me."

"But they didn't tell you how to do it?"

"They don't know how, Elaine," Katie said. "But they seem to think I'll figure it out."

"You can burn sage," Elaine said.

"Where?"

"In the house. It drives ghosts away, but it doesn't always get rid of them. They might come back when the air clears."

"We've got plenty of sage in the garden."

"Let me be in charge of it," Elaine said.

"Can't hurt, I guess. Maybe that's all we'll need to do. Hopefully he disappears, and we'll be done with this."

Elaine popped up from her chair and started for the garden to harvest some sage.

"One second, Elaine," Rachel said, her voice booming.

Elaine froze and turned around sheepishly, sure that she had done something wrong.

"What?" she said.

"You're not going to tell anyone about this, right?" Rachel said.

"I promise," Elaine said.

"No one, Elaine."

"I understand. Can I go now?" Elaine didn't wait for an answer. She scampered away.

"You can't say anything either, Katie. You know how far-fetched all of this sounds. People will think you've become unhinged."

"Some people already think that."

Rachel frowned. "And make sure Rob doesn't tell anyone either."

"I'm going inside to join the therapy session," Katie said, getting up from her chair.

"This is going to get out," Rachel said, sounding resigned.

Katie shrugged her shoulders. "You wanted to bring back Dorothy Bradford," she said. "Here she is."

CHAPTER ELEVEN

Propane and Lobster Rolls

Rob and Danny stood on the deck of the house and stared at the grill in that way men do when meat is cooking on an open flame. Rob held a beer in one hand and a spatula in the other. He pressed down on the hamburger patties, and fat dripped down onto the burners, causing flames to shoot up through the grill. They were cooking for just the two of them. Katie was having dinner with Rachel and the residents at the Bradford House. Rob and Danny were debating the existence of ghosts.

"I saw that blond Norwegian guy," Rob said. "Or whatever they call him. Just like Mom described him. He was walking on the beach."

"You were stoned."

"That was later. The guy's a contractor who lives on Corn Hill during the off-season. He's renovating a house there now. And he knows about the 1620 marker. He's the guy Mom saw. Not a ghost."

Danny had a beer of his own that he nursed gingerly. "But then she saw him again on the beach with those other ghosts, right?" he said.

"She was dreaming. Or maybe *she* was stoned."

"Mom doesn't smoke pot. Maybe it was an acid flashback?"

"I don't know. Can you have acid flashbacks two years later?"

"Have you had any?"

"None involving dead people." Rob turned down the gas as the flames threatened to create an inferno. He shifted the hamburgers to safety at the edge of the grates. "Rachel came by this afternoon. She's worried about Mom's dreams. Mom told her and Elaine this morning that Sammy Boland is dead and that we've been seeing his ghost. Apparently Boland is a bad ghost, and the other ghosts want Mom to get rid of him."

"What?"

"I know."

"Do we need to worry about Mom killing Sammy Boland?"

"I don't think she really believes this stuff, Danny. At least I hope she doesn't."

"What about Rachel? I could see her whacking Boland."

"Rachel said no one's doing anything until they can confirm Boland is dead. Which they can't."

"He looked fine when I saw him."

"You've seen him, I've seen him, and Tim Desmond has seen him."

"So has Martha."

"Who's Martha?"

"At the Bradford House. The other day." Rob frowned and held his hand over the grate. "Oh, shit."

"What is it?"

"The gas died." Rob punched the starter on the grill a few times, but the burners didn't reignite. The tank was only half-empty. He turned off the propane, then turned it on again. Still nothing.

"Why is everything not working all of a sudden?" Rob said, remembering he had to fix the ice maker.

"We have a charcoal grill, don't we?"

"It's in the garage."

Danny put down his beer and went to look for the grill and some charcoal. Rob moved the half-cooked hamburgers onto a plate. He had the urge to take the grill apart and diagnose the problem, but decided to leave it for tomorrow. He'd already had two beers and didn't want to risk blowing himself up.

While he waited for Danny to come back with the grill, he saw Elaine Snow carefully making her way up the driveway. She was cradling a bowl in her hands, holding it out in front of her like some kind of holy relic. As she got closer, Rob saw that whatever was in the bowl was smoking.

"What have you got there?" Rob said. Elaine had taken a lap around the house before coming onto the deck.

"Sage," she said, her eyes still fixed on the bowl. "It will drive out the evil spirits."

"You're not going to take that inside, are you?"

Elaine did exactly that. She opened the screen door, went inside the house, and placed the bowl on the kitchen counter. Then she brought her hands together, as though giving thanks or praying to the Almighty.

Rob thought the sage bundle looked like a dried-up dog turd. It was brittle and white and had a pungent smell, like the inside of a spice shop. Or a head shop. He thought of his leftover joint lying on top of the dresser in the bedroom. He'd smoke more of that later.

"Why are we doing this?" he said.

"To keep Sammy Boland's ghost away."

"Sammy's not dead, Elaine. There are no ghosts out there or in here."

Elaine gave Rob a hard look, like a foreign object was stuck to the side of his face.

"What's that smell?" Danny said, coming inside with a small grill and a bag of charcoal. "Are you burning something?"

"Sage," Rob said. "Wards off evil spirits."

Rob explained. Elaine breathed deeply. Danny coughed.

"Jesus Christ," Danny said. "I'm going outside." He set the grill down on the deck and dumped in the charcoal.

"How long do we have to keep it burning?" Rob said.

"Until the evil spirits have gone," Elaine said. "Be gone, spirits!"

The smell quickly filled the house and wafted out onto the deck. Elaine stayed close to the sage, and Rob wondered if she meant to stay until the evil spirits flew up the chimney.

"Do you want a hamburger, Elaine?" he said.

"I have to get back to the Bradford House."

"Are you burning sage there, too?"

"Absolutely."

Elaine left. Then Danny left again, having forgotten the lighter fluid. Rob poked at the smoking sage bundle. The house was unusually quiet. Nothing was running, clanking, or burping. All the appliances were at rest. Rob went out to the deck and opened the valve on the propane tank. Out of curiosity, he pressed the ignition button. Still nothing.

◆ ◆

Rob snuffed out the sage, smoked some more pot, then climbed into bed and slept for ten hours. It was the first time he could remember sleeping through the night without getting up to go to the bathroom. Perhaps sage, or the pot, was also good for relaxing the prostate.

Katie hadn't come home from the Bradford House until after Rob had gone to sleep, and she had gotten up well before he did. A gentle breeze was blowing through the open windows, ballooning the shades into the room and flushing out the lingering smell of sage. Rob slept for another half hour and then rolled out of bed. He stood at the toilet and looked out the window. The window had a top-down shade that prevented anyone from seeing him with his dick in his hand. Anyone, of course, was Helen Schantz. Through the pine trees, he saw a yellow tent in Helen's side yard. This was curious. He had never seen a tent in Helen's yard before.

"Did you see the tent in Helen's yard?" he said, coming into the kitchen. Katie was behind the refrigerator, which she'd pulled away from the wall.

"Did you shut off the water line?" she said.

"Yesterday. It was leaking on the floor." Her hair was down, and Rob noticed a single braid on each side of her head. This was also puzzling. "Are those braids?"

"Martha did them last night."

"Which one is she? Is she the one Danny's running with?"

"That's Fat Agnes."

"I need to talk to you, Kay."

"About Helen's tent?"

"That and Sammy Boland."

"Let's go get lunch. We can talk there."

"Lunch? What time is it?"

"Almost noon."

Rob got some coffee and decided to go outside for a closer look at what was going on in Helen Schantz's yard before talking about ghosts again. The tent was a small dome-shaped enclosure, sized to sleep two. The flap was closed, and there was no way to tell if anyone was inside. Rob moved a little closer and then saw Helen Schantz sitting in a beach chair a few feet from the tent. She was staring off into the trees, smoking one of her joints.

"Are you camping?" Rob said.

Helen turned to look at him for a moment, as if trying to place him, and said, "I needed to get out of the house."

Rob didn't want to ask why. He was worried she was going to say that the house was haunted, and he'd have to go fetch some more of the sage dog turds.

"I see," he said finally. "Where'd you get the tent?"

Helen Schantz didn't bother to answer. Rob had the impression she didn't know or had forgotten. The tent didn't look new. He went back inside to get washed up.

◆ ◆

They drove to Wellfleet for lunch. Passing the Transfer Station on Route Six, Rob imagined a large mushroom cloud of sage smoke rising up from the open field behind the trash containers. What a Board of Selectman meeting that would be, he thought.

"First order of business—an open fire permit. Mr. Crosley, the floor is yours."

"Thank you, Mr. Chairman. We are asking permission to burn several bales of sage at the Transfer Station."

"Who's we?"

"My wife and I. She's a witch."

"And the purpose of the fire?"

"To exorcise a ghost."

"Very good. All in favor?"

They ordered lobster rolls and sat outside with cups of water while waiting for their number to be called.

"Why didn't you tell me about Sammy Boland?" Rob said, scanning the faces of the few patrons to see if he knew any of them.

"I was going to. I was just too exhausted last night."

"Not last night. The night before."

"Right. Sorry."

Rob leaned in close to Katie's ear, wanting to be sure no one else would hear. "You don't really believe we've been seeing Sammy Boland's ghost, do you?" he said.

"We don't even know if he's dead."

"But if he is dead, you have to get rid of him?"

"I know it sounds ridiculous. But the problem is, if I ignore it or if I pretend it will just go away, I start getting anxious. I worry the panic attacks will come back if I don't do something."

"You did do something. You burned sage. Just tell yourself that. You burned sage. The ghost is gone. It's over."

"Not if he isn't dead."

"If he isn't dead, then he's not a ghost, and the Blond Horseman, or whatever the fuck you call him, is full of shit."

Katie sipped her water. The idea that Erik might be full of shit bothered her. She didn't want him to be full of shit. "It's weird," she said. "But it kind of felt like he was watching over me. Like a guardian angel. I kind of liked him."

"He's still around. You can find him renovating houses on Corn Hill."

♦ ♦

After lunch, Rob walked to the bike shop next door to buy the box of inner tubes he needed. Katie got some ice cream and sat on a bench. There was a graveyard across the street, full of souls who died three hundred years ago—people Dorothy Bradford might have known at one time. She saw a young boy dart out from behind a tree. He ran a slalom course through the gravestones, tapping the top of each stone as he passed by. The boy had dark hair and reminded her of Dak. He was on his own, apparently; there was no sign of his parents. Every so often, he'd stop to call out the names on the gravestones, as though he knew them by heart, as though he was making sure they were still at peace, as though he was guarding their graves against intruders who might disturb their eternal rest. Katie wondered if there was a gravestone somewhere for Sammy Boland.

CHAPTER TWELVE

Animal Skins and the Garden of Eden

When Dorothy Bradford fell off the Mayflower and plunged into the icy waters of Cape Cod Bay, there was no boat to search for her. Her husband, William, and the rest of the scouting party had taken the ship's only longboat across the bay to explore the inland coastline. Some of the crew dove in to see if they could retrieve her, but the water was too cold and there was no sign of her anywhere.

William Bradford and Myles Standish, along with the others in the scouting party, had decided against settling on Cape Cod.

The land was barren and rocky, and there were no signs of game. They did find an abandoned campsite on their first expedition and stumbled upon a large cache of corn. The natives, apparently having moved inland for the winter season, had buried the corn there to seed the next planting season. The scouting party dug up the corn and took it back to the ship, where the starving passengers and crew feasted on the spoils. Dorothy would not eat the corn, though. She had become increasingly depressed over the final weeks of the voyage and had lost her appetite. Like many of the passengers, she lay in her cramped quarters, battling homesickness and depression, holding a blanket over her head to keep the leaking seawater from dripping on her face.

On the second excursion, the scouting party dug for more corn and came upon the remains of a man and a small boy. The man was large and had blond hair with the features of a Nordic trader. The boy had dark hair and appeared to be Indian. Unnerved at having disturbed an Indian burial site, the men quickly tossed a thin layer of sand on the bodies and ran back to the ship, praying they had not brought more bad luck upon themselves. The next day, the scouting party gave up on Cape Cod and headed west to explore the coastline across the bay.

◆ ◆

When Dorothy heard the story of the unearthed man and boy, her depression deepened. She thought of her own son, whom she had left with her parents in Amsterdam, and felt sure she would never see him again. The next day, after her husband left with the scouting party to explore possible inland landing sights, Dorothy fell off the ship and was given up for dead. Two days later, the Mayflower set sail for what would become Plymouth Colony, leaving Dorothy Bradford at the bottom of Cape Cod Bay.

But Dorothy Bradford was not at the bottom of the bay. She was lying in the sand, a few feet from the water. Her clothes were wet, and her hair and face were plastered with sand. Though she had just come out of the freezing water, she was not cold. She opened her eyes and saw a flock of seagulls circling overhead, ready to dissect the lifeless carcass below them. She sat up, and the birds flew off. She brushed the sand off her dress and wiped the sand from her face. After clearing her eyes, she looked out across the water. There was no sign of the Mayflower, but separation didn't distress her. She was glad to be rid of the ship. She despised the decrepit heap and had begun to loathe the self-righteous people aboard it, including her husband. Wherever they ended up settling, she would not be among them. It was not her intention to drown, but she needed to get off the ship. She would either survive or not, but she would be free of the Mayflower's perdition, at least for a little while.

That the ship was nowhere to be seen meant, she assumed, that she had been swept a great distance from it. But the hook of land to the north looked no further away than it had from the ship's rail. Perhaps the Mayflower had finally succumbed and become so full of seawater that it sank to the bottom of the bay. The ship had drowned, but not Dorothy Bradford.

She got to her feet and found a path leading away from the beach, winding through tall grasses and into the woods. Each step on the sandy soil brought her relief, a welcome transition from pacing the heaving, water-logged floorboards of the May-flower. She had taken off her shoes and left them on the beach. Her coif, shift, and apron had come off in the water. She had a strange desire to remove all of her sodden clothes and wander the woods in the nude—Eve in the Garden of Eden.

She came to a clearing that was dotted with several small, dome-shaped shelters covered in bark. The camp looked deserted. No fires were burning. She looked inside a few of the shelters. Clearly, whoever had lived in them had left. At the edge of the camp, she came across an open pit, six feet in diameter and as many feet deep. At the bottom, she saw kernels of corn strewn across the floor. A pile of fresh dirt sat next to the pit.

It was then that she noticed the woman kneeling at the edge of a smaller pit. She wore an animal hide, and her long black hair was tied up in a braid. She was pushing dirt into the pit. Dorothy came closer and saw that the woman was crying. All at once, the woman stopped what she was doing and turned to see the white-skinned woman in stocking feet. Dorothy came closer. The woman spoke in words that Dorothy did not understand. She pointed into the hole. Dorothy looked where the woman was pointing and saw the outline of two bodies, one large and one small. She knelt and placed her hand on the woman's arm, thinking the woman was burying her husband and child, which she was, though not for the first time. The woman's expression softened. Dorothy motioned to the dirt at the edge of the pit and reached over to push an armful into the hole. The woman nodded and resumed.

When they were done filling the grave, the woman led Dorothy into one of the shelters and pointed at her dress. Dorothy was all too happy to take the thing off. She stripped down to her undergarments, and the woman draped an animal skin over her, tying it at the waist with a leather belt. Next, she undid Dorothy's hair and combed and braided it. The woman patted her chest and said, "Catori." Dorothy smiled and said her own name. She had found the new world.

CHAPTER THIRTEEN

Ear Infections and Tennis Balls

Katie yelped as Rob's hand came down on her head. It wasn't the first time her husband had jolted her from sleep in this way.

"Sorry," he said. "I was checking to see if you were there."

"Jesus, Rob, why can't you just look?"

Rob moved the offending hand down to her back and tried to salvage the moment with some massage.

"That's better," she said.

"Were you up last night?"

"No. Slept through the night." She yawned and stretched

her arm out, slapping Rob's head. "There, we're even." She left her hand there and played with the unruly mass of hair. "You need a haircut."

Rob got out of bed, hopeful that another uneventful night meant that Katie had gotten the ghosts out of her head. He put on shorts and a t-shirt and went into the kitchen. He was rinsing out the coffee pot when he saw the chocolate lab tied up on the deck. The dog was sitting with her hind legs splayed out behind her. She watched Rob at the sink and sat up a little straighter, her tail wagging, when Rob came to the door.

"Brie?" he said, looking around for her owner, the woman named Natalie. He hadn't heard from her since their meeting on the beach and was surprised that she would just stop by, especially at such an early hour. But there was no one else on the deck. There was no car in the driveway. There was only a large bag of dog food with a note tucked under it. Rob read the note while Brie licked his feet.

Thanks for taking Brie. We both knew immediately that you were the right person to be her new owner. I can now go to London, knowing she is in good hands. I've left you a bag of food and a printout of her medical record. You'll see she is in the best of health. Other than the occasional ear infection, you shouldn't have any problems with her. Thank you again. I know Brie will be the perfect companion for you. And I know you and she will have a happy life together. I left my number in case you have any questions. Be well.

Brie looked up at Rob and held out her paw. Rob took it and, in that moment, became the proud owner of a fourteen-month-old Labrador Retriever.

"Did you know she was going to do this?" Rob said to the dog. She was licking his hand now.

"Who's this?" Katie said, coming onto the deck. Brie left Rob's hand to dry and nuzzled against Katie's legs. "What a beautiful dog. Is this the lab you were telling me about?"

"Brie," Rob said. "Her owner left her here. Apparently, she's ours now."

"You already bought her?"

"No. She gave her to us."

"That's odd, isn't it?"

"Yeah, but most of what goes on around here is odd."

"She just left her dog?"

"There's a note."

Rob called Natalie to make sure of her intentions. She answered and asked if everything was okay. "I'm here until tomorrow," she said. "If things don't work out, just give me a call." She thanked him again and hung up.

They decided to take the dog for a walk on the beach. While they got dressed, Brie deposited herself in the middle of the bed and promptly fell asleep. Lying down, she looked much bigger. Rob sat next to her and ran his hand along her flanks. She snored gently.

"Should I wake her?" he said.

"Leave her. Let her get acclimated."

"I think she already is."

A car came up the driveway. Katie looked out the window.

"Who is it now?" Rob said.

"It's that private investigator, I think," she said. "The bourbon guy."

"Why is it nobody calls first?"

Mike Van Winkle sat in his car, checking his cell phone. Rob watched him for a minute and then went outside when he finally got out of the car. Rob wasn't sure about inviting a private investigator into the house—they could talk in the yard—but he did anyway. He still believed there might be a bottle of Pappy Van Winkle in it for him. And he also felt bad for Van Winkle, who, in the course of the investigation, had been shot in the arm by Tim Desmond.

"How's the arm?" Rob said.

"A little sore," Van Winkle said as he followed Rob into the house. "I'm fine."

Katie and Brie, who had hopped off the bed, greeted Van Winkle at the door. Katie offered him some coffee, and Brie licked his hand, as though she could sense his pain. They sat down in the living room and the dog lay down at Van Winkle's feet.

"Nice-looking puppy," Van Winkle said, sounding knowledgeable. "How long have you had her?"

"An hour," Rob said.

"Seriously? She looks right at home."

"Labs are like that," Rob said. He had no idea if labs were like that. "So what can we do for you, Mike?" Rob hadn't called him Mike before. He wasn't sure he'd called him anything before. "Any news on the investigation?"

"Not yet," Van Winkle said, looking down at Brie. Rob noticed that the dog was actually on top of Van Winkle's feet now.

"She's not bothering you, is she?" Rob said.

"Not a bit," Van Winkle said. "Makes me feel at home. I grew up with four Retrievers."

"Where's home?" Katie said.

"Kentucky, ma'am," Van Winkle said. "Big old house in the country. Lots of history, lots of animals."

And lots of whiskey barrels, Rob wanted to add.

"Yes, I think Rob mentioned that to me."

"I came to ask a few questions," Van Winkle said. "And then I'll be out of your way." He asked Rob to tell him about the man he had seen on the beach at Race Point. Rob rehashed all of it, including the bare-breasted sunbathers and the coyote.

"I went up there yesterday," Van Winkle said. "It's pretty hard to get to. There's only one or two ways in or out, and hardly any place to hide. Not like the woods. How come you didn't call the police?"

"I wasn't sure it was him. And I'll bet the police are getting plenty of calls now from people claiming to have seen Boland."

An amused look crossed Van Winkle's face. "I heard a rumor that Boland is dead."

There was an uncomfortable silence. Katie looked directly at Van Winkle, not diverting her gaze. Somebody had said something, she thought, most likely Elaine.

Rob looked at Katie, thinking she would respond. But Van Winkle hadn't asked a question. No response was necessary, but Rob didn't like uncomfortable silences.

"Where'd you hear that?" Rob said.

"Donut shop. I stopped to get a coffee this morning and overheard two women in line talking about Boland."

Rob cleared his throat. Katie remained silent.

"He didn't look dead to me," Rob said. "Lots of crazy ideas out there. But then this investigation has been going on for a long time."

Van Winkle nodded and sighed. He reached down to pet Brie, who had started snoring.

"Sorry," Rob said. "I didn't mean your investigation."

"No, I get it," Van Winkle said. "Conspiracy theories are going to spread until we bring him in."

"It's actually not a new theory about Boland being dead," Rob said. "After he disappeared, a lot of people thought he'd been knocked off by the cartel, and his body dumped in a landfill."

"Or the bottom of the bay," Van Winkle said. "That's where the women at the donut shop thought he ended up. Oh, and they also think that everyone is seeing his ghost."

Rob threw up his hands. "Well, that explains it, then," he said dryly.

"I understand ghost stories are popular around here," Van Winkle said.

"I've heard one or two," Rob said.

"Do you believe in ghosts, Mr. Van Winkle?" Katie said.

"Me? No. My mother does. Supposedly, there's one in our house back in Kentucky. Old black woman by the name of Mary. No one else has ever seen her, though. Just Mom. The house was built before the Civil War, and Mary was a cook for the original owner, a guy by the name of Rufus Barksdale."

Brie sat up and started sniffing the air. Rob was reminded of the sage dog turd remnants that were still sitting in a bowl on the kitchen counter. He wondered if Van Winkle had noticed it.

"But I didn't come here to waste your time with ghost stories."

"No, go on, Mr. Van Winkle. I'd like to hear it," Katie said.

Rob didn't want to hear any more ghost stories and was bothered by Katie's eagerness to have Van Winkle continue. He didn't need anyone putting more ideas in her head about paranormal activity. He relented, though, if only because he was still feeling bad about Van Winkle's arm.

It became apparent that Van Winkle enjoyed telling the story of the family ghost, even though it cast his mother as something of a quack. Mary had been a slave who belonged to Rufus Barksdale. Barksdale was not a good person. He treated his slaves poorly, and his family not much better. He was concerned only with himself. Barksdale went off to fight in the war and never returned, which was generally a good thing for all concerned. Mary stayed on after the emancipation and continued to work as the family's cook. When she died, Mrs. Barksdale had her buried on the property. Barksdale's son, who took after his father, was incensed by this, and after his mother's death, he dug up the grave and moved Mary to an Enslaved Persons Cemetery.

"According to Mom, Mary's ghost stayed behind," Van Winkle said.

"And she's still there?" Katie said.

"Apparently."

"Are there others?"

"Barksdale's ghost came back at one point, according to Mom, but she got rid of him."

"Did she burn sage?" Rob said.

"You know about sage?" Van Winkle said.

"Not really."

"Why did Barksdale's ghost come back?" Katie said.

"Mom said he was trying to drive Mary away. She heard him roaming the halls, yelling at her to get out, calling her a... You know."

"How did she get rid of him?" Katie said. Rob noticed she was becoming more interested in the story now.

"This strange woman came to the house one night. My dad thought she was a witch. She had this small bag of dirt with her. She said she had taken the dirt from Barksdale's grave. She summoned the ghost and chanted some spells. Seemed like a lot of craziness, but it was enough to get Mom to believe that the ghost was gone. She didn't see him again after that."

"That's quite a story," Katie said.

"Completely off the wall, but harmless. Mom's a good soul."

"I'm sure she is."

Rob thought to ask if the witch was a white witch, but he'd had enough.

"One last thing," Van Winkle said. "Not about ghosts." He reached down and scratched Brie behind the ears. When he stopped, she pawed his hand for more. "The girls staying at the Bradford House, Martha and Fat Agnes, I think they call themselves?"

"Haley and Kristin are their real names."

"Right. They're the ones who bought drugs from Boland, correct?"

"Yes."

"I didn't want to bother them until I talked to you first, Mrs. Crosley, but have they said anything more about why they think Boland was sneaking around the house the other day?"

Katie shrugged. "Haley said that Sammy once told her that if she ever cleaned herself up, he would be interested in seeing her. Something like that."

"He liked her?"

"It would seem."

"But not Kristin."

"I don't get that impression."

"Does Haley think he might come back again?"

"Well, I'm not sure about that, Mr. Van Winkle. You'll have to ask her."

◆ ◆

Rob and Katie took Brie down to the beach for a walk. Katie brought her oars with her. She planned to take the boat out after Rob and Brie went back to the house. Rob brought along a tennis ball for Brie.

"She looks just like a seal," Rob said, watching Brie swim after the ball. When she caught up with it, she snatched the ball out of the water, much like a shark snatches a seal, and paddled back to shore. She shook herself dry, then dropped the ball in the sand and nudged it toward the water with her nose. Rob threw the ball again, but not quite as far this time.

"Do you think Van Winkle wants to set up a stakeout at the Bradford House?" Rob said.

"He better not. I don't need anyone else lurking in the woods."

"What did you think of his ghost story?"

"He seemed to enjoy telling it to us."

"I hope you didn't get any ideas."

"About what?"

"About banishing bad ghosts."

"No ideas. Just information," she said. Katie flipped a rock into the water, and Brie charged after it. The rock sank to the bottom, but Brie kept swimming away from shore.

"Brie! Turn around!" Rob yelled, but the dog kept going. Rob lobbed the tennis ball over her head so she had something to retrieve. "I guess she's not a very bright dog."

"She's fine. I'll take her over to the Bradford House after lunch. The girls will love her."

Brie returned with the ball and started running sprints at a frantic pace along the shore. She went back and forth several times, then collapsed, panting heavily.

"Maybe Danny should take her running," Rob said, thinking the dog might need more exercise.

"He's been taking Kristin running lately."

"Which one is she?"

"Fat Agnes. Come on, Rob, we just talked about her with Van Winkle."

"She's the skinny one, right? He should take her out for a burger instead."

"I think they like each other."

"Is that allowed?" Rob said, sounding annoyed. "I mean, isn't she supposed to be rehabbing?"

"She's not in confinement, Rob."

Brie hopped up and started plowing the side of her head through the sand. When she was done, she sat down on her haunches and stared at the water.

"So, we'll keep her then?" Rob said. "Brie, I mean. Not Fat Agnes."

CHAPTER FOURTEEN

Dog Ticks and Cruise Ships

Katie woke with a stir. The anxiety was back, bubbling beneath her rib cage. Rob snored, each rattling breath making her feel more uneasy.

"Dammit," she said, her eyes now open wide. She tried to calm herself without getting out of bed, but the fear began to build. She kicked off the covers and got up before the panic set in; otherwise, she knew she might never come back.

She went outside on the deck and stood at the railing. "This isn't the Mayflower," she said. "I'm safe here." She closed her eyes and focused on her breathing. The fear subsided gradually, and after a few minutes, it was gone. The self-relaxation techniques were working, but she was having to use them more often than usual. Something more needed to be done. The ghosts had not left her. She took a deep breath and went back to bed.

◆ ◆

Rob woke up with what felt like a burn or a scrape on his left hip. He thought he might have scratched himself in his sleep, or maybe the dog had swiped him with one of her paws. The sun was up, but the room was dark. Katie was fast asleep.

He went into the bathroom and turned on the light. Before he could examine his hip, he heard a thumping noise behind him that sounded like an angry neighbor pounding on the wall. He looked around, wondering if the flapper he had installed in the toilet had caused some kind of plumbing catastrophe, and found Brie lying on the floor, nuzzled up against the closet door. Her thick, beaver-like tail was wagging furiously, thumping the door like a bass drum. The rest of her body was inert, her head lying between her paws, and her eyes focused squarely on Rob. Once she had his attention, her head came up and her tail beat faster. Out came her tongue.

He had forgotten about the dog. She had hopped on the bed during the night and curled up between him and Katie. At some point, she jumped off and slept on the floor. Rob leaned down and petted her. She lay back down, rolled on her back, and pawed the air, beckoning him not to stop.

He felt another shot of pain in his side and turned to the mirror to get a look at what was causing the problem. "Son of a bitch," he said when he saw the black tick lodged in his skin. He used a pair of tweezers to grab the tick, then pulled it out cleanly. He set the parasite down on a tissue and had a closer look. It was a dog tick, less of a concern than deer ticks, and was not engorged, which meant it had not yet tapped into his blood stream. "No more sleeping on the bed for you, young lady," he said to Brie, her head popping up off the floor once again.

"What's that banging noise?" Katie said, when Rob came back to bed.

"That's Thumper," Rob said. Brie followed, getting up on her hind legs and placing her front paws on the bed. She started making whimpering noises. "Our new dog has a mallet for a tail."

"You should take her out."

"It's only six."

"Take her out."

Katie rolled over and went back to sleep. Rob sighed and got out of bed again. Brie pivoted and headed for the door, tail wagging. Rob covered himself in bug spray and walked the dog down the driveway on her leash. In a few weeks, he'd let her roam freely, but for now, she was still a flight risk and needed to be restrained. She did her business and took note of the turkeys foraging in the brush. She dropped her nose to the ground, trying to catch their scent, and then lifted her head. She made a feeble sort of yipping noise, as if she wasn't sure whether to play with or retrieve the odd feathered birds.

"Those are turkeys, Brie," Rob said. Brie sat down in the driveway and studied them. Rob tightened his grip on the leash in case she decided to give chase. He looked back toward the house and watched the early morning sun vaporize the dew on the roof, sending spirals of steam into the air. The plastic owls stood sentry on either end of the roof, warding off woodpeckers and other avian pests.

Brie started making whimpering noises, and Rob turned to find Danny and Fat Agnes coming down the steps from Danny's apartment.

"Whose dog is that?" Danny said. He was dressed for his morning run, somewhat earlier than usual. Fat Agnes was also wearing running shoes along with a pair of stretch pants and a long-sleeved shirt. She had added weight to her narrow frame.

"Ours," Rob said.

"She's beautiful," Fat Agnes said, coming alongside and giving Brie, who was up on her hind legs now, a hug.

"Where did you get her?" Danny said.

"Long story," Rob said.

"Does she have a name?"

"It's Brie."

"Like the cheese?"

"Yes, like the cheese."

"Did you pick the name?"

Rob looked down at Fat Agnes's running shoes. They were brand new. He found it curious that she had gone up to the apartment to meet Danny. Or perhaps she had spent the night?

"Does she run?" Danny said, as if he were talking about an old car or a nag.

"Brie? I don't know. I guess so."

"Should we take her? We're just going out for a mile or so."

Rob gave the leash over to his son and watched the three of them head up the road. Danny held the leash in his left hand, and Brie happily trotted alongside. As they reached the top of the hill, he reached over and gave Fat Agnes a playful hug. She laughed and slapped Danny on the butt.

◆ ◆

"Fat Agnes is sleeping with Danny," Rob said, coming back into the bedroom.

Katie was still in bed, lying on her stomach with her eyes

closed. It had taken her a while to calm down after the latest bout of panic, but she'd finally managed to get some sleep. Her dreams were benign, except for one unsettling interlude. Tom Ridley appeared, looking tired and ill, behaving more like a ghost than a spirit. His head and lips were swollen, and his face was covered in leaking pustules. Eventually, he became completely unrecognizable. He collapsed on the ground, and his headstone appeared. As he sank into his grave, he said, "You haven't forgotten about us, have you, Dorothy?"

Katie took a deep breath, trying to clear her head of the dream but knowing she couldn't ignore the message. She pushed herself up from the mattress, resting on her elbows now. "How do you know they're sleeping together?"

"They came out of the apartment together. They took Brie for a run."

"That doesn't mean they're sleeping together."

"Fat Agnes looks like she's twelve."

"She's twenty, Rob."

"She's also a heroin addict."

"*Was* a heroin addict. Don't be an ass."

"I'm not being an ass." Rob poked at the red spot where the tick had bit him. It didn't hurt anymore. "Check yourself for ticks before you get dressed," he said. "I found one on me this morning. I think it was from the dog."

◆ ◆

Katie rowed into Pamet Harbor. A layer of clouds had moved in from the west, and a breeze was blowing, creating a light chop in the water. She turned the boat north along a tributary of the Pamet River that ran along a sandy spit of land bisecting the river and the bay. On a sunny day, she might expect to see a handful of people on this part of the river. But today there was no one.

There were a few landing spots along the spit, and she picked one closer to the end of the tributary. A blue heron landed in the grass along the shore and gazed into the distance.

Katie opened her backpack and took out the Ziploc bag. She'd cut out another strawberry tab that morning, resolving to combat her relapsing panic disorder aggressively so that it wouldn't overtake her, as it had done before, and send her back into isolation. "Lysergic acid will reshape your mind," Maggie Mason had told her. "You'll get back in touch with who you are and who you were, and your fears will disappear." It had worked two years ago. It would work again now.

Katie had broken her rule by taking the rowboat, but she knew from the last time that the acid trip didn't last very long and the effects weren't that intense; she'd be fine rowing back to the house later in the day. The possibility that she might hop into the boat while under the effects of the acid didn't concern her. Still, she sat several yards away from the boat to avoid temptation.

Within a few minutes of dissolving the tab on her tongue, the blue heron was no longer blue, and the sky was no longer gray. The heron became several colors, and when it flew off, it left a trail of ice particles behind, like the exhaust from a jet engine. As with the previous trip, none of the images Katie saw were threatening, and she felt she was able to distinguish between what was real and what wasn't. She knew, for example, that the large cruise ship coming into the tiny harbor was imaginary. The boat, seven stories high and three football fields long, pulled up to the pier and disgorged several hundred passengers, who set up tables in the parking lot and played canasta. But the man who came over the dunes from the bay and started dragging Katie's boat toward the water posed more of a challenge. She recognized the man but wasn't sure if he was really there. The man was Sammy Boland.

"What are you doing?" Katie said. She was lying in the sand, propped up on her elbow. A box turtle lay next to her, its head and legs hidden inside its shell. Boland wore a bathing suit and a t-shirt, and carried a backpack that he tossed into the boat.

Sammy Boland smiled. "I got your boat, Dorothy," he said. A large neon-colored fish jumped out of the boat and flopped around on the sand until it found its way into the water. Katie thought the fish had slithered out of Boland's backpack. The water had become crystal clear, and Katie was able to follow the fish as it swam off toward the harbor.

The turtle stuck its head out of its shell and said to Katie, "Be careful."

Boland climbed into the boat and set the oars in the oarlocks. Then he started rowing toward the harbor, moving very quickly over the water, the oars bending violently with each stroke.

"Hey, wait a minute!" Katie said, trying to get up. She seemed to be moving very slowly. Even the turtle was outpacing her as it inched its way toward the tall grasses.

"That's my boat!" Katie said. She was on her feet now and running along the shore, trying to keep up. But Boland continued to accelerate and quickly disappeared around a bend. Katie climbed the low dunes that bordered the river to see if Boland was heading into the bay. But the cloud cover had grown so thick and dropped so low that it looked as if a massive glacier had overtaken Cape Cod Bay.

Katie returned to the spot where she had left the boat, wondering if it might still be there. Maybe Sammy Boland had never really stolen it. But there was no boat, and the sand looked strangely undisturbed, like nothing had recently been dragged out of or into the water. She stood there for a few minutes, or possibly longer, thinking the boat would reappear. Other things appeared, but none of them were boats.

No longer sure she had even brought the boat in the first place, Katie picked up her backpack and walked over the dune to the bay beach. The air was much colder now, and the wind howled. Massive blocks of ice had been pushed up onto the beach, and Katie had to pick her way through them like a hiker in a Himalayan icefall. The entrance to the Corn Hill Beach parking lot was just a few hundred yards away, and Katie was able to get there before the glacier overtook her.

The parking lot was empty except for an ice cream truck. There was a large horn-shaped speaker on top of the truck, playing some sort of medieval Gregorian chant. Katie walked up to the window, and a small man appeared. The man asked her if she had a reservation.

"Do you have any water?" Katie said.

"It's our specialty," the man said, pulling a gallon container from under the counter.

"Anything smaller?"

"No."

Katie left the food truck and walked down the shell-covered path that led to the Corn Hill monument. This was where she had first met Dak and Erik, the Blonde Norseman. The strong wind rattled the lines running up the bare flagpole, making it seem like she was standing on the deck of a ship in a storm. Katie sat down on one of the benches and set the gallon container of water down next to her. She closed her eyes for a moment, and when she opened them, Erik and Dak were sitting on the opposite bench. They smiled, looking happy to see her, as if they were expecting good news.

"Hello, Dorothy," Erik said. Dak hopped off the bench and came to sit next to her. He lay down and put his head in her lap.

"I was hoping I'd find you here," she said.

"How are you coming along with Mr. Boland?"

"I was just with him. He stole my boat."

"Why didn't you extinguish him?"

"I don't know how." The word stuck in her head—*extinguish*. Was that the correct term? Was she meant to snuff him out like an open flame?

"I thought maybe that's why you have all that water."

Dak hopped off the bench and ran over to the flagpole. He grabbed on with both hands and let the wind lift him off the ground so that he was horizontal—a ghost flag.

"Are you sure he's dead?" Katie said.

"Oh, yes."

"Do you know where his body is?"

"Will you be needing that?"

"Maybe. Again, I'm not sure."

"I expect you will have seen the burial site in a dream, just like you've seen all of ours."

"I don't think so," Katie said.

"He can't be far," Erik said. "Spirits stay close to their remains."

"I'll remember that," Katie said. She looked up and saw that Dak had shimmied up to the top of the flagpole, holding on with just one hand now.

"After he died, Dak sat on top of a tree for ten years," Erik said. "I could never get him down. He still likes climbing things, but he comes back to earth every now and then. I often wonder what kind of person he would have become had he lived."

Dak let go of the pole and flew off into the gray skies above the cottages across the street.

"But we spirits aren't given to melancholy," Erik said. "Tell me, Dorothy, what is it you'll do once you've found Boland's body?"

"I'm not clear on that part," Katie said. "I'm not clear on any of it, really. I just need to find my boat."

"Search your memories, Dorothy. I'm sure it will come to you. Now, if you'll excuse me, I need to go find Dak."

◆ ◆

"Nice run?" Rob said when Danny came back to the house with the dog. Fat Agnes had gone back to the Bradford House.

"Fantastic," Danny said.

Brie lapped up two bowls of water and lay down on the kitchen floor, water dripping from her jowls. She looked happily spent.

"She's young, isn't she?" Rob said.

"Brie?"

"Fat Agnes."

"What are you talking about?"

"You two seem to have a thing for each other."

"So? I like her."

"Fine, okay," Rob said. He went to the sink and started washing dishes. He never washed dishes.

"What's the problem?" Danny said.

"You shouldn't lose focus on your running."

"You're worried I'll get distracted?"

"Maybe."

"You sound like my coaches."

"You should listen to your coaches."

"I'll be all right."

"Just be careful, okay?"

"The only person I need to be careful of is the guy pulling into the driveway."

It was Steve Ridgeback. He'd come with news from a literary agent who said that he could get an advance of a hundred thousand dollars from a publisher for Danny's autobiography. The agent was ready to go to work immediately but needed a synopsis of the book that he could present to the publishing houses.

"Kristin has to be in the first chapter," Danny said.

"Who's Kristin?" Ridgeback said.

"His new friend," Rob said.

"What's that mean?" Ridgeback shot a confused stare at Danny. Brie got up from the floor and started licking Ridgeback's shoes.

"She's staying at the Bradford House for a few weeks," Danny said. "We started seeing each other. We hit it off immediately. We love each other."

"My son is full of shit," Rob said.

"She can be in a later chapter," Ridgeback said. "Listen, Danny, are you ready to do this? The agent said he'd come out here to meet with us. He thinks we can have a book deal within a week."

"You can write it," Danny said. "Make it a biography."

"The publishers will want your name on it. We're not going to get that kind of money otherwise."

"Fine."

"Really?"

"No."

"What?"

"I'm not writing a book."

"I already wrote a synopsis." Ridgeback pulled three typewritten pages from his jacket pocket and waved them at Danny. Brie lay down on top of Ridgeback's feet and yawned. Ridgeback looked down as though he was noticing the dog for the first time. "Who's this?"

"Brie," Rob said. "She's new. You can write a chapter about her, too."

"I'll leave the synopsis here," Ridgeback said, seeing that Danny wasn't going to take it from him. "You can read it over." He looked for someplace to put down the pages, but his feet were immobilized by the seventy-pound dog, and there were no flat surfaces within reach.

"Give it to Brie," Danny said. "Maybe she'll eat it."

Ridgeback folded the pages and tossed them on the couch, nearly falling over in the process. "It's a lot of money, Danny. Six months from now, it won't be available. People will have forgotten about the Olympics."

"Until the next one."

"You can write it then," Rob said. "Then he'll have two gold medals. You can get two hundred thousand dollars."

"Sure." Ridgeback stared dejectedly at his feet, still obscured by the large brown puppy. The dog was snoring softly now. Ridgeback wiggled one of his feet, seeing if he could dislodge it without waking the dog. "Hey, have you guys heard anything about Sammy Boland? There's a rumor going around that he's dead, and people are actually seeing his ghost."

Rob rolled his eyes. Danny went into the kitchen for some water. A bird shrieked outside the window. "Who came up with that idea?" Rob said.

"Some ghost aficionado, I guess. We have a lot of those around here."

"He didn't look like a ghost to me," Rob said.

"He was wearing a sheet when I saw him," Danny said.

Brie jumped up and lumbered over to the window. She stared at a spot in the trees and started growling.

"Brie doesn't like ghosts," Rob said.

"Maybe she can chase him down," Ridgeback said. "No one else seems to be able to."

"Brilliant idea," Danny said, heading for the door. "I'm going for another run."

"In this weather?" Ridgeback shook his head and watched Danny run down the driveway. "What is it with this generation?" he said. "They don't seem at all interested in money or fame."

Rob joined Brie and Ridgeback at the window and watched the weather jostle the trees.

"You don't believe in ghosts, do you, Rob?" Ridgeback said.

"Well, I've never seen one. Have you?"

Just then, a thirty-foot oak bent violently in the wind, and the ground gave way. The tree uprooted and crashed onto the driveway, narrowly missing the garage and Ridgeback's car.

"Holy shit!" Ridgeback said. "My Subaru!"

◆ ◆

Katie didn't get up from the bench at the Corn Hill monument until the Gregorian music stopped and the food truck disappeared. The gallon container of water was gone, too. She walked back to the river, hoping to find her boat there, but saw nothing. Someone had taken it. She thought about calling the police to report the theft, but answering questions about what she saw, not to mention the condition she was in when she saw it, deterred her. She didn't need the police anyway. Once the Dorothy Bradford Society learned that Dorothy's boat had been stolen—a holy relic if ever there was one—the members would lay siege to the beaches and waterways until they found it.

She walked home on the street, stopping in Truro Center to get a real bottle of water. The music in the store was decidedly not Gregorian. There were several people in the store, and Katie felt a little apprehensive about going in, but she was parched and needed the water. Once inside, she was fine, but it bothered her that she'd thought twice about going in. Cracks were opening, and the fear was seeping through.

When Katie arrived at the house and saw the tree lying across the driveway, she kicked it a few times to make sure it was real. There was a large hole where the tree had stood, and the severed roots fanned out from the base of the trunk like snakes from Medusa's head. There was something familiar about the fallen tree, and all at once she knew why. She had seen it in a dream.

CHAPTER FIFTEEN

Casters and Ugandans

Rachel heaved the keg onto the folding table in the front yard of the Bradford House. The keg had only recently been reintroduced into the Bradford Society meetings after the fallout from the LSD microdosing ordeal. Tending to the beer kegs had been one of Rachel's responsibilities when she was Maggie Mason's assistant. Beer was what the Pilgrims drank—in large quantities—so the society had adopted it as their drink of choice. When Maggie had the meetings in her Provincetown backyard, everyone was plastered and a little bit trippy from the acid by the time the meetings were over. Rachel knew nothing of the special ingredient that had been added to the beer. Only Maggie and her supplier, Sammy Boland, knew about the LSD. After Maggie went to jail, the society continued to serve beer at their meetings, but only the store-bought kind. Homemade beer was no longer allowed.

This particular meeting had been hastily arranged. It was not on the calendar. When Katie told Rachel about the stolen boat, Rachel was furious. "It's time we find this guy," Rachel said. "Enough." To that end, she sent out notices to the members, asking them to come to the Bradford House that evening for an important meeting.

Rob was frustrated with Katie when she told him what had happened. He wanted her to call the police. "This isn't just a case of someone seeing him or thinking they've seen him," he said. "He stole your fucking boat!"

Katie wasn't going to say that she was tripping at the time and that it could have been anyone who hopped into the boat. And what could the police do, anyway? Keep an eye out for it, just like they were keeping an eye out for Boland? "It's not like a stolen car, Rob," she said. "The police aren't going to find it. Our members stand a better chance of finding the boat than they do."

Rob had to call somebody, so he called Mike Van Winkle instead. Van Winkle couldn't understand why Boland would want to steal Katie's rowboat. Rob explained the importance of the boat to the Dorothy Bradford Society. Van Winkle asked if Boland held some sort of grudge against them. Rob had no idea. He only worried that Boland might hold a grudge against Katie, but that made no sense. They had never met. Rob invited Van Winkle to come to the society meeting that evening. "You're sure to hear a lot of theories," Rob said. "You and I will be the only two guys there."

Katie came outside to help Rachel set up chairs. Rachel noticed that she seemed anxious. She'd set a chair, then stand staring at it with her hands clasped together.

"Let me kick things off," Rachel said. "I called the meeting."

"Why?" Katie said, not wanting to surrender to the anxiety. "I'm all right."

"I know. But let me do it anyway. I can get them fired up, and that's what we need right now."

Katie knew she was right. Rachel was the person to call the membership to action, whether it was a pledge drive or a political cause. Katie was the more calming influence, better suited to education and training and walks in the woods.

"Let's be careful, though," Rachel said. "We know someone's going to bring up Boland's ghost at some point. Let's try not to engage in that, okay?"

"Have you told Elaine that?"

Fat Agnes came outside. She had blow-dried her hair and put on makeup. She looked entirely presentable. Katie thought she had made herself up for the meeting, but Fat Agnes had other plans.

"Danny and I are going out for dinner," she said. "I hope that's okay. Should I have asked first? I signed out."

"It's absolutely fine," Katie said.

"I will be in good company, after all."

"You let me know if he isn't!"

Fat Agnes wished them luck with the meeting and went across the street to Danny's apartment.

"Is she ready to go back into the world?" Rachel said, continuing with the chairs, unfolding two at a time. She was a strong woman.

"She's doing really well."

"She told me she doesn't want us to call her Fat Agnes anymore."

"I never liked that name."

"She and Danny are hitting it off."

"It would seem so," Katie said. Her voice thinned out a bit. Rachel heard the drop in tone and knew it didn't have to do with Danny and Kristin. Katie was dealing with nerves. She'd be standing up in front of a crowd in an hour.

"You need to be Dorothy Bradford now," Rachel said. "Right?"

"I'm okay."

"Who are you?"

"Dorothy."

◆ ◆

The meeting started promptly at five o'clock. Ninety-five members showed up, and as Rob had predicted, he and Mike Van Winkle were the only two men. They stood by the keg while the rest of the crowd sat down with their beers and listened as Rachel opened the meeting. She stood next to an easel on which she had placed the poster-sized photo of Dorothy Bradford in her rowboat, the one stolen by Sammy Boland.

"Sammy Boland stole Dorothy's rowboat!" Rachel said indignantly, and that was all it took to get everyone's attention.

Katie sat in the front row and listened to the yelling and hollering that ensued. There was no more important symbol to the Dorothy Bradford Society than the rowboat—far more important than the Mayflower or a beer mug. Stealing the rowboat was akin to stealing a beloved mascot.

"Is Dorothy okay?" someone shouted. "Did he hurt her?"

"She's fine," Rachel said, motioning for Katie to get up. Katie stood and faced the members. She felt the weight of their attention bear down on her, causing her pulse to quicken. Her thoughts swirled in her head, difficult to retrieve and more difficult to convert into words.

"He didn't do anything to me," she said, her voice shaking, then quickly returned to her seat.

"What did he do to her?" someone demanded to know, convinced that Dorothy Bradford was not all right.

Rob saw the panic in Katie's eyes and knew immediately what was wrong. He went quickly to the front of the assembly and sat down in the empty seat next to her. He leaned over and asked if she was okay.

"Just a little anxious," she said.

Rob squeezed her hand and said, "Find Dorothy Bradford."

She stood again but wouldn't let go of Rob's hand, so he was forced to get up with her. They faced the audience, hand in hand, like a pair of newlyweds having just repeated their vows, and Katie declared resolutely, in a strong voice, "I need all of you to help me get it back." This elicited a loud roar from the audience and a sigh of relief from Rachel.

"What about Boland?" someone said when the noise had died down. "What do we do if we find him?"

Several suggestions were offered, one of which involved castration.

Rob waved to Mike Van Winkle, thinking it might be helpful for him to intervene. Katie thought so, too, and she made the introduction. Van Winkle counseled caution if anyone saw Boland and advised that no one engage him in any event.

"Call the police," Van Winkle said. "Or you can call me."

"The police are useless," someone shouted.

"And what if he's a ghost? What do we do then?" someone else said.

Elaine Snow, who was also sitting in the front row, raised her hand, eager to chime in. Rachel shot her a stern glance and shook her head.

"Sammy Boland is not a ghost," Rachel said. "Let's put that one to bed right now."

But the audience wasn't having it. One woman said, "Are you sure he's not a ghost?" Another said, "You can't arrest a ghost." To which someone responded, "You have to exterminate him, like vermin."

Katie leaned over to Rachel and said, "Let them get it out of their system."

What followed was a discussion of the various ways to exterminate a ghost. The first step, the members agreed, was to find Boland's body. Once that was accomplished, the skeletal remains were to be ground up and mixed with different substances, like animal blood, pig vomit, or cranberry juice. One woman thought this was bad form and said that if they found the body, they were obligated to notify the authorities and return the remains to Boland's father, Jerry, for proper burial. After further discussion, the crowd determined that the entire skeleton wasn't required, just a small fragment, like a lock of hair or a fingernail. Wondering what he had gotten himself into, Van Winkle said that no one should mutilate a corpse under any circumstances. "That'll land you in jail," he said.

Ignoring Van Winkle, the audience began to discuss possible incantations to chant over the Boland concoction, or hell broth, as someone called it. One woman yelled out a four-line verse that she apparently composed on the spot.

Ghost, ghost, ghost be gone!
Back to which ye belong!
Back to the caster!
Take your disaster!

"I don't know what a caster is," someone said.

"Does the ghost have to be there?" someone else said.

"Who chants the spell?"

Having heard enough, Rachel held up her hand. "Let's focus on finding the boat," she said. "If we find Boland in the process, then we'll let the authorities deal with him."

"And if he's a ghost?"

Elaine, who could remain silent no longer, stood up and said,

"Dorothy Bradford needs to chant the spell. It has to be Dorothy."

"No ghosts!" Rachel said. She grabbed the photo of Dorothy Bradford from the easel, held it over her head, and said, "Storm the beaches, ladies! Find the boat!"

No longer needed at the front, Rob worked his way back to the keg and drew another beer, inadvertently chanting the caster/disaster incantation to himself as he waited for his mug to fill. He'd learned a while ago that the only way to get through the society meetings was to drink plenty of beer, much the same way the Pilgrims got through their ordeals.

The incantation lady was standing behind him, and having heard Rob's recitation of her previous offering, she served up another one:

> Smoke of air and fire and earth
> Cleanse and bless this home and hearth
> Drive away all harm and fear
> Only good may enter here

"Earth and hearth don't rhyme," Rob said.

"They don't have to," the lady said.

Rachel got the members to finally focus on the boat search, and it was decided that a fleet of kayaks would be deployed on the Pamet River, since that was where the theft occurred. The kayakers agreed to meet the next morning, and then the meeting broke up, sending everyone back to the keg for more beer.

Mike Van Winkle, who may have been the only one not drinking beer, wanted to see the spot where the boat had been stolen and asked Rob if he was a kayaker.

"Me? No," Rob said. "I have problems on the water. I have problems in the water."

"Can we get there on foot?"

♦ ♦

Kristin and Danny drove back to the Bradford House after their date night in Provincetown. The society meeting had long since broken up, and Martha and Lady Agnes were hanging out in the living room. Kristin had eaten a piece of haddock for dinner, along with a potato and a non-alcoholic mojito. She was becoming more and more comfortable with keeping food in her stomach, and Danny in her company.

"Let's do something," she said.

"You just did do something," Lady Agnes said. "You went to dinner."

"I know what we can do," Kristin said. She turned on the TV and asked Danny to find the video of his gold medal run. Kristin had never seen the run or any of the last Olympics, given that she was strung out on drugs at the time. Danny, who was uncomfortable reliving past glories, explained that the ten-thousand-meter race was not really a viewer-friendly event, lasting nearly half an hour. The most popular events were the ones that took less than four minutes. The shorter, the better. He tried to convince her to watch just the last few laps, but Kristin wanted to see all of it. Danny relented and put on the YouTube version from the beginning. Then he lay on the floor and hid under a pillow.

"Stop being ridiculous," Kristin said, flipping the pillow off his face with her foot.

"I'm taking a nap," Danny said. "I've seen it before."

Lady Agnes and Martha watched, too, though Lady Agnes hung back near the bedroom owing to her continued discomfort around men. Rachel came in toward the latter part of the race. She'd seen it in real time, on the very same TV.

"Why are you on the floor, Danny?" she said.

"He's being a baby," Kristin said.

"I'm being a baby," Danny said.

"How many laps are left?" Martha said, looking altogether bored.

"Too many," Danny said.

"Don't you get tired of running in circles for so long?"

"I hate running in circles. It makes me run faster."

With four laps to go, Danny had lapped everyone else on the track, with the exception of two runners from Uganda. One of them was within striking distance, lending some uncertainty to the outcome. Danny was on world record pace. The video superimposed a moving green band on the track, showing where he was in relation to the record. The Ugandan was four or five seconds behind but looked to be in good form.

"Does he get any closer?" Martha said.

"You have to wait and see," Kristin said.

"He's fast."

"Danny's faster!"

The gap between Danny and the Ugandan had not changed by the time they reached the bell lap. Though they all knew the outcome, the girls found themselves growing anxious, wondering if Danny would really pull it off.

"Go, Danny!" Kristin said, jumping up from her seat.

The Ugandan picked up his pace, further closing the gap. The eighty thousand spectators roared as the two runners rounded the first turn of the final lap. When it seemed like he might be caught, Danny kicked into a higher gear and ran away from the Ugandan, overtaking the world record pace in the process. By the final turn, the race was over. The only question was whether Danny would break the world record. In the home stretch, the green band disappeared from the screen, and only the time was visible. The crowd noise was deafening, and the announcer, a former American runner himself, was losing his mind. He said that all the little hairs on his skin were standing up.

All the girls were on their feet now, and even Lady Agnes had inched further into the room when Danny broke the tape. His time was twenty-six minutes and nine seconds, two seconds faster than the previous world record and four seconds ahead of the Ugandan. The camera found Rob and Katie in the stands, jumping up and down with their arms around each other. Somebody gave Danny an American flag, and he took a victory lap with the Stars and Stripes fluttering behind him.

"So exciting," Kristin said, kneeling down to give Danny a hug.

"Were you tired?" Martha said. "You didn't look tired."

"I was tired later," Danny said.

The girls wanted to see the gold medal ceremony, so Danny had to play that, too.

"How come you're not crying?" Lady Agnes said. "I'd be sobbing."

"Hey, look who's talking to a guy!" Kristin said.

"It's only Danny," Lady Agnes said, smiling sheepishly.

"Exactly," Danny said, having curled up into more of a fetal position.

"Don't sell yourself short, Agnes," Rachel said. "This is the first time in a while you've been in the same room with a man. I'm proud of you."

Lady Agnes took a deep breath and nodded. Danny clapped his hands from his spot on the floor and said, "Lady Agnes is the real hero here."

Rachel beamed and said, "Lady Agnes has no fear of men."

"Lady Agnes has no fear of men," she said, repeating the mantra.

Kristin, formerly Fat Agnes, got up and gave Lady Agnes a hug. Then she announced that she was going to the bathroom to pee. She was now in the habit of declaring her reasons for going to the bathroom so as to be clear to herself and others that she was not going there to vomit.

"Too much excitement?" Lady Agnes said.

Kristin went into the bathroom. A moment later, she screamed.

◆ ◆

"What is it?" Danny said frantically, leaping to his feet and racing to the bathroom door. "Are you okay?"

Rachel didn't wait for a response. She opened the door and found Kristin standing by the toilet, looking shaken. Her gaze was on the window, but she quickly shifted her attention to a spot on the floor.

"A mouse," she said. "I think it was a mouse."

"Where did it go?" Danny said.

"I don't know."

Martha stuck her head in. "Jesus, I thought it was Boland again," she said.

"Just a mouse."

"I'll get some traps," Rachel said. "Why don't you use the other bathroom?"

"I'm okay now," Kristin said. "Now, if you don't mind?"

"It might still be in here," Danny said.

"It's just a mouse."

They left, and Kristin sat down on the toilet, keeping a close eye on the window the entire time.

CHAPTER SIXTEEN

Off Days and Bodily Fluids

There was no rain forecast, but it rained that morning anyway. The Bradford Society kayakers pushed their search, which had to be synchronized with high tide, to the following day. Rob and Van Winkle, on the other hand, planned to meet that afternoon, regardless of the weather, to visit the site of the theft. Van Winkle had a meeting in the morning, after which he'd meet Rob at the Corn Hill Beach parking lot.

After the society meeting, Rob had the feeling that Katie didn't want to talk about her anxiety, so he waited until breakfast to bring it up. She had slept peacefully through the night, as far as he knew. The fact that she was in bed with him the next morning was always a good sign. He asked her if she'd been feeling anxious in other situations or if what had happened at the meeting was an isolated event. He asked her how she was feeling now. She waved it off and said that she had things under control. "I'm allowed to have an off day every now and then, aren't I?" she said. Rob couldn't argue—he had off days all the time. With Katie, though, the worry was that the episodes would become more frequent and intense, causing her to avoid activities with other people, including those with Rob.

Katie got up to clear the dishes, signaling an end to the conversation. She glanced out the window at the fallen tree. She'd cut and cleared the section of the trunk that lay across the driveway, leaving the other two sections for later.

"What are you looking at?" Rob said, thinking another unexpected visitor was coming up the driveway.

"The tree," she said.

"I hope you'll wait until it stops raining to cut up the rest of it."

Water had ponded in the hole where the tree had stood. The exposed roots had turned brown. There had to be thousands of downed trees across the Outer Cape, Katie thought, but most of those snapped in two, leaving the roots intact. Finding trees blown clean out of the soil like the one in the front yard, like the one in her dream, might not be that hard to find.

"I'll be working downstairs this morning," she said, "then at the Bradford House this afternoon." She finished rinsing the dishes, then went over to Rob and gave him a kiss on the cheek.

"What's that for?" Rob said.

"That's for being there for me yesterday," she said. Then she went downstairs and disappeared into her workshop.

◆ ◆

The rain didn't stop Danny and Kristin from going out for their morning run. Danny ran no matter the weather, and he had no trouble convincing Kristin to come along in the lousy conditions. Afterwards, they showered together at Danny's place. Danny wrapped Kristin in a towel and carried her over to the bed. "You're getting heavier," he said, pretending to labor under the weight. Horizontal exercise ensued, followed by a second trip to the shower.

After breakfast, Kristin returned to the Bradford House. Lady Agnes and Martha were sitting with Rachel in the living room. They were discussing ways in which Lady Agnes could continue to overcome her fear of men.

"Maybe I should go running with Danny," she said, causing some laughter. The girls had begun needling Kristin about all the time she'd been spending with Danny of late. Kristin knew they were probably just jealous, but the attention bothered her nonetheless. Sensing her irritation, Rachel asked her about what she might do after leaving the Bradford House.

"She'll be doing Danny," Lady Agnes said, causing Martha to laugh hysterically.

"At least I've got someone," Kristin said. Ordinarily, the two of them traded barbs in a good-natured fashion, but Kristin now felt she was being attacked.

"Easy, girls," Rachel said. "Take a breath. We're here to help each other."

"I was just kidding around," Lady Agnes said.

"Well, I'll be gone soon. You'll have to find someone else to kid."

"What *will* you do?" Martha said, trying to relieve the tension.

"Maybe get a job at a gym where I can work out for free," Kristin said. Everyone thought this sounded fantastic, and they expressed their support without any ribbing. "And Danny," she added.

◆ ◆

In Provincetown, Mike Van Winkle sat in his hotel room and watched the rain pound the parking lot. He had a meeting with his client in an hour and was hoping the rain would let up before he had to leave. Not only was Van Winkle a private detective who didn't drink, but he was also a private detective who didn't own a raincoat.

The rain was ponding on Route Six, leaving Van Winkle to slalom around the water hazards, which was made more difficult by the car's awful wipers that skidded across the windshield and left just a sliver of clear glass to see through. The rain seemed to let up when he pulled off of Route Six, but more likely it was just the decrease in speed that reduced the intensity. The road he turned onto went right past the Truro Police Station and then meandered its way toward the bay. The house was not on the bay but sat atop a crest that offered a partial view of the water. Van Winkle parked in the driveway, next to the sign with the name and house number on it. The name, printed in neat white letters, was "Boland."

Van Winkle knocked on the door, but there was no answer. There were also no gutters, and the rain slid off the roof and dumped onto the ground, splattering sand and pine needles onto Van Winkle's pants. He peeked in a few windows on the sides of the house, away from the eaves, but didn't see anything. Jerry Boland's car was in the driveway, and a light was on somewhere on the second floor. He tried the door again and heard a dog barking. It was a feeble bark, and the dog sounded as though it was in distress. Van Winkle had met the dog the last time he met with Sammy Boland's father, some form of mutt who had barked much louder than the dog he now heard through the door.

The door was secured with a deadbolt lock. Van Winkle carried a tension wrench and pick on his key chain, and after knocking a third time and calling out Boland's name, he picked the lock and opened the door. The first thing he saw was the dog sitting by the door, panting and looking dehydrated. But it was the smell that alarmed him—the stench of rotting eggs and feces. He'd smelled it before—it was the smell of a decomposing corpse.

The walls of the living room were covered with Sammy Boland's photos, most of them pictures of birds skimming across the water or scavenging along the shoreline. But there were no signs of disruption here or anywhere else on the first floor, except for the dog urine and feces. Van Winkle found the dog's water bowl in the kitchen and filled it up. He brought it to the dog, then went up the stairs to the bedroom, the room with the light on.

◆ ◆

Owing to the proximity of the police station, Don Hill and three officers were there five minutes after receiving the call from Van Winkle. Hill asked one of the officers to call the county's animal rescue squad and have them handle the dog.

Hill climbed the stairs slowly, bracing himself for what he was about to see. Van Winkle had only said that Jerry Boland was dead, but from the tone of his voice, he could tell the scene was disturbing. One of the officers who followed him upstairs stopped and vomited over the railing, adding to the piles of excrement in the first-floor hall.

Van Winkle stood by the bedroom window. He had wanted to open it and get some air into the room, but he knew that could contaminate the crime scene, especially with the blowing rain outside. Don Hill would later say that Van Winkle was white as a ghost.

When the officer came to the bedroom door, he vomited again. Don Hill told him to go back downstairs. There were enough bodily fluids to examine without having to pick through a policeman's puke. Hill was glad he hadn't eaten lunch yet; otherwise, he might have thrown up as well. On the bed was a body. Hill could only assume it was Jerry Boland. His face had been chewed off.

CHAPTER SEVENTEEN

Witches and Hijinks

Every Sunday, Elizabeth Hatch, the spinster schoolteacher who Thomas Ridley called one of the most beautiful women on Cape Cod, went for a long walk on the ocean beaches. She wore a white cotton dress and a wide-brim hat to keep the sun off her face. She always brought a book along, and after a few miles, she'd sit at the base of the dunes and read.

Elizabeth only ever saw a handful of other people during her walks. On this occasion, a warm day in June, she was sitting with her book when another woman appeared, walking along the shoreline. She was barefoot and had on a white pleated dress. Her hair was long and blond and hung down to her waist. She looked as though she was getting ready for bed. The woman's gaze was fixed mostly on the waves, but every so often she looked down at the sand in front of her. Elizabeth noticed that her lips were moving. She might have been reciting a poem or singing a song. All at once, the woman stopped and turned to look at Elizabeth, her eyes squinting from the bright sun hovering over the dunes.

"Good afternoon," Elizabeth said politely. The woman no longer seemed so far away and was easily within earshot. Elizabeth noticed a resemblance. The woman looked just like her. They could have been sisters.

"I know who you are," the woman said.

Elizabeth closed her book and stood up, brushing the sand off the backside of her dress. "I'm Elizabeth Hatch," she said.

The woman came nearer. Her feet barely left an impression in the sand. "And you must know who I am," she said.

Elizabeth looked closer, thinking at first that the woman might have been the mother of one of her students, but she would have remembered a woman that looked just like her. "I do not," she said. "Please tell me."

"You must have come here to find me. Well, here I am." The woman held out her arms. She held a rock in each of her hands, as if to provide ballast. They were smooth and thin and appeared almost to be a part of her palms.

"I'm sorry," Elizabeth said. "I walk this beach regularly and can say that I have never seen you here before, or in town either, for that matter."

"Why do you walk the beach? Are you searching for someone?"

"I walk for solitude, for pleasure."

The woman sneered. Her eyes narrowed. "I cannot be sure of your motives. Your beauty is unsettling, though. We look the same, you and I. You could be a threat."

"A threat? To you? I don't even know who you are. Please stop this charade."

"You should not be here when Samuel returns. He might mistake you for me." The woman held her hand up to Elizabeth's face, fingers outstretched. The rock remained in her palm. Elizabeth took a step backward as the woman began to recite what sounded like an incantation.

"What are you doing?" Elizabeth said. "Are you insane?"

"Do not move, please," the woman said, now waving her hand at Elizabeth's feet. "I am banishing you from this place."

"Are you a witch?" Elizabeth said.

"I shall banish you from this place for two hundred years. Samuel will have returned by then. In the meantime, you may go anywhere else you like and practice your hijinks there."

"My hijinks? I'm a schoolteacher."

"No one will miss you." The woman held her hand up to Elizabeth's face again. "Now, I need you to speak the names you are known by. Please tell me."

Elizabeth tried to move away, but her feet felt sluggish. She swung her book at the woman's head and hit her in the temple. The woman was unaffected.

"I would have expected you to be a more formidable opponent," the witch said. "Perhaps you have no powers of your own? The names, please." The witch murmured a new incantation. "This will go a lot easier if you cooperate."

"I have told you my name," Elizabeth said.

"Never mind. It doesn't matter." The witch circled behind Elizabeth and held up both of her hands now, as though she meant to push Elizabeth Hatch into the sea. "I could banish you forever, but I am not uncaring. One day you will be back here walking this beach, and I will be gone, reunited with my Samuel. Perhaps we will meet again. Perhaps we will be friends."

And then the witch began her chant. It went like this:

Behold what is left

No matter how odd

For two hundred years

Set no foot on Cape Cod

Nothing happened. The witch waved her hands and recited the spell again. Elizabeth sighed and rolled her eyes.

"Shit," the witch said. "I used the wrong spell. That one was for a ghost, not a witch. I haven't had cause to banish any witches lately."

"As I've said, I am a schoolteacher," Elizabeth said. "Now, please leave and let me go about my business." She took another swipe at the witch, this time grazing her forehead.

"Please stop doing that," the witch said. "It's getting annoying." Her eyes went wide, and she started a new chant. This one went like this:

> There can be only one witch
> On the land that we trod
> Until I depart
> Be you gone from Cape Cod

A strong gust of wind kicked up a cloud of sand that enveloped both the witch and Elizabeth Hatch. The witch's eyes closed, and she began dancing in a circle, her head thrown back. When the wind died down, Goodie Hallett said farewell and continued on her way down the beach. That was the last anyone saw of Elizabeth Hatch on Cape Cod.

CHAPTER EIGHTEEN

Fire Roads
and Rabbit Holes

When Mike Van Winkle met Rob in the Corn Hill Beach parking lot and told him about Jerry Boland's face becoming dog food, Rob thought of the coyote ripping the flesh off the seal carcass at Race Point, its hind legs braced, its jaws locked, and its head jerking until the flesh came free.

"The whole face?" Rob said.

"Most of it," Van Winkle said. "His nose and cheeks were gone. Grisly stuff. When a dog is starving, it will eat whatever's available."

Jerry Boland had died in his sleep and lay in bed for three days before Van Winkle arrived. The EMTs, who had seen this type of thing before, said the dog began by licking its master's face, trying to get him to wake up. Two days later, the dog's basic instincts took over, and the licks turned into bites.

"So Jerry was your client, then?" Rob said.

"He paid me half up front," Van Winkle said. "The other half was due when I found Sammy. Actually, I get paid even if it's not me who finds him. I guess I need to find out who Jerry's attorney is."

The rain had finally stopped, and the sun was carving up the cloud cover. Van Winkle was late to their meeting at Corn Hill owing to the grisly scene at Jerry Boland's house.

"So are you going to keep looking for him?" Rob said.

"I guess I should talk to Boland's attorney first, but if I want to get paid the balance of the fee, I need to see this thing through."

Rob led Van Winkle south along Corn Hill Road and then wandered off into the sand and brush. A few feet later, they came to the terminus of the northern branch of the Pamet River, which looked more like a drainage ditch at this point than a river.

"This is the river?" Van Winkle said, sounding unimpressed.

"It gets bigger," Rob said.

They continued south, and the river widened. The sun was out now, as was the tide, which had shallowed the river appreciably. Birds picked through the leavings along the narrow shore.

"This must have been where she was," Van Winkle said. "We're running out of beach." Up ahead, the grasses overtook the land between the river and the dunes to the bay. There was nowhere else to land a boat or to walk.

"Not much else to see, I guess," Rob said.

"How far is the bay?"

"Maybe a hundred yards."

"Is there a path somewhere? Katie said Boland came from the bay beach."

They found a path that cut through the grasses to the bay. Rob had never walked through this area before, and he kept his focus on the ground in front of him, ever vigilant for poison ivy.

"Hey, what's that?" Van Winkle said. They were just a few yards from the river, and there, resting in the grass, was a rowboat, though Van Winkle had never seen a rowboat like this one before.

"Jesus," Rob said. "That's Katie's boat."

♦ ♦

Once the rain stopped, Katie picked up Elaine Snow, and the two of them drove to the fire road that ran through the woods between Collins Road and the ocean. Elaine believed that if someone wanted to bury a body in the woods, they'd most likely drive down a fire road at night and dig a shallow grave near the side of the road. That way, the killer could unload the body from the trunk of the car and dump it right into the grave. They chose this particular fire road because it was close to the spot where Danny had seen Sammy Boland, and Katie knew from the Norseman that ghosts tended to stay close to their remains.

Katie had decided on this new course of action as the best way to treat her relapsing anxieties. She was beginning to doubt the effectiveness of the LSD, and rather than take more of it, which remained a possibility, she was convinced now that her fears wouldn't subside until she dealt with Sammy Boland. So she decided to operate under the assumption that Sammy Boland was, in fact, a ghost and that she was meant to get rid of him. To that end, she would go and find his body, as a few of the society's members had suggested, and chant a few cryptic words that may or may not rhyme. Sammy Boland's ghost was eliciting her fears, as ghosts were wont to do, and once the ghost was gone, her fears would leave with him.

Elaine had readily agreed to come along on the excursion. Rachel thought it was crazy to think they were going to stumble upon an unmarked grave. "But it's not unmarked," Elaine said. "There's an uprooted tree there. Dorothy saw it in her dreams."

"I thought we agreed not to chase ghosts," Rachel said.

"We're not chasing ghosts. We're looking for Boland's body," Katie said.

"And what if he's not dead?"

"Oh, he's dead," Elaine said. "They would have caught him a long time ago if he wasn't."

The fire road had a chain across the entrance; only emergency vehicles were allowed to enter. Though, if someone wanted to—someone with a body in the trunk—they could have maneuvered a car through the trees and onto the fire road. Katie wasn't about to drive onto the fire road, so she parked the car and grabbed the shovels from the back seat. She gave one to Elaine, who held the thing out in front of her like a dead animal.

"Put it over your shoulder, like this," Katie said, demonstrating.

Elaine lifted the shovel onto her shoulder with great effort, and the two women marched down the fire road.

◆ ◆

Rob took the oars but left the boat. The tide was too low to row back to the harbor, and Rob wasn't going to row anything anyway. He and Van Winkle drove straight to the Bradford House, expecting to find Katie there. Rachel met them instead.

"She's not here, Rob," she said.

Rob told her about the boat, pointing to the oars sticking out of the car's rear window.

"Boland brought it back?"

"It looks that way."

"One less thing to worry about, I guess," Rachel said, sounding concerned.

"Is there something else?" Rob said. "Where's Katie?"

Rachel groaned. "She and Elaine went out looking for Boland's grave," she said.

Rob stared at Rachel, looking puzzled.

"Where?" Van Winkle said, bothered that he hadn't been included. "Did someone tell them where to look?"

"They're looking for a downed tree, like the one in your front yard."

"I think I'm missing something," Rob said, still confused.

"She said she's had dreams about an uprooted tree and thinks that's where Boland's body is buried."

"So he's dead now? She just saw him yesterday."

"Did she?"

"She's gone down the rabbit hole," Van Winkle said. Rachel and Rob didn't react, and he worried they'd heard it as an insult. "Sorry," he said. "That's what my dad says about my mom when she starts chasing ghosts."

"I thought you were making an LSD reference," Rachel said.

"Me, too," Rob said.

"Sorry. I hadn't thought of that. I forgot you have a history of LSD use here."

"Involuntary use."

"I wonder," Rachel said.

"What?" Rob said, though he knew where she was going.

"These visions and dreams of hers... you don't think they have something to do with LSD?"

"Where would Katie get LSD? I thought it was all gone."

"Maybe the police missed something when they cleaned out Maggie's place."

"Well, Katie wouldn't take acid voluntarily," Rob said. "If anyone went down a rabbit hole, it was Elaine, and she pulled Katie along with her."

"Do you know where they went, Rachel?" Van Winkle said.

"A fire road somewhere off Collins Road."

"Let's go," Rob said.

◆ ◆

"How about that one?" Elaine said, pointing to another downed tree. There were a lot of them. The same wind storm that knocked over the tree in the Crosleys' yard had brought down several trees along the fire road. One of them had even fallen into the road and been cut away since.

"This may have been a bad idea," Katie said.

"Don't be silly, Dorothy," Elaine said, and then covered her mouth. She'd called Dorothy Bradford silly. "I'm sorry. I mean, we just started looking."

They continued down into a swale where the tree damage was less severe. Elaine started taking pictures of the downed trees, dropping her shovel each time, scolding herself for not having documented all of them.

"Wait a minute," Katie said.

"What?"

"That tree that was cut away from the road."

Elaine dropped her shovel again and thumbed through her photos. "I don't think I got that one," she said.

Katie turned and headed back up the road while Elaine continued to scroll through her pictures.

"Come on, Elaine!"

The dimensions of the oak tree were nearly the same as the one in Katie's yard, taking into account the lengths of the three segments. The crown was similar, but it was the base of the tree that was almost identical. The severed roots looked like brown carrots, and the water in the hole where the tree had stood was murky and still.

"I think this is it," Katie said.

Elaine caught up and started snapping pictures from all angles. Katie started probing the ground with her shovel.

"Elaine, put down your camera and help me," Katie said. She'd found a bare, soft spot in the soil next to the fallen trunk and started digging. Elaine joined in but had to take a break after each shovelful. Katie did most of the work.

Their backs were turned when Rob and Mike Van Winkle came jogging down the fire road. Rob called out as they approached. Elaine spun around and held out her shovel in front of her like it was some sort of martial arts weapon.

"Jesus," Rob said. "You're up to your ass in poison ivy, Elaine."

Elaine looked down at the ground, her feet covered by the shiny green leaves. "I'm not allergic," she said.

"Well, stay away from me, please." He hadn't put on his flannel shirt and long pants, but he had the gaiter in his pocket.

"Rob, what are you doing here?" Katie said.

"That was my question for you," Rob said.

"Rachel told you?"

"We found your boat, Kay. It was where you left it, more or less."

Katie was bent over her shovel, knee-deep in the hole. She stood a little straighter upon hearing the news.

"Really?" she said. "Did you bring it back?"

"The tide was too low. I took the oars, though."

"I'll get it later. Do you want to help me dig? Elaine could use a break." Katie started digging again, tossing large mounds of soil out of the hole with each volley. As with any effort she undertook, Katie looked as though she'd been doing it her whole life, however long that may have been. Each motion was supremely efficient—arms swinging, legs lifting, hips pivoting. Van Winkle was astonished by her strength and agility.

"You're expecting to find Sammy Boland down there?" Van Winkle said.

Elaine picked up her shovel and offered it to Rob. Rob stepped back.

"Keep away from me, Elaine," he said, swatting at a mosquito. All the rain had brought on another brood of flying insects.

"It's a very promising tree," Elaine said. "Dorothy's seen it in her dreams."

Rob looked at his hand and found the exploded mosquito on his palm, lying in a splotch of blood. "So who did you see yesterday, Kay?" he said. "Who took your boat?"

"I'm not sure what I saw," she said, flipping another shovelful of soil out of the hole.

"Half the trees on Cape Cod look like this one."

"Humor me, Rob," she said, pausing for a moment. "I need to play this out."

Rob looked at Van Winkle, hoping he might have something

useful to add. Van Winkle shrugged. His cell phone rang.

"How do you get any reception out here?" Rob said.

Van Winkle answered the phone and then said nothing for an uncomfortably long period of time. Then he said, "You're kidding."

"Who was that?" Rob said when Van Winkle ended the call.

"That was Don Hill. They just fished Sammy Boland out of the Pamet River."

CHAPTER NINETEEN

DNA Tests and Road Rage

Sammy Boland's remains were found at the mouth of the river, just a hundred feet from the Ballston Beach parking lot. Early that morning, a local man returned to the lot after walking his dog on the beach. The dog was not on a leash at the time and, for some unknown reason, tore off into the bramble west of the lot. It was very unusual behavior for the dog, a ten-year-old Golden Retriever whom the owner said rarely tore after anything anymore. The owner was only able to track down the dog because he wouldn't stop barking. The man found him by the edge of the river, just a narrow, overgrown stream at this point, barking his head off. The man struggled over the last few yards, battling thick vegetation, mosquitoes, and an uprooted tree that lay across the river. When the owner appeared, the dog calmed down and started digging in the mud. What surfaced made the owner's stomach crawl.

◆ ◆

"Did he drown?" Rob said.

"Hard to know," Van Winkle said. "Hopefully the medical examiner can find a cause, but it might be difficult."

"Why?"

Van Winkle looked at Katie, who now stood motionless in the grave that wasn't a grave. A breeze came up and blew the water off the trees. Elaine covered her head with the blade of her shovel.

"Because all they found were bones and hair."

A pine cone, thick with moisture, fell from a tree behind Rob, landing with a thud that sounded much louder than it should have. Rob thought it might have been a clumsy squirrel at first, something more substantial than a pine cone.

"Oh, that is so awesome," Elaine said. "That means he's been dead a long time."

"Then how do they know it was him?" Rob said, kicking the dank pine cone.

"He was wearing the vest," Van Winkle said. They'll do a DNA test to confirm."

"So who the hell have we been seeing?" Rob said.

"You've been seeing his ghost," Elaine said.

"Or maybe it wasn't him at all," Van Winkle said.

Katie climbed out of the hole and brushed the dirt off her pants. "Where's the body now, Mike?" she said.

"Medical Examiner's Office. Why?"

"She needs it to get rid of the ghost," Elaine said.

Katie ignored Elaine's comment and began shoveling dirt back into the hole. Elaine joined in, pushing the dirt rather than shoveling.

"Here, give me that," Rob said, taking the shovel from Elaine, who was happy to surrender it.

"What are we doing, Kay?" he said, trying to keep up with her shoveling pace. She was much more proficient with tools.

"I don't need the whole body, Rob," she said. "Just a piece of it."

"Like a finger or an eyeball?" Elaine said, standing close behind.

"Why?" Rob said.

"Hold what is left, no matter how odd," Katie said.

"Is that part of the incantation?" Elaine said. "Hold what is left, no matter how odd?"

"Maybe she said, behold what is left. I'm not exactly sure."

"Who?" Rob said.

"The witch."

"The witch?" Elaine said. "Was it Goodie Hallett?"

Rob turned and gave Elaine a cold stare.

"Sorry," Elaine said, taking a step back.

"You're going to do what those women at the meeting said to do? Chant some incantation over Boland's remains?"

"I'm not doing it for them," Katie said, shoveling faster now. "And I'm not doing it for the Norseman, or Tom Ridley, or any of the rest of them. I'm doing it for me."

Rob slowed his shoveling, hoping Katie would slow down too, but she kept up her frenzied pace.

"Kay, stop," he said, and he saw that there were tears running down her cheeks. He put his hand on her shovel—he was still stronger than she was—and held it in place. She looked at him the way she did when she was fighting off a panic attack, trying to maintain her composure so she could spend a few more minutes with him.

"Help me, Rob," she said.

Rob nodded and took his hand off the shovel. "Hey, Mike," he said, giving his neck gaiter to Katie so she could wipe her face. "Do you think we can get in to see the body, or what's left of it?"

"Only if you're next of kin," Van Winkle said. "And Boland doesn't have any next of kin anymore."

Rob thought for a moment. "I've got another idea."

◆ ◆

"I'm on my way there right now," Ridgeback said, racing west on Route Six. Rob could hear car horns blaring in the background. Someone yelled, "Asshole!"

"Where?" Rob said.

"Medical Examiner's Office. Mashpee."

"Can we meet you there?"

"Who's we?"

"Katie and I. Maybe Van Winkle?"

"Why?"

Rob didn't have an answer to the question, at least not one he could share with Steve Ridgeback. He stammered a bit, then said, "I guess we're curious to see the remains. Van Winkle heard from Don Hill that it's just bones and hair."

"I've heard that, too," Ridgeback said.

"And?"

"And, how come you, Danny, and all these other people claim to have seen Boland in the last few weeks when it sounds like his body has been in the ground for over a year?"

"I don't know."

"Sure you do."

"What do you mean?" Rob said, worried he was somehow being implicated in a cover-up of some kind.

"Shithead!" Ridgeback yelled, making Rob think he was yelling at him when, in fact, it was just another driver. Ridgeback laid into his horn. Another horn answered. One day, it would be gunfire. "People don't use their turn signals anymore. It's too much trouble. Assholes are everywhere. What was I saying?"

"You think I know who it is we've been seeing."

"Of course!" Ridgeback said. "You've been seeing his ghost!"

"I thought you said you didn't believe in ghosts."

"No, I said that I'd never seen a ghost. How can anyone who lives on Cape Cod not believe in ghosts? You're living with a four-hundred-year-old Pilgrim, for Christ's sake. What does Dorothy have to say about all this?"

"Leave Katie out of this, okay?"

"Okay, but you're not going to get to see the remains unless you're next of kin."

"That's what Van Winkle said."

Katie finished filling the hole and summoned Elaine to tamp it down. Elaine danced on the loose dirt while chanting, "Behold what is left, no matter how odd; get off my land, or I'll stuff you with cod!"

"Can you do me a favor, then?" Rob said. He was wary of asking Ridgeback for favors, knowing there'd be a need for repayment in the future.

"You want pictures?"

Even though Rob had not put the call on speaker, Katie and Van Winkle could hear every word Ridgeback was saying. Rob looked at Katie. She shook her head.

"We need a piece of him," she said.

There was silence for a moment. Then Ridgeback honked his horn. "Fuck you, asshole!" he yelled, pounding his fist on the steering wheel.

"You okay?" Rob said.

"The passing lane is for passing, cocksucker!"

Rob held the phone further away from his ear.

"Someone's going to shoot that guy in the head," Van Winkle said. "Too many people with guns now."

"Is that Katie?" Ridgeback said. "Hi, Katie! What do you mean by a piece of him?"

"I don't know. Anything. A lock of hair, a piece of bone."

"You want a souvenir?"

"Yes."

"Why?"

Katie looked at Rob. Rob widened his eyes and shook his head.

"Bring me a souvenir, and I'll talk to Danny about writing that book you want, okay?"

"Deal!"

CHAPTER TWENTY

Clam Rolls and Morphine

Ridgeback had promised he would call after he'd viewed the remains, but more than two hours had passed since he'd hung up with Rob, and there was still no word.

"Maybe he got caught trying to snap off one of Boland's toes," Rob said.

Katie had started sweeping the floors when they got home and was still sweeping. Brie thought it was some sort of game and chased after the broom, barking and snapping at the bristles.

"Why don't you sit down, Kay?" Rob said, knowing she was

on edge. "The dog needs a break." Brie had begun an endless cycle of running up to the broom, trying to bite it, then racing to the opposite end of the room.

"You're sure you want to do this?" Rob said, trying to engage her. "And I'm not talking about sweeping."

Katie stopped and looked up. She swept the floors with the same sense of purpose she had when digging the hole in the woods. At times, her behavior could evolve from dutiful to obsessive. She looked at him curiously, as though she hadn't been aware he was in the room.

"Mike told me about Jerry Boland," she said. "That poor man. That poor dog. I guess they'll have to put him down." Brie growled at the now-idle broom, trying to revive its spirit. "And I don't want to do this; I need to do this. I can pretend there's a ghost, just like I can pretend to be Dorothy Bradford."

Rob found some consolation in knowing that Katie did not believe in Sammy Boland's ghost. But who was it she'd seen stealing her rowboat, and who was it he'd seen at Race Point?

"So once you have Boland's toe and chant your spell, it'll be over?"

"I hope Steve doesn't bring back a toe. That's a little too morbid, and we've had too much morbidity today."

When, at last, Steve Ridgeback called, he was not on the road or at home; he was at the Cape Cod Hospital.

"I rolled the Subaru," Ridgeback said. "Broke my back. I'm in traction!"

"Jesus. Are you okay?" Rob said.

"Of course not! I broke my back!"

Ridgeback had, in fact, been trying to call Rob when he drifted across the median. Horns blared, and Ridgeback veered hard back into his lane, but the wheels came up and the car flipped over, tumbling off the road and into the pines.

"They had to cut me out of the car," Ridgeback said. "The jaws of life!" For someone who had just suffered major trauma, he was having no trouble making himself heard.

"Do you need anything?" Rob said, knowing Ridgeback didn't have any family close by. He really wanted to ask about Boland's remains, but he didn't want to seem insensitive.

"They've got me on morphine. What else could I need?"

Rob looked over at Katie, who was struggling for control of the broom. Brie had clamped her jaws on the handle and was trying to tug it away from her. "What happened?" she said.

Rob shook his head and said, "He's in the hospital. Wrecked his car."

"And I broke my back!" Ridgeback yelled through the phone. Katie heard him and covered her mouth with her hand. Brie broke free with the broom and raced into the bedroom.

"Did this happen on the way back from the coroner?" Rob said.

"Of course! But I got what you asked for. I'm not sure where it is now, though."

"What do you mean?"

"It was in an envelope on the passenger seat. I assume it's still in the car, but I don't know for sure. I don't even know where the car is right now."

"We should go see him," Katie said. She went to the bedroom to try and salvage the broom before Brie turned it into splinters.

"We're coming down there," Rob said. "We'll find out where the car is."

"Can you bring me a notepad?" Ridgeback said. "I don't have anything to write on."

"Sure. We'll be there in an hour."

"I'll try and hang on."

"You're making jokes?"

"It's the drugs."

"What's in the envelope, Steve?"

"A tooth!"

♦ ♦

Traffic was light on the trip down to Hyannis. Rob's eyes kept scanning the trees on the opposite side of Route Six, looking for signs of Ridgeback's wreck. He had no idea where the accident had occurred. He only knew it happened while Ridgeback was heading home.

"What are we going to tell Ridgeback?" Rob said. "We can't tell him you're banishing a ghost."

"Yeah, we can," Katie said. "We'll just tell him that some of the members of the society want to stage an exorcism. That's almost the truth anyway."

"He'll want to be there, though. He'll want to write about it."

"I don't think we'll have to worry about that."

"Why not?"

"Because he's in the hospital, Rob."

Ridgeback was admitted to the surgical wing of the hospital, but he didn't need any surgery. As was typical of Steve Ridgeback, he had embellished the consequences of his accident. Technically, he did have a broken back, but it was just a small crack in one of the vertebrae. He had suffered no neurological damage, just some numbness in his legs. And he wasn't in traction.

"I thought you said you were in traction," Rob said.

"Did I say that? Must have been the morphine."

"Was there a lot of pain?" Katie said.

"Of course! Though I don't feel anything now."

"But you're going to be okay?"

"That's what the doctors tell me, but I have to stay in bed for a few days, and then I'll have to wear a brace for a month."

"Here," Rob said, tossing the spiral notepad he'd brought on the bed.

"Jesus, Rob," Katie said. "Don't throw things at him."

"Thanks," Ridgeback said. He opened the notebook and began writing things down.

"What are you writing already?" Rob said.

"All sorts of things have come to mind since the accident, and I haven't had anything to write them down on. I asked the nurse for some paper, but she never brought me any. They're not very caring here. Bastards."

"Is there anything you need?" Katie said.

"I need you to find my car. See if it's a total loss. And find the tooth, of course. My other notebook is in there, too. That's where I have all my notes about the remains. And you're still going to talk to Danny about the book, right?"

"Only if we find the tooth," Rob said.

"Of course I'll talk to him about the book," Katie said.

Ridgeback told them about what he'd seen in the Medical Examiner's Office. Boland's skeleton was largely intact. Everything except the bones and the hair had decomposed. Most of his clothing, including the vest he was fond of wearing, had survived the elements.

"There were no signs of trauma to the skeleton," Ridgeback said. "No blows to the head, no broken bones. There were blood stains on his shirt and pants. The coroner thinks he was either shot or stabbed, though he didn't find any bullet fragments. The police didn't find a knife either."

"It doesn't sound like a mob hit. The mob wouldn't stab someone, would they?"

"They'd strangle him or shoot him in the head," Ridgeback said. He extended his thumb and forefinger to mimic a gun and said, "Pop!"

"How'd you get the tooth?"

"The coroner had them in a plastic bag on his desk, for DNA testing, I guess. He had to step out for a minute, so I opened the bag and helped myself. It's fine. There were five teeth in there. How many do you need for a DNA test? They'll never miss it. There's plenty more." Ridgeback shifted in the bed as best he could and grimaced.

"You okay?" Rob said.

"I'm not okay!"

"Right. Sorry. You broke your back. You know, you really shouldn't be allowed to drive."

"I'm not driving anywhere for a while." Ridgeback tried to reach behind himself to adjust the pillows. Katie went over to help.

"So how do we find your car, Steve?" she said, helping to get him situated.

"The police told me it's in a lot in Yarmouth. I have the

address. I called them and said you'd be coming to get my stuff. But you won't be able to do it until tomorrow. They close at 4:30."

Rob checked his phone. It was 5:45. They'd have to drive back down in the morning.

"Rob and I were thinking of grabbing dinner down here," Katie said. "Can we get you something and bring it back?"

"Yeah, a bottle of scotch," Ridgeback said.

"You can't drink," Katie said. "You're on morphine."

"I was never on morphine."

"What?" Rob said.

"They gave me some ibuprofen and anti-inflammatories. Everyone in the medical profession is terrified to prescribe morphine anymore. If my spine was in two pieces, they'd give me morphine."

Rob and Katie went out and got clam rolls and a bottle of scotch, and the three of them ate dinner together in the hospital room. Rob had been hoping for a quiet dinner with just the two of them, but Katie wouldn't hear of it.

"So, tell me what you're going to do with the tooth, Dorothy," Ridgeback said, looking squarely at Katie. He knew it had nothing to do with Rob.

In a very convincing fashion, Katie explained that the society was going to stage an exorcism of Sammy Boland's ghost and needed "a piece of him" to include in the ceremony.

"That sounds very witchy," Ridgeback said, his eyes widening. "Like a coven or something." He wrote down some notes and then, as predicted, said, "Can I come?"

"This is all off the record, Steve," Rob said. "It's just a game, like Dungeons and Dragons."

"You guys are too old for Dungeons and Dragons."

"You get the idea."

"Listen, I've got to finish the story about Boland's murder before I write about anything else. It'll be in the papers tomorrow. So, can I come to the witch thing?"

"You're in the hospital, Steve. You've got a broken back. Where are you going to go?"

"Can you FaceTime me?"

CHAPTER TWENTY-ONE

Wrecked Cars
and Boland's Tooth

Danny and Kristin ran to Ryder Beach that morning and walked back along the water. The first weekend in July—the holiday weekend—crept closer, and the waterfront properties stirred to life as owners readied their homes for the summer season. Kristin tied her shoes together and slung them over her shoulder, stuffing the socks inside. Danny kept his shoes on—his feet were too important to risk stepping on a jagged shell or a sharp rock.

"We should run on the beach sometime," Kristin said.

"Too uneven," Danny said. "You're on an angle the whole

time." Danny picked up a flat rock and flung it into the water. "Jesus, I'm beginning to sound like my dad."

"He won't run on the beach either?"

"He'll walk on it, but mostly for the dog."

"Have you ever hurt your foot walking on the beach?"

"No."

"You're like a soldier, never taking his boots off."

"You've got to take care of your feet."

"*You* do, Mr. Track Star." Kristin veered off into the surf and let the water come up to her knees. She used to hate going into the water. It was always too cold. She didn't mind now. She was better insulated.

"Did you hear they found Boland's body?" Danny said.

"Rachel told us last night."

"Sounds like he's been dead a while."

"Whatever."

"I guess the guy I saw wasn't Boland. It sure looked like him, though."

"Who?"

"The guy I saw in the woods last week. The guy who ran away from me."

"Somebody else, I guess," she said, her voice dropping off, barely audible over the six-inch waves lapping at the shore.

"We don't have to talk about it," Rob said, sensing Sammy

Boland was still a sore subject for her. "I have to go to Boston for a couple of days."

"Why?" she said, sounding irritated. Danny was surprised by her tone.

"I leave later this morning," he said. "Meeting with my coaches."

"Oh." She turned her back and looked down at a stray bit of seaweed wrapping around her leg.

"Are you okay?"

"Sure."

"You sound bothered. Are you bothered?"

"A little, I guess."

"Tell me why," he said. Sometimes he needed to remind himself that she was still in recovery.

"Shit." She started to cry.

"What is it?" He didn't want to go in the water, but he took off his shoes and went in anyway, putting his arm around her.

"I'm sorry, Danny. I don't mean to sound so needy. I can get a little crazy about the things I like."

"Does that mean you like me?"

"Shut up," she said, managing a smile.

They held hands for the rest of the walk home, and Danny even kept his shoes off. On the way up the stairs to the house, they met Helen Schantz coming down to the beach. She stopped midway and studied the man and woman approaching. Danny knew enough of Helen Schantz to know that the woman didn't recognize him. She certainly didn't recognize Kristin.

"Hello, Helen," Danny said as they prepared to squeeze by.

"Are you visiting someone?" she said. She was wearing only a one-piece bathing suit, no robe or hat, and large sunglasses that dwarfed her nose. Her feet were bare.

"It's me, Danny Crosley."

Helen looked more closely. Her gaze settled on Kristin.

"You're very skinny," she said.

"I am," Kristin said.

Helen Schantz narrowed her eyes, and Danny became concerned that she was going to make an inappropriate comment about heroin use. She didn't say anything, though. She remained squarely in the middle of the steps, blocking their way. Her eyes were glassy. She was clearly stoned.

"We'll be heading up," Danny said. "Enjoy the beach."

Still, she didn't move.

"Is she okay?" Kristin said. "She looks wasted."

"Relax," Helen said finally. It may well have been the first time Helen Schantz ever told anyone to relax. "How nice to be young," she said, and then stepped aside and let them continue up the stairs.

◆ ◆

Katie was feeling anxious that morning, so Rob offered to drive down to Yarmouth himself. She'd had a restless night, and after much tossing and turning, she moved into one of the spare bedrooms. Rob worried that he was the cause of the anxiety, and fearing a full-blown panic attack, he thought she should stay home and let him retrieve the tooth.

"Are you sure?" she said.

"It's probably better this way. There might be other journalists out there looking for a Dorothy Bradford story. Stay here. I'll call you."

Rob started the car and revved the engine a few times, wondering what would happen if he didn't find the tooth. There were sure to be human teeth available for sale on the internet, he thought. He could also stop at a dentist's office and see if they had any stray molars lying around. No one would know it wasn't Boland's tooth, and why did it matter? It was just a prop.

Rob looked through the trees toward Helen Schantz's house, wondering why the engine noise hadn't brought her out onto the deck. Any time there was a loud noise, Helen Schantz came outside to investigate. Perhaps she had already gone down to the beach? Or perhaps she was just too stoned to care anymore. Rob put the car in gear and rolled quietly down the driveway.

On the way to Route Six, he stopped to pick up newspapers at the market. All of them had stories about Sammy Boland being dug out of the Pamet River. Even the Boston papers devoted column space to the story. Any time a body was found anywhere on the Cape, it was big news, especially in Truro. Truro had a history of gruesome murders, some of which were mentioned in the articles. The most famous one happened in 1970, when Tony Costa murdered four women and buried their mutilated bodies in a field of marijuana plants. Costa never admitted to the crimes and was convicted on overwhelming circumstantial evidence. He received a life sentence, serving five years before he hung himself in his cell.

Steve Ridgeback's story included a few paragraphs on the recent sightings of Boland and how they conflicted with the body's advanced stage of decomposition. "The medical examiner will confirm an approximate time of death, but it appears from the remains that Sammy Boland was murdered approximately two years ago," Ridgeback wrote. He cited the places where Boland had reportedly been seen, including Tim Desmond's home and the Dorothy Bradford House. If he'd written anything about the ghost theory, his editors had struck it out. But he didn't have to write anything—his readers would come to that conclusion themselves.

After being pulled out of the trees along Route Six, Steve Ridgeback's Subaru had been towed to an auto parts store in

Yarmouth. Ridgeback said that the car was pretty banged up and likely beyond repair. This particular auto parts store was the beneficiary of most of the mash-ups on Route Six and got to strip the cars once the insurance companies decided they were goners. Rob turned off his phone to eliminate distractions and drove slowly the whole way, constantly checking his mirrors for any sign of trouble. He did not want to end up in the trees, too.

The manager of the auto parts store was skinny and bald, and his arms were covered with tattoos. At first, he was reluctant to discuss the car with Rob, claiming not to have any knowledge of Ridgeback's prior authorization. Rob told the manager to call Ridgeback. The manager didn't want to call Ridgeback, so Rob did and handed the manager the phone. The manager listened to Ridgeback for what seemed like a full minute, then said, "Okay," and handed the phone back to Rob.

"Are we good?" Rob said. The manager ignored the question and disappeared into a back office. A moment later, he returned with a cardboard box.

"This is what we took out of the car," he said, dropping the box on the counter. Rob looked through the box, hoping to see an envelope, but all he found was Ridgeback's notepad, the car key and registration, a jacket, and the owner's manual.

"That's it?" Rob said.

"Except for the trash," the manager said. "We threw that away."

"How did you know it was trash?" Rob said, annoyed.

"You want to see empty soda cans and food wrappers?" the man said.

"I'm looking for an envelope," Rob said.

"I didn't see an envelope," the manager said.

"You cleaned out the car?"

"I clean them all out."

"I'd like to see it," Rob said.

"Out the door and to your left," the manager said. "Back of the lot against the fence."

Rob fished out the Subaru key fob from the box.

"You won't need that," the manager said.

"What do you mean?"

"Doors don't close."

There were five wrecked cars at the back of the lot. Most of them were unrecognizable as far as make and model were concerned, the logos lost in the chaos of twisted plastic and metal. The Subaru was in the best condition of the group, having retained some of its original shape, though no part of the car was undamaged. In addition to rolling over, the car had apparently rammed into a tree or an abutment of some kind; the engine compartment was partially collapsed. All four of the doors were ajar; none of them were able to close completely. Though it wasn't his car, Rob felt a sense of loss when he opened the passenger-side door. He had been sitting there just a few days ago, bouncing through the Provincetown dunes. The seat itself was undamaged, but there was a gash in the floorboard through which Rob could see the pavement below. "Shit," he said, picturing the envelope sliding through the gash like a letter disappearing into a mail slot. Boland's tooth was back in the woods again.

"What are you looking for?"

The voice came from inside the car. Startled, Rob banged his head on the ceiling, or what was left of it, and turned to find a man lying in the back seat. He had long, ratty hair and wore an unzipped parka. He looked like he had been sleeping.

"Are you supposed to be in here?" Rob said, backing out of the car. He wasn't about to get murdered in a car lot over a lost tooth.

"Don't mind me. I sometimes sneak on the lot and sleep in the wrecks. Owner don't care, long as I'm gone before they open. Guess I overslept." The man laughed and then coughed. Rob noticed he was missing a few teeth.

"Would you mind getting out now?" Rob said.

"You still haven't told me what you're looking for."

Rob raised his hands in frustration and looked back toward the office, wondering if the manager was related to the derelict in the back seat.

"Okay, an envelope," Rob said.

"White or vanilla?" the man said.

"I think you mean manila."

"Sure."

"I don't know."

"What's in it? Money?"

"It's not money."

"What then?"

"A tooth."

"Don't fuck with me. I'm not as stupid as I look."

"I'm not fucking with you."

"Will you give me five bucks if I find it?"

"I'd rather just look for it myself, if that's okay with you."

"Be my guest," the man said, and dropped his head down on the seat.

Rob bent down and looked under the passenger seat. There was a foul odor in the car. He gagged. Finding nothing under the seat, he checked the sliver of space between the seat and the center console. He found a pen and some loose change. Then he went around to the driver's side and checked there. No envelope. He was now faced with having to look in the back seat—something he wasn't about to do with the man lying there, along with whatever he might have excreted on the upholstery.

"Okay," Rob said to the man. "I'll give you five bucks if you find the envelope. But it has to have the tooth in it."

"You're on!" the man said, pulling himself up from the seat with startling alacrity. He combed every inch of the vehicle, including the trunk and the engine block. He even stuck his head under the car to check the bruised undercarriage. After fifteen minutes, Rob told him to stop. There was nowhere else to look. The envelope was gone.

"How about one of my teeth?" the man said, cramming his hand in his mouth. He mumbled something that sounded like five bucks. Rob seriously considered it but told the man it wouldn't be necessary.

"You can have the five bucks anyway," Rob said, handing the man the money.

"Thanks, buddy," the man said. "Sorry about your envelope."

"Yeah, me, too."

◆ ◆

Rob drove to the hospital to deliver the box of stuff from the car and to tell Ridgeback about Boland's tooth, or the lack of Boland's tooth.

"Do you think we can get another one?" Rob said.

"How am I going to do that?"

"I could go."

"Rob, the guy didn't give me the tooth; I stole it. What

am I going to do? Ask him to put one of Boland's teeth in an envelope and leave it at the front desk?"

"We're running out of options," Rob said. He looked out the window and saw a plume of exhaust pouring out of a vent on the side of the building. It reminded him of a column of ash rising to the sky. "Hey, what do they do with Boland's body once the autopsy is done?"

"That's a good question. If he doesn't have a will and there's no one to claim the body, I expect they'll cremate him." Ridgeback reached for his cell phone.

"Who are you calling?"

Ridgeback held up a finger. "Hello, Jim?" he said. "Are you cremating Boland's remains?" He tapped the speaker icon so Rob could hear.

"Well, no one's claimed the body yet," Jim said. Rob assumed Jim was the medical examiner. "But it's only been a day. If no one claims it, he'll be cremated."

"Have the DNA results come back yet?"

"Tomorrow, maybe. But it's definitely Boland. We found a tag on the inside of his vest with his name on it."

"Can you tell me how he died?"

"Knife wounds to the thoracic region. The lacerations in his clothing and damage to the ribs are consistent with that. How are you doing, by the way? I hear you're in the hospital."

Ridgeback scribbled a few notes and explained his condition to Jim, much less melodramatically than when he described the accident to Rob and Katie. Rob grabbed the pen from Ridgeback and scribbled a question on his notepad. It read, "What happens to the ashes?"

CHAPTER TWENTY-TWO

Cemeteries and Christmas Trees

Kristin stood at the foot of the driveway and looked up at Danny's apartment. He was expected back that afternoon. Why did it matter to her so much? Was she so hung up on him that she had to count the hours until he returned? So what if she was? Wasn't he hung up on her too? Hadn't they talked on the phone for two hours last night? He'd told her how much he missed her and that he'd be back soon. "Next time, you'll take me with you," she told him. He said he liked that idea.

"Get out of the road, Agnes!"

Kristin turned to find Lady Agnes standing in the front yard of the Bradford House. She had just gotten up, still dressed in the sweat pants and t-shirt she wore to bed.

"Did you forget how to run?"

"Funny," Kristin said. "You know, you used to be a lot quieter."

"Do you need me to go with you?"

"Even funnier." She waved and ran up the road at a faster pace than usual, showing off her newfound athletic ability.

"I can run!" Lady Agnes called out.

Kristin ran to Truro Center, then turned onto South Pamet Road. She slowed, already having gone two miles, and walked for a while. Her home, or her parents' home, was about a mile away, but she wasn't planning to go that far. She wasn't ready for that yet. There was no one there anyway. Her parents were never home.

Cars flew by, heading toward Ballston Beach. Kristin had resumed running when a jeep, heading in the same direction, slowed down to match her speed. There was just the driver in the car. He wore a baseball cap and no shirt. His bare left arm hung out of the window like a shank of beef, his fingers idly tapping on the door panel. She knew who he was—a man from her past. He smiled deviously and motioned to the backseat, then let go of the steering wheel and brought his right hand to his left arm, feigning an injection.

"Fuck you," Kristin said under her breath, careful not to look at him.

The man sneered and started slapping the door, barking like a seal.

"Please go away," Kristin said. Becoming frightened, she turned around and ran away from the jeep, back toward Truro Center. She ran as fast as she could and was grateful when another man appeared by the side of the road—someone who could offer assistance if she needed it. But as she got closer and saw his face and his outfit—the boots and the vest—she panicked and darted off the road and into the woods.

♦ ♦

Katie was in the basement when Rachel called to tell her that Kristin hadn't come back from her run. She had left around eight o'clock, and it was nearly eleven now. Katie wasn't working in the basement; she was sitting by the tool cabinet, wondering what to do about the acid. Her anxiety levels were still up, even though she'd committed herself to banishing Boland's ghost. Should she take more or leave it alone? The drug had certainly produced plenty of fantastical images, but it had done little to quell her anxiety. She wondered if the tabs were losing their potency, having exceeded their shelf life. A quick check of the internet told her that even under ideal storage conditions, LSD will lose potency after two or three years. Katie's storage conditions were not ideal. Perhaps the tabs had turned to trash. Or perhaps she needed to take more of them.

Her own state of mind became secondary now. Kristin's well-being took precedence. She raced out of the house and jumped in the car. Rachel and the girls were searching the beaches. Katie was going to drive along the roads that Danny typically ran on and some of the back roads, too. She called the police station to ask if there had been any accidents that morning involving a pedestrian. She was relieved to hear that none had been reported. She gave them Kristin's name and a description and asked that they keep an eye out for her.

◆ ◆

Rob sat in the front seat of Mike Van Winkle's rental car with the box of Sammy Boland's ashes on his lap. The ashes were sealed inside a heavy-duty plastic bag with Boland's name written in permanent marker on the side. The bag sat inside a white box with a red lid, looking like something meant to be stashed under a Christmas tree. Rob had never held a box of human ashes before, only a dog's ashes. He was surprised at how heavy they were—close to six pounds, according to the medical examiner. Apparently, this was less than normal since all the internal organs had already been spoken for prior to incineration.

He was still astounded that they had been able to get them so quickly. Actually, it was Jerry Boland's attorney, the next best thing to a family member, and something of a son of a bitch, who had persuaded the county to release them.

Rob had asked for Van Winkle's help after Steve Ridgeback learned from the medical examiner that Boland's ashes would end up in a mass grave if no one collected them within a year. "Actually, it's a mausoleum now," the examiner explained. "The county doesn't like to bury things anymore." Rob wondered if Jerry Boland's attorney might be able to claim the ashes on behalf of Jerry's estate. "I take it you never found the tooth?" Van Winkle said. He was calling the attorney anyway to discuss payment of the balance of his fee and was happy to ask him about the ashes, too. The attorney admitted he had thought about the ashes since there was no one else to claim them, but wasn't sure what to do with them if he did get them. "A lot of cemeteries won't take criminals," he explained. "And I'm not in the habit of storing my client's ashes." Van Winkle offered to find a place for the ashes and even to go pick them up if the attorney took care of the necessary paperwork. The attorney was curious as to why Van Winkle would want to do this. "I feel like I owe it to Jerry," he said. "All he wanted to do was get his son back."

"I guess I owe you one," Rob said as Van Winkle pulled the car onto Route Six. Rob had spent entirely too much time on the road over the past few days. There was nothing pleasant about Route Six during the summer. At least this time, he wasn't driving.

"It's okay," Van Winkle said. "I've got to do something to earn my fee. And I'm kind of interested to see how this all plays out anyway, if only to give me a good story to tell my mom when I get home."

Rob's cell phone rang. It was Katie calling to give him the news about Kristin.

"She can't have gone far," Rob said. "Danny told me she doesn't run more than two miles."

"I'm hoping she just stopped somewhere."

"Maybe she's having her own Dorothy Bradford moment, wandering through the woods somewhere." He drummed his fingers on the box of ashes and said, "Hey, we got the ashes."

"I can't think about that right now, Rob. I've got to find Kristin." Rob heard the worry in her voice. He knew she felt responsible.

"We'll help find her, Kay," Rob said, glancing out the window at the angry mass of black clouds hanging off the coast. A storm was coming. "Van Winkle said he'd help."

"Before you do, can you stop at home and check on Brie? I left in a hurry and forgot to put her in the kitchen."

By the time they pulled into the driveway, the rain was coming down in sheets, and a cold wind blew hard out of the northeast. Rob ran inside, leaving Boland's ashes in the car. He worried about getting them wet, even though they were sealed in a sturdy plastic bag. But more than that, he found the idea of bringing them into the house unsettling. He might just as well pull a body out of the trunk and lay it out on the dining room table, he thought. Van Winkle didn't seem to mind leaving the ashes in the car, either, even though they were technically in his charge. He followed Rob inside to use the bathroom.

Rob found Brie asleep on the couch. She opened her eyes when Rob came in but made no effort to get off the couch. Rob snapped his fingers and said, "Off!" and the dog bolted upright and jumped down. Then Rob went through every room in the house to make sure Brie hadn't left a trail of destruction. She was still young enough to gnaw on a furniture leg every now and then. But there was nothing out of order that Rob could see, other than the door to the basement being left open. He didn't think Brie would go down there, though, and Katie was always good about cleaning up her workshop, not leaving any pieces of wood or power cords lying around for Brie to chew. Rob went downstairs anyway and took a quick look around. Everything was in its place, except that the middle drawer of the tool cabinet was open. He went to close it, but as he did, he noticed a Ziploc bag peeking out from under a tray of hardware. He could see the edge of a piece of paper inside the bag with what looked like small red stickers on it. He lifted the tray and saw that the paper was filled with stickers. They looked like little strawberries.

Rob had no idea what he was looking at. He thought it was some kind of colorful marking system for woodworking projects. But what did strawberries have to do with carpentry?

"You down there?" Van Winkle said. He came down the stairs and was immediately impressed by the array of tools lining the walls.

"Are you a woodworker, too?" Rob asked.

"Yeah, but I think I'm out of your league," he said. "I didn't know you were into this stuff."

"I'm not. This is Katie's thing."

Rob had yet to close the tool cabinet drawer. Still curious about the stickers, he pulled out the Ziploc bag and asked Van Winkle if he knew what they were. "The drawer was open," Rob said, as though he needed to convince Van Winkle he wasn't rifling through his wife's possessions. "Is this something carpenters use?"

Rob offered the bag to Van Winkle for closer examination, but he didn't take it. He raised his eyebrows and gave Rob a worried look.

"What?" Rob said, seeing the concern in Van Winkle's face.

"You really don't know what that is?" Van Winkle said.

Rob now had the feeling that the stickers had nothing to do with woodworking. He realized they were something Katie didn't want him to see. That's why they were down here, tucked under a tray of hardware inside a drawer that was normally closed.

"Oh, shit," Rob said, quickly stuffing the bag back under the tray. "Wait, you don't need to confiscate this, do you? Are we in trouble? Dammit."

"I'm not the police, Rob."

"I didn't know. They're LSD tabs, right?"

"Strawberries are a popular image."

"What the hell is she doing?" Rob said. He fumbled for his phone and called Katie, worried she was driving around town while high on acid.

◆ ◆

Katie had driven up and down every main road within a three-mile radius of the Dorothy Bradford House. Usually there were any number of people running, walking, or cycling, but with the deteriorating weather conditions, most everyone had taken shelter. Even the number of vehicles had thinned out because of the weather. Katie could hardly see out of the windows from all the rain. If Kristin was still outside, she'd be soaked. Two scenarios, both equally worrisome, played out in Katie's mind: first that Kristin was lying in a ditch somewhere, and second that she had relapsed and was sitting in someone's basement shooting heroin.

"Where are you, Agnes?" Katie said, checking again to see if the windshield wipers were on their highest setting. Katie called Rachel, who was still on the bay beaches, asking anyone she saw if they had seen a skinny young female runner. The other girls had gone back to the Bradford House. Katie told Rachel to do the same. The weather was just too awful.

"Have you called Danny?" Rachel said, her voice booming over the howling wind. "You should let him know."

Danny was in the car when Katie called. He had just set out from Boston, where the traffic was much worse than the weather. Katie had debated whether to tell him that Kristin was missing, worried he would drive too fast. "We're out looking for her now," she said.

"Shit," Danny said. "Did you call the police? Did you call the hospital?"

"I called the police. I haven't checked with the hospital."

"Call them. I'll be there as soon as I can."

Katie told him not to drive too fast and then called Cape Cod Hospital. She was put on hold three times before being told that there were no patients named Kristin Harris who had been seen in the emergency room or admitted to the hospital.

Rob called just after Katie finished the call with the hospital and she hoped he had news about Kristin. He didn't.

"Is everything okay?" Rob said. "I mean, is Kristin at the hospital?"

"No. I was just checking to see if she was there. I've looked everywhere, Rob." The windshield was fogging. It was hard to see anything in front of her. She pulled off the road and turned on the defroster, then the hazard lights. "I called Danny. He's on the way. Are you home?"

"Where are you, Kay?"

"Old County. Not far."

"Are you all right?"

"I'm frustrated. Why? Is something else wrong? Is Brie okay?"

"She's fine. No damage done." He paused. The words escaped him even though he'd rehearsed what he was going to say. "Listen..."

"Uh oh. This doesn't sound good."

"Yeah, well, the basement door was open, so I went downstairs to make sure Brie hadn't gotten into anything."

"Did she? You told me she was okay."

"She is. I don't think she went down there, but I noticed one of the drawers in the tool cabinet was open."

Katie knew immediately what had happened. She'd forgotten to close the drawer, and Rob had found the tabs.

"Did you find the strawberries?" she said.

"Jesus, Kay, I thought we were done with that. Are you high now? You shouldn't be on the road if you are."

"One of the members gave me those two years ago. I didn't know how to throw them away, so I stashed them in the tool cabinet."

"But are you taking any?"

"I've taken a couple to help with the anxiety."

"Did you take one today?"

"I don't think they work anymore."

"Katie, the drawer was open, and the tabs were sticking out."

"Before this week I hadn't taken any."

"And how many this week?"

"I don't know. Two, three? Count the missing tabs. I can't hear you so well. Are you in the basement, or is it the cell reception?"

"I'm coming to get you. Tell me where you are."

"I have to find Kristin. I'm fine, Rob. Really. I don't think they work anymore."

"I don't want you driving."

Katie finally relented. She wasn't sure what she was seeing out of the windshield anymore. She had to open the door to get her bearings and got soaked in the process. Up ahead, she saw the sign for Pine Grove Cemetery, a convenient landmark. She told Rob where to find her and ended the call.

She hadn't looked in the cemetery. The turn-off was only about a mile from the house, and Kristin could have easily taken it. Katie didn't wait for Rob. She left the hazard lights on and pulled the car back onto the road.

Katie knew plenty of women, many of them from the Dorothy Bradford Society, who refused to go down Cemetery Road, particularly if they were on foot. Pine Grove, one of Truro's oldest cemeteries, was an unremarkable tract of land that had been cleared and planted with the dead in 1794. Located a mile into the woods, it was reminiscent of Thomas Ridley's secluded gravesite, though much larger and a lot easier to find. There were no flowers or manicured lawns here. A rutted dirt road led to the graveyard and then circled around the tombstones. But it wasn't the graves that scared people away. It was the mutilated body of Susan Perry, who was found here in 1970, having been cut up by her boyfriend, the serial killer Tony Costa.

The picture of a mutilated woman wasn't what Katie needed to have hanging in her head right now. The image became terrifyingly real, and she found herself pumping the brakes as she drove into the cemetery. The rain continued to make it hard to see anything, so Katie stopped the car and got out. She grabbed the lightweight rain jacket that she kept in a survival kit in the rear of the SUV and continued on foot.

The boundary road was filled with water, so Katie walked on the grass. The ground was so wet that she thought the gravestones might lose their footing and collapse in the muck, leaving the dead to percolate to the surface. She was halfway around the loop when she thought she saw something move. She pulled the hood of her jacket tighter around her head and headed for an upright marble slab near the center of the cemetery. Katie stopped and waited. Before long, a dark-haired boy peeked out from behind the stone.

"Hello, Dak," Katie said. Dak looked at her and smiled. He was wearing only a bathing suit. The rain ran down his dark skin and puddled around his bare feet. "What are you doing out here in the rain?"

"Visiting," Dak said. He sat down, crossed his legs, and began picking at a soggy weed. "Are you looking for Sammy Boland?"

"I'm looking for a girl," Katie said anxiously. "Her name is Kristin. Do you know where she is?" The air grew colder, and the wind whipped harder.

"It's going to get bad," Dak said.

"What is?" Katie said.

Dak looked up and pointed to the sky. There was no lightning, but Katie imagined the boy had probably died in weather like this.

"Maybe the girl is with Sammy Boland," Dak said.

"Well, I have to find her. I thought she might be around here somewhere."

"Is she dead? There are only dead people in here. Except for you."

"She's not dead," Katie said emphatically, closing her eyes against the rain. When she opened them, the boy stood up and pointed to the top of the tombstone. Katie leaned in closer. The letters had shallowed over time, and she wondered if the stone had been etched by the same stone carver who had butchered Tom Ridley's name. She wiped away the water with her hand and was able to make out the family name at the top of the stone. It read, "Ballston."

CHAPTER TWENTY-THREE

Flooded Lots
and Boland's Bag

Van Winkle drove past the sign to the cemetery. He was leaning forward, hugging the steering wheel, and trying to get a better look out of the windshield. Katie's car was nowhere to be found.

"Where is she?" Rob said, fumbling for his cell phone. "Your wipers suck, by the way."

"Yeah, well, it's not my car."

Katie answered Rob's call after the first ring. "I'm just pulling into the Ballston parking lot," she said. Her voice was stronger and more animated than before. She sounded like

Dorothy Bradford again.

"You were supposed to wait for me."

"I think Kristin is down here somewhere."

"Why?"

"Let's call it a hunch. Do you still have the ashes with you?"

"They're in the trunk."

"Good. Bring them with you."

"In the rain? I thought we were focused on finding Kristin."

"I think they're connected."

"What does that mean?"

"Just come quickly. Okay?"

"As long as you wait for me. No more driving, okay?"

◆ ◆

Katie had stopped at Ballston Beach earlier in the day when she first started looking for Kristin. The weather was much calmer then, and there were people walking on the beach, though none of them were Kristin. The weather now was fierce. The wind blew hard off the ocean, driving sand and saltwater over the dunes and into the parking lot. The river basin, normally dry, was also filling with seawater, rushing across the Cape toward the bay.

She parked the car at the far end of the lot, near the entrance to the beach. With the engine and wipers turned off, she was cloaked in a cocoon of fog and water that made it impossible to see anything outside of the car. She tightened the Velcro on the hood of her jacket and then pulled the lever to open the car door. At first, she thought there was something blocking the door, but it was only the wind holding it in place. By using her shoulder and right hand, she was able to shove the door open enough to get out of the car. Once she was clear, the door closed itself, though not before the driver's seat took a soaking. Turning her head away from the wind, she made her way over the dune toward the beach, where she expected to find Kristin and quite possibly a ghostly presence, too.

Mike Van Winkle's rental car was no match for the storm. The windshield wipers had become nearly ineffective, and the air-conditioning system was doing a lousy job of clearing condensation from the windshield. The rear window on the driver's side was also leaking.

"Do you get storms like this a lot here?" Van Winkle said, struggling to keep the car on the road.

"Only in the winter," Rob said, wishing they were driving a car with a higher wheelbase, something less likely to get squashed like a tomato if a tree came down on top of it. "Unless it's a hurricane. I don't think this is a hurricane."

When they reached the Ballston Beach parking lot, they were barely able to see Katie's car parked at the far end of the lot. Van Winkle parked next to it, just in front of the big sign with the picture of a hungry-looking shark. The car was facing the wind, and Rob was sure the windshield would collapse.

"We should have taken my car," Rob said, straining to see if anyone was inside Katie's car.

"Do you think we're safe here?" Van Winkle said, watching the seawater spill across the low point in the dunes and into the river. There was a berm between the lot and the river basin, though not a substantial one. The water was muddied with rocks and sand, and it looked as though the basin could easily be breached by a storm surge.

"Safe from what?" Rob said. There were any number of risks out there—violent surf, heavy rain, hungry-looking sharks. Possibly ghosts.

"It's a lot of water."

"Don't you have water in Kentucky?"

"Not like this."

Rob pushed open the door and stepped out into the weather. He didn't have a rain jacket and quickly became drenched. He looked inside Katie's car but didn't find anyone there.

"I'm going to the beach!" Rob yelled into the wind. Van Winkle didn't hear any of it, but he knew what Rob had in mind. He got out of the car, bracing the door with his foot.

"Do we take the ashes?"

Rob got Boland's bag out of the trunk. The box stood no chance in the rain, but the bag was sealed and looked waterproof. All the same, Rob tucked the bag under his shirt.

"What's the point of doing that?" Van Winkle said. "Your shirt is soaked."

But Rob wasn't comfortable walking around with Boland's ashes in plain view. Even though there was no one around to see him, what would they think? *Why is that man spreading ashes in a nor'easter?* More than that, the cold, sticky feeling of Boland's bag against his skin was creepy, and maybe just a little obscene.

"Here, hold this for a second," Rob said. He gave the bag to Van Winkle, then took off his shirt and fashioned a sling suitable for carrying the ashes. This also gave him the use of both of his hands should the wind knock him down.

"You're not cold?" Van Winkle said. "Why don't you put your shirt back on, and I'll carry the ashes?"

Rob squinted his eyes against the rain and held open his shirt satchel, prompting Van Winkle to insert the bag. "Let's find Katie," he said.

Rob led Van Winkle up the dune, and when the beach came into view, he stopped. The scene was both fantastic and terrifying. It was nearly impossible to distinguish between the land, sea, and sky. All of it was a violent, grayish-white panorama of fury. The beach had been overrun by massive waves that slammed into the defenseless dunes. The low-hanging clouds, as angry and gray as the surf, moved nearly as fast, dumping their moisture onto an already obliterated landscape.

"Where is she?" Rob yelled, unsure of how anyone could survive on the beach.

"There!" Van Winkle shouted, pointing to the high dune south of the entrance. Halfway up the hill, just beyond the reach of the exploding surf, were two women trying to scramble up the collapsing face of the dune. The sand was so unstable that it was difficult for them to gain traction, and they seemed to slide two feet for every foot they climbed.

"Is there a path along the top of the dune?" Van Winkle said.

"There's a house up there," Rob said.

They ran back to the parking lot and splashed their way to a point just beyond the entrance, where a driveway climbed toward a house at the top of the dune. Rob had no idea if there was anyone home to witness the half-naked man running up their driveway, but in this weather, who was going to rush outside to chase him off their property? At worst, they'd call the police, and maybe that's what was needed right now anyway.

A path led from the house to the top of the dune. From there, they could see Katie and Kristin almost directly below. Kristin was lying in a fetal position now, having surrendered to the storm, while Katie sat next to her, trying to shield her from the rain. Rob shouted as loud as he could and waved his arms. The shirt-satchel came loose in the fierce wind, and the ashes fell to the ground with a thud.

"I'm going down there to help!" Van Winkle said.

"I got it!" Rob said. He picked up the ashes and hurtled down the dune, taking large chunks out of the face—something that was utterly taboo as far as dune erosion control was concerned and would have elicited hysterical shouts of indignation from the locals on the beach, had there been any locals on the beach. He got to the two women quickly, nearly overshooting them, his momentum threatening to send him tumbling down into the maelstrom below. Katie looked up at him, her eyes bleary from the wind and water, and maybe the acid, too. She'd taken off her rain jacket and put it over Kristin, though she was struggling to keep it there in the teeth of the wind.

"Where is your shirt?" she said.

"I used it to carry the ashes," he said, looking back up the dune. Van Winkle was coming down now, stepping gingerly, and creating his own path of destruction. "Is she okay?"

"She's scared."

"I'm scared, too. This is end-of-world shit. Let's get out of here." He bent down, intending to help Kristin to her feet.

"Not yet, Rob," Katie said. "Give me the ashes and hold the jacket over Kristin.

"You're doing it now?"

"It won't take long. Sit."

"I don't see him anywhere."

"I don't think we have to."

He sat down and took the jacket from Katie. "Did she?" he said, not sure how to word the question. "Shoot up?" He tapped the veiny part of his forearm, nearly losing the rain jacket in the process.

Katie shook her head and nestled Boland's bag between her legs.

"What about you?" he said. "The LSD? Are you still seeing things?"

"I'm seeing a half-naked man in a storm."

"Can I help?" Van Winkle had reached them. He stood in a crouch, as though worried the dune was on the verge of collapsing into the sea.

"Sit there, Mike," Katie said, pointing to a spot just upwind of her. "You can block the wind for me."

"What are we doing?" he said, sitting down as instructed, with his back to the wind. He dug his left foot into the sand to keep from sliding into the abyss.

"Finding some peace, hopefully," Katie said. She plucked two smooth stones from the sand and placed one in each palm.

"He's here?" Van Winkle said, looking behind him.

"Kristin thinks he is," Katie said. "She says he's here for her."

"Why?"

Katie didn't answer. Rob was nearly lying on top of Kristin now, trying to keep the jacket in place but also trying to keep warm. The wind seemed to pick up, if that was possible, and it got even colder. Kristin moaned.

"Rob, not so close," Katie said.

Rob sat up and shivered. The wind was blowing so hard that it began to howl. He wondered if it was Boland who was howling.

"Sit tight," Katie said. "Let's see what happens."

Dorothy Bradford closed her eyes and held up her hands. The wind pressed the rocks into her palms, keeping them from falling, and she began the incantation. "Behold what is left no matter how odd!" she said, her voice rising above the wind. She wasn't sure what the rest of the spell would be, but perhaps it didn't matter. *Cod* rhymed with *odd*, and the rest came easily. "For all eternity, set no foot on Cape Cod!"

There was a rumbling in the distance, then a loud thunderclap that nearly dislodged Van Winkle from his sandy perch.

"We need to get out of here!" Van Winkle said.

Dorothy Bradford didn't move. She was perfectly still, except for the hair whipping around her face. There was a calmness in her expression that seemed to ease the fears of those around her.

Rob noticed it and found that he was no longer shivering. The wind shrieked a final time, and then the anger in the sea and sky fell away. The waves continued to crash on the shore, but the surf retreated from the dunes, leaving a scarred and ravaged beach in its wake. Dorothy let her hands fall to her sides, and the stones slid from her palms, dropping into the sand.

Kristin pushed herself up from the dune. She was covered in wet sand. Tears were streaming down her face, but it was impossible to distinguish them from the rain.

"Is he gone?" she said.

"You're safe," Katie said. She stood up and got Kristin to her feet, helping her into the rain jacket.

Barely audible, Kristin turned towards the sea and said, "I'm sorry. I didn't know what I was doing. It was an accident."

Van Winkle got on the other side of Kristin, and he and Katie helped her climb the rest of the dune, using the footholds he and Rob had left during their descent. Rob brought up the rear, having resumed responsibility for Boland's bag.

"Rob, where is your shirt?" Katie said when they got to the top of the dune. The wind had faded to a stiff breeze, and the sting had gone out of the air. Rob found his shirt draped over a thatch of beach roses. A small pool of water had ponded in the center. He set down the ashes and picked up the shirt, careful not to touch the underside until he had inspected the vegetation more carefully. Once he was sure there was no poison ivy, he wrung his shirt out and put it on.

Katie led Kristin down the driveway and back to the cars. Mike Van Winkle stayed back with Rob while he made himself more presentable.

"Did Katie just change the weather?" he said, looking up at the sky, which had become far less turbulent.

"That wasn't Katie," Rob said. "We should get out of here before the owners come after us."

Van Winkle picked up Boland's bag and shifted it back and forth in his hands, as though assessing the weight. "Kristin was pretty traumatized," he said.

"I guess she thought Boland was after her."

"Boland was Kristin's heroin dealer, right?"

"Boland was everyone's dealer."

"Why would she think Boland was after her? I heard her say something about it being an accident. What was 'it'?"

"What are you getting at?"

"Did she kill him?"

CHAPTER TWENTY-FOUR

Roast Beef and Cereal Bowls

Katie climbed into the back seat of the SUV next to Kristin. Kristin had stopped crying and regained some of her composure. Rob started the engine and opened the windows. The water in the parking lot had receded, but a thick carpet of wet sand blanketed the pavement. Mike Van Winkle attended to his shitty rental car, opening the doors to let the upholstery dry out. He walked around the car several times, as if deciding whether it was worth the risk of getting back inside. Rob wasn't so sure about getting inside Katie's car either, now that Van Winkle had suggested that Kristin might be a murderer.

"You guys okay?" he said, turning around. Kristin was wiping the sand and snot off her face with her shirt sleeve. She looked sad and pathetic, and not at all like the type of person who was capable of killing someone. But then she wasn't a heroin addict anymore. Heroin addicts were entirely capable of killing someone, particularly when they needed a fix.

"We're fine, Rob," Katie said. "Let's go home."

Rob couldn't turn his attention away from Kristin, though. He wasn't sure what she was capable of. He felt like he was at the zoo waiting for some pacing animal to make a run at the perimeter fence. "Glad we got out of here in one piece," he said.

Kristin looked as though she was going to cry again. "What is he saying?" she said, turning towards Katie, her voice shaking. Rob hated it when people referred to him in the third person.

"Let's go, Rob," Katie said. "We can talk about it later."

Mike Van Winkle, who still couldn't bring himself to get in his car, stuck his head in the window and said, "This is where they found Boland's body, right?"

Kristin started to cry again, becoming more pitiful. "Can we go back to the house now?" she said.

"Why did you come here, Kristin?" Van Winkle said. "In the middle of a storm?"

"I didn't kill anyone!" Kristin said.

"Nobody said you did."

Just then, a fire engine and a police car roared into the lot. A police officer got out and approached Rob's window while a crew of rescue workers raced out to the beach. Boland's bag was lying on the passenger seat. Rob reached over and quickly knocked it to the floor.

"We had a report of a woman trapped on the dunes," the officer said. "Were you on the beach?"

"She's okay," Rob said. "She's in the back seat." He pointed, trying to shift the officer's attention away from the front seat.

"Don't tell him anything!" Kristin screamed. She jumped out of the car and ran down the parking lot toward the road. The policeman took chase.

◆ ◆

Kristin fought with the officer and was put under restraint. She was taken to the Truro police station. Rob and Katie followed in the SUV, with Van Winkle trailing in his shitty rental car. She was processed, then taken to a room for questioning. Don Hill, the chief inspector, came out to talk with Katie first. Hill already knew from Katie's call to the station earlier in the day that Kristin had been missing.

"I thought you left town," Don Hill said to Mike Van Winkle. "How are you involved in this?"

"I was leaving, but Rob asked me to stay and help find the girl."

"And are you getting paid for this, too?"

"Go easy on him," Rob said. "He was doing us a favor."

"Besides, I didn't want to leave the Cape," Van Winkle said. "I like it here."

"Lots of people do. Tell me about Kristin, Mrs. Crosley."

Katie explained what little she knew about the circumstances of Kristin's disappearance. "We found her at Ballston, trapped on the dune by the storm," she said. "We managed to get her down and back to the parking lot."

"Can you tell me why she ran from the car and then fought with the officer?"

"She was scared," Katie said.

"Of what?"

"The storm."

"She grew up here. She's seen storms before. Did something happen to her out there?"

Katie hesitated, not sure how to answer. Rob and Van Winkle exchanged glances.

"She thinks she saw Sammy Boland," Rob said finally.

"I don't want to hear any ghost stories," Don Hill said. "This isn't a camp fire."

Katie gave Rob and Van Winkle a stern expression, making

it clear she didn't want them saying anything more about Sammy Boland.

"Listen, guys," Hill said. "I was expecting to hear you say that Kristin Harris panicked out there in the parking lot. I know there are a few women at the Bradford House who suffer from that sort of thing. Like you used to do, Mrs. Crosley. So, tell me, did Kristin have a panic attack?"

"You could say that," Katie said.

"The arresting officer said Kristin screamed at you not to tell him anything. What was that about? She wasn't using, was she?"

"No," Katie said sternly. "You won't find any heroin on her, and there's none in the car. You can take a look if you like."

Rob thought about Boland's bag, which he'd stuffed under the passenger seat. It looked just like a giant bag of heroin.

"Thanks, that won't be necessary."

Just then, Danny rushed into the police station, looking out of breath, something Danny rarely was.

"Danny Crosley!" Don Hill said. "You didn't run here, did you? Ordinarily, I'd say it's not a good idea to run into a police station."

"Where's Kristin? Is she okay?" Danny said. He had been heading to the Bradford House when he got the call from his mother, telling him where they were.

"And what's your relationship with Ms. Harris?" Don Hill said.

◆ ◆

They sat in the waiting room for nearly two hours without any sign of Kristin or Don Hill. While they waited, Danny and Van Winkle peppered Katie with questions about what had happened to Kristin. Rob listened in earnest, but his thoughts were more on driving home and getting Boland's ashes out of the police station parking lot.

"I don't understand," Danny said more than once, wanting to know where Kristin had been before Katie found her on the beach.

"I don't know, Danny," Katie said. "She told me she'd seen Sammy Boland's ghost and that he was after her. I guess she was trying to get away from whatever she'd seen or thought she'd seen. She ended up on the beach, and the storm came in."

"But after the thing with the ashes, she was okay?"

"She was better."

Van Winkle asked Katie what she thought Kristin had meant when she screamed at them not to tell the police anything. "It sounds to me like she's hiding something," he said.

"What could she have to hide?" Danny said.

"She was scared," Katie said. "The police probably trigger a lot of bad memories for her."

Rob got up and suggested they go home and change into

dry clothes. Van Winkle, whose clothes seemed weirdly dry, could stay at the station. Katie wasn't about to leave, though.

"I'm not leaving either," Danny said. "I didn't get wet."

"Maybe you should go," Rob said.

"What's that mean?"

Rob motioned for Danny to follow him.

"Where are we going?"

He led Danny to the public restroom just off the lobby. Inside, he pulled a wad of paper towels from the dispenser.

"What are you doing?" Danny said.

"I need to dry out the inside of the car," Rob said.

"You don't need me for that."

"Listen, Danny. Mike thinks Kristin might have been involved in Sammy Boland's murder."

Danny's eyes widened, and he shouted, "What?" loud enough that people outside the restroom, some of whom carried sidearms, probably heard him.

"I don't think it's a good idea for you to be involved with her right now. I mean, until this gets resolved."

"What evidence does he have?"

"None. It's a hunch. Kristin said Boland was after her and then said something about it being an accident."

"What was an accident?"

"That's the question."

"It's horseshit, Dad. Van Winkle sounds just like Steve Ridgeback. People are too quick to judge these days. Don't you be one of them."

"Not judging, just making you aware." Rob grabbed another wad of towels from a second dispenser. He had never been comfortable with Danny dating Fat Agnes, though he wasn't sure why. Was it the illnesses she was recovering from, or was it the possibility she could shift Danny's priorities away from running? Probably the latter, he thought. The argument became moot, though, if Kristin had murdered someone.

"What does Mom say?"

"I haven't said anything to her about it. I don't want to upset her."

"What about me? You've upset me."

"It's different. Mom's close to Kristin. She cares a lot about her."

"I care a lot about her."

Rob muttered, "Yeah, well," and tucked the two wads of paper towels, nearly a foot high, under his arm.

"You're really going to walk out of here with all that?"

"I pay enough taxes. I can take a few paper towels."

"They've got cameras, you know."

Rob left the police station without incident and wiped down the interior of the SUV. He left the ashes under the front seat, not wanting one of the police cameras to also record him in possession of a suspicious-looking bag. The car wasn't as wet as he'd thought, and it only took half the towels to soak up the water. He'd bring the rest of them back inside the police station and return them to the restroom. First, though, he hopped in the car and drove down Route Six to pick up some sandwiches. He was starving and expected Katie, Van Winkle, and Danny were hungry, too. He had no idea if Kristin Harris was hungry or, if she was, what she'd eat, assuming she regained her freedom.

There were few signs of the violent weather from earlier in the day—just some wind-blown debris and downed tree branches on the sides of the road. The pavement was nearly dry now. He ran into Helen Schantz, sitting at one of the tables outside the sandwich shop. She was devouring a hot roast beef wrap with melted cheese and onions and a bag of chips. He had never seen Helen Schantz anywhere outside of their neighborhood before. He almost didn't recognize her. She most certainly didn't recognize him.

"It's me, Rob Crosley," Rob said. Helen had on her sunglasses even though it was still overcast.

"Oh," she said. "Are you staying?" She had an entire picnic table to herself and may have thought Rob wanted to join her.

"I'm just picking up."

"New strain," she said.

Rob thought she was talking about her sandwich at first, like it was a recent addition to the menu.

"It makes me hungry all the time," she went on. "I don't think I'll stick with it."

It was all about the weed with Helen Schantz. Rob nodded and, for some reason, asked if there was anything else she needed, as though she were a guest at his house.

"You look wet," Helen Schantz said.

"Got caught in the storm," Rob said.

"Was there a storm?"

◆ ◆

Rob returned to the police station to find Katie, Danny, and Van Winkle waiting outside, looking tired and uncomfortable. Rob was feeling uncomfortable, too. Despite all the water he'd soaked up with the paper towels, the interior of the car had taken on a mildewed smell that made him nauseous and less interested in eating sandwiches.

"What happened?" Rob said, pulling up next to them.

"She's coming out in a minute," Katie said. "They asked us to wait outside."

"They're letting her go?"

"Finally," Katie said.

Rob looked at Van Winkle, hoping he might verbalize what Rob was thinking—was it really such a good idea to take custody of a suspected killer and bring her back to the Bradford House? Or Danny's apartment, for that matter?

When Kristin came out of the station she ran straight to Danny. She had cleaned herself up and even been given dry clothes to wear. She emitted an exasperated cry when she fell into Danny's embrace, sounding like a hostage released from captivity. They hugged for a time, and then Kristin, very uncharacteristically, said in an angry voice, "Let's get the fuck out of here."

Kristin rode back to the Bradford House with Danny. Rob and Katie took the SUV, and Van Winkle followed in his shitty rental car. Rob had invited him back to the house for lunch.

"She's a mess," Rob said to Katie as they pulled onto Route Six. Katie held the sandwiches in her lap. Boland's ashes were still under the seat.

"She's been through an ordeal," Katie said. "She needs our help."

Rob wanted to say something about Van Winkle's theory but decided to wait until there was more to go on, if there ever was more to go on. If Don Hill hadn't come up with anything incriminating after two hours of questioning, what was there for Rob or Van Winkle to find?

"What about you? How are you feeling?" Rob said.

"Me? I'm fine."

"So, you feel like it worked then? We're done with Sammy Boland?"

"I think so."

"Even if you didn't see him there?"

"He was around somewhere, according to Kristin. She said he chased her up the dune."

"She was hysterical."

"She was scared."

"It's hard to make sense of any of this."

"Just give yourself over to it, Rob. It's easier if you suspend disbelief, just like you did for Dorothy Bradford."

"I'm still working on that one." Rob yanked on the seat belt, tightening it around his waist. "You weren't on acid today?"

"No. I thought about it, but then Rachel called about Kristin."

"We're going to throw the tabs away—however that's done—when we get home, right?"

"I think they've expired anyway."

"We're throwing them away."

"You can do it. Drop me off at the Bradford House first."

"I don't know how to do it. Do you flush them down the toilet?"

"Look online. I'm sure you'll find instructions."

Rob was becoming increasingly unsettled. The car in front of him was going thirty-five in a fifty-mile-per-hour zone. He wanted to honk like Steve Ridgeback, holler a few vulgarities out the window, and maybe bang his hand on the steering wheel.

"You okay?" Katie said, noticing his discomfort.

"I'm worried about the girl," Rob said. "I think she's unstable."

"I'm worried about her, too. But she'll be okay. Danny will help settle her down."

"That's what I'm worried about. I think she's becoming too dependent on him. She'll fly off the rails anytime he goes away. And what happens when Danny breaks things off with her?" His voice had gotten louder. To add emphasis, he honked the horn. A line of traffic had formed behind him. It was his responsibility to prod the sluggish vehicle ahead.

"Why don't you get off here?" Katie said, suggesting Rob take an earlier exit. Rob wanted to continue harassing the slow driver, but he relented and pulled off of Route Six. "Listen, I'm sorry about the LSD," she said, knowing her drug use was part of his frustration. "I should have told you. I never intended to use any of it."

"We're getting rid of it."

"But we're not getting rid of Kristin, okay? She didn't kill Sammy Boland."

♦ ♦

Rob and Van Winkle sat at the kitchen table and ate their sandwiches. Sammy Boland's ashes remained under the passenger seat of the SUV, apparently having served their purpose. At some point, someone was going to have to deal with their disposition. Amused by the irony, Rob wondered if they could be mixed in with the LSD tabs and disposed of jointly.

"So, why do you think they held Kristin for two hours?" Rob asked Van Winkle. "They had no reason to suspect this had anything to do with Sammy Boland. Unless she said something."

"You told Don Hill that Kristin thought she saw him."

"I did?"

"It doesn't matter. I think they just wanted to give her time to cool off. Make sure she wasn't on anything. Do you have any beer?"

"I thought you didn't drink?"

"How does a private investigator not drink?"

Rob got beers for the two of them and a treat for Brie, who was wagging her tail furiously.

"If you wanted to find evidence that Kristin killed Boland, where would you start?" Rob said.

"Do you know where she lives?" Van Winkle said. "Or where she lived before coming to the Bradford House?"

"With her parents, I think."

"Where?"

"Somewhere in Truro."

"That's where I'd go, then."

◆ ◆

The Harris family lived in a house off of South Pamet Road, about a half-mile from Ballston Beach. Kristin was the only child. Her parents owned an art gallery in Provincetown. Oddly, the Harris Gallery was where Sammy Boland once exhibited some of his bird pictures. Boland never knew that the Harris's were Kristin's parents. The Harris's never knew that Boland sold their daughter heroin. They spent most of their time in the gallery and were mostly oblivious to Kristin's activities outside of school. It wasn't until Kristin was found lying on the floor of a bathroom in an Eastham gas station in full respiratory arrest that they became aware of her addiction. Kristin spent several months in rehab and was then placed in the Bradford House, both to ease her transition back into society and to give her parents more time at the gallery curating artwork before they had to come home and babysit their daughter.

So it was that the following morning, there was no answer at the Harris residence when Van Winkle rang the doorbell. Rob still wasn't clear on what they would say if one of the Harris's came to the door. Would they explain that they suspected Kristin of murder and wanted to poke around the house to see if they could find any evidence?

"Now what?" Rob said, aware that he was standing directly behind Van Winkle, out of the line of fire.

"We go around back," Van Winkle said.

"What's around back?"

"A back door, usually."

They went to the back of the house, with Van Winkle in the lead. The grade fell away, and a set of steps led up to the back door. Van Winkle climbed the steps and knocked again.

"There's still nobody home," Rob said.

Van Winkle looked up, checking for security cameras, then tried the door. It was unlocked.

"We're going inside?"

"Sure."

"Are you allowed to do that? As a private investigator, I mean."

"No. Listen, Rob, if you're not comfortable with this, you should go wait in the car. You don't have to be here."

"What about a warrant? Can we get one of those?"

"We're not the police," Van Winkle said, and then stepped into the house.

Rob stood at the bottom of the steps, one foot tentatively planted on the first step, his hand clamped around the rickety railing. "You don't have to be here," he repeated to himself, nearly ready to head back to the car. If only he'd worn a hat and some sunglasses, maybe his gaiter to hide his face. There was no one to see him, though, and no line of sight to any of the neighbors' homes. And the door was open. No breaking was involved, only entering. He climbed the stairs carefully, as though any creak might give him away.

The back door led into a dated kitchen, full of linoleum, Formica, and dull green fixtures. Rob noticed a single cereal bowl in the sink. Dried flakes clung to the sides of the bowl, and a puddle of milk sat at the bottom. Katie always yelled at Rob for not rinsing out his cereal bowls. Did Mrs. Harris yell at Mr. Harris, too, or was she the cereal-eater in the family? Rob didn't know any women who ate cereal.

Rob reconnected with Van Winkle, and the two of them went upstairs to the second floor in search of Kristin's bedroom. Rob looked in the master bedroom. The bed was unmade, and a large flat-screen TV hung on the opposite wall. Two sets of pillows were propped up against the bed board, and empty coffee cups rested on the side tables. There was a large bookcase on the wall, but instead of books, the shelves held a huge array of dolls, neatly lined up, many of them sitting with their legs dangling. Each one exhibited frozen, corpse-like stares that followed you around the room, daring you to get a good night's sleep.

"Over here," Van Winkle said, having found Kristin's room.

"How do you know this is her room?" Rob said.

Van Winkle pointed to a pillow on the bed that had Kristin's name embroidered on it, then started opening drawers. Rob looked in the closet. It smelled like mothballs.

"What are we looking for?" Rob said. There was a psychedelic poster on the inside of the closet door with the words *Get Out of Your Head* written across the top.

"Anything that seems out of place, anything hand-written."

"Like a diary?"

"Girls don't keep diaries anymore. They have Instagram. But if you do find one, let me know."

Rob was uncomfortable sifting through someone else's things, particularly a young woman's. The hangars held mostly blue jeans and flannel shirts. He pushed a few hangers out of the way to see what was behind.

"What if we find something?" Rob said. "Since we don't have a warrant, doesn't that mean we can't use it in court?"

"That only applies to the police. And we won't be taking anything with us anyway."

Why are we here, then? Rob wanted to say. There was a stool at the bottom of the closet, and Rob stood on it to get a look at what was on the shelf above the pole. He found a number of balled-up sweatshirts and a few baseball caps of teams in the Cape Cod Summer League.

"Shouldn't we be wearing gloves?" Rob said, poking at some of the sweatshirts to see if there was anything stuffed in the front pockets. Van Winkle didn't answer. Rob found a scarf and wrapped it around his hand. Underneath one of the sweatshirts he saw a small black case of some kind with a strap on it. At first he thought it was a cell phone case, the kind runners wear on their arms, but it was longer and thinner than any cell phone. He picked it up with his scarf-covered hand and looked at it more closely. "What's this?" he said turning towards Van Winkle. He was sure it would be important. Van Winkle was sifting through the drawers of a small desk that stood beneath a window overlooking the backyard. Rob got down off the stool and laid the case on the bed.

"What did you do to your hand?" Van Winkle said, picking up the case with his bare hand.

Rob pulled off the scarf and tossed it back in the closet. "Nothing," he said.

"This is a sheath for a knife," Van Winkle said. There was no knife inside, though.

"What's the strap for?"

"You wear it on your leg. Under your pants. Or your dress."

"Kristin doesn't have any dresses."

Van Winkle opened the sheath and looked inside. "This could be very helpful," he said.

"That's right. Boland was stabbed, wasn't he?"

"Where did you find this?"

Van Winkle had Rob put the sheath back on the shelf where he found it and then took a couple of pictures. Then he got up on the stool himself and pulled everything off the closet shelf. There was no knife.

"She would have gotten rid of the knife, wouldn't she?"

"You watch a lot of TV crime dramas, don't you?"

"Katie does."

"We may not need it. Chances are, she put the knife back in the sheath after killing Boland. There was no sign of it anywhere at the crime scene."

"So?"

"So, there's a good chance there's dried blood in there." Van Winkle closed the closet door and then returned to the desk.

"We're leaving it here?"

"Can't take it with us."

"Why?" Rob said, not sure he wanted to hear the answer.

"Because we're trespassing."

They spent another few minutes in Kristin's room, then went to the basement. They found nothing else of interest in the house, and Van Winkle decided to have a look in the toolshed in the back yard. On the way out of the house, Rob stopped at the kitchen sink and rinsed out the cereal bowl, his way of atoning for the intrusion and because he also felt bad for Kristin's parents. They had lost their daughter to heroin addiction, and now that she was nearly recovered and ready to return home, she could well be arrested for murder. Doubt crept into his mind, and he wondered if going to the police with news of the sheath, or whatever it was that Van Winkle intended to introduce, was the right thing to do. There didn't seem to be anyone left in the Boland family who needed to find justice for Sammy. Who would benefit from Kristin's arrest? She may only have been defending herself when she killed Boland—if she killed Boland. Rob may not have liked that Kristin and Danny were dating, but that didn't mean she needed to be locked up in prison.

Rob pulled the back door shut and followed Van Winkle to the shed. There were no knives in there, either; just a lawn mower, an old ten-speed, and a rake.

"What if we don't say anything about the sheath?" Rob said. "Pretend we never found it."

"Having second thoughts?" Van Winkle said.

"Do you think she's a threat to anyone?"

"No. But that's not for me to say."

"Are we obligated to tell the police?"

"If we don't, we're both accessories after the fact."

"That doesn't sound good."

"Jail time, for sure."

CHAPTER TWENTY-FIVE

Wet Dogs and Smack

Sammy Boland's last day on earth ended on a cool, clear summer evening in the Ballston Beach parking lot. He had walked there from the nearby home of one of his clients, who was traveling abroad for the summer. Though he stored drugs in some of his clients' homes, he never sold them there. He preferred to do business in beach parking lots later in the evenings, after the campfires had been doused and the clam bakers had gone home. On this particular evening, he was meeting a young heroin addict named Dixie, though he knew that wasn't her real name. Most of his clients didn't use their real names.

Sammy couldn't stand Dixie. She was belligerent and demanding and took him for granted, as though she had a choice of dealers and he was lucky to get her business. The only reason he kept selling to her was that money was never a problem. She never needed an advance. He knew she lived with her parents and expected she stole from them routinely.

She was always there, waiting for him when he arrived. He had no idea how she got to the parking lot and didn't much care. She could have lived in the dunes for all he knew. He found her sitting in the strip of sand along the side of the lot, smoking a cigarette. She was thin and poorly dressed for the weather. She was shaking, but not from the cold.

"Give it to me," she said, getting up from the sand. "I feel like a wet dog."

"You smell like a wet dog."

"Asshole."

"What did you call me?"

"An asshole." Dixie reached into her pocket and pulled out a wad of cash. "Here," she said, shoving it into Sammy's hand. "Now give it to me!"

"Easy," he said. "Don't wave cash around like that."

"No one's here. Give it to me!"

"Keep your voice down, or I'm leaving."

"Now!" she yelled and punched him in the shoulder.

Sammy lost his temper and slapped her in the face. Though he had been dealing drugs for three years, he rarely had to hit anyone. Dixie fell back into the sand.

"I'll kill you!" she screamed.

"I'm through with you, bitch," Boland said. "Find your shit somewhere else." Sammy turned and started back toward the road. He didn't see Dixie pull the knife out of the sheath she wore under her pant leg. He heard her chasing after him, though, and when he turned to confront her, she plunged the knife into his stomach.

"How's that, asshole?" Dixie said. Sammy looked down at the blood seeping onto his jacket, and Dixie stabbed him again. He fell to his knees. He tried to speak, but there was blood filling his throat. He crawled toward the bushes, attempting to escape, but collapsed in the sand. Dixie rolled him over while he gagged and grabbed the bag of heroin from his jacket pocket. She laid out a line of powder on her forearm and snorted it. Then she laid out another. Sammy was drowning in his blood.

"Oh, shit," Dixie said, now realizing what she had done. She threw sand on his face to soak up the blood that was spilling out of his mouth, then snorted another line. She lay down next to him and looked up at the stars as the heroin took effect. "Look at that dipper, Sammy," she said. "Can you see it? Is that the big one or the little one?"

Sammy Boland's chest and abdomen filled with blood. He saw the stars, too, but they were all shooting across the sky, like some furious meteor storm. He thought to take a picture of the spectacle but hadn't brought his camera. He had one final moment of clarity before dying, and in that moment he looked over at Dixie and whispered through the blood, "You'll be dead soon, too."

Dixie didn't hear it, of course. She was lost to the beast. She lay next to Boland's stiffening corpse for two hours, then sat up and looked around. The lot was deserted and lit by the stars and a half moon. She looked at Boland. His face was caked with red sand. "I'm sorry, Sammy," she said, then went through the pockets of his jacket, taking the cash out of his wallet. She also found some coke and snorted a few lines to wake herself up. "What do we do with you?" she said, wondering if she could just leave him there. She hastily wiped off the knife on his jacket and returned it to the sheath on her leg. Then she got up and scouted the woods to the west of the parking lot. She quickly found herself in a marshy area and thought she might be able to drag the body there and let it sink in the muck. She did another line of coke and felt instantly energized. Boland was much lighter than she imagined, and she had no trouble dragging him into the marsh. She laid him out in the grasses, and the water swelled up around him. His face rose out of the water and lay motionless on the surface. Dixie shivered. Cold air rushed past her, as though a freezer door had been flung open. Boland's face was ashen and luminescent. Bubbles surfaced around him as his corpse gave up its gases. Dixie found a large rock and dropped it on Boland's face. Then she waded into the muck and stuffed smaller rocks inside his jacket and pants pockets. Eventually, he disappeared into the depths of the marsh. "Nothing else to do," Dixie said, and then walked back to the parking lot. She made sure there were no red stains anywhere in the sand. Then she went out to the beach and walked south toward Wellfleet, putting as much distance between her and Ballston as possible before she decided it was time to lie down and snort some more smack.

CHAPTER TWENTY-SIX

Fireworks and Sweatshirts

The end came quickly for Kristin Harris. After the visit to the Harris home, Mike Van Winkle went to see Don Hill at the Truro Police Department and told him that he had information about a sheath belonging to Kristin Harris, a sheath that may have held the knife used to murder Sammy Boland.

"And where is this sheath?" Don Hill said.

"I'd look in her bedroom," Van Winkle said.

"You would?"

Don Hill got a warrant, recovered the sheath, and sent it

to the lab. The results came back the next morning. Traces of blood were found, and the pathologists extracted DNA samples. The DNA belonged to Sammy Boland.

Don Hill also tracked down some of Kristin's classmates to ask if they had ever seen her wearing the sheath. "Hell, yes," one of them said. "She was suspended once for wearing it to school."

When Don Hill and the two officers pulled up to the Dorothy Bradford House, Kristin saw them and went out the bedroom window. She didn't get far.

Rachel, Martha, and Lady Agnes watched her being handcuffed and read her rights. Rachel and Lady Agnes were crying. Katie ran down from the main house. She asked Don Hill questions, but he wasn't forthcoming. She already knew about the sheath. Rob had told her about his trip to the Harris house with Van Winkle. "We had to do it, Kay," was all he could say, seeing the shock overtake her. She was silent for a time and then said, "That's awful." Rob wasn't sure whether she was referring to the news about Kristin or the fact that he had broken into the Harris's home. "They might not find anything," he said, trying to console her. "It might just be a sheath. I went along for the ride." Katie closed her eyes and said, "Enough," as Rob offered up more excuses.

Kristin said nothing as she was being arrested. She stared off into the woods, and eventually the muscles in her legs let go, and she collapsed. The officers hauled her back up and led her to the patrol car. She looked at Katie as one of the officers placed a hand on her head to keep it from banging on the door frame. She mouthed the words, "I'm sorry."

♦ ♦

Danny was out on a training run when the police came to arrest Kristin. Rob and Katie hadn't told him about the sheath. As far as Danny was concerned, the possibility that Kristin had murdered Sammy Boland was still just a private investigator's wild conjecture. "Danny doesn't need to know about our involvement," Van Winkle told Rob. "Let him think the police conducted the search as a result of their interrogation. Or an anonymous tip." But Rob didn't like keeping things from his son any more than he did his wife. He might not tell him right away, but he would tell him. He didn't want to be an accessory to anything after the fact.

Danny saw the police car drive by. He slowed and stepped off the road, even though the cruiser's lights weren't flashing. He waved. Most of the officers in the department knew him and always waved back when they passed by. In this case, however, the officer didn't wave and kept his eyes straight ahead.

The woman in the back seat didn't see the runner. Her head was between her legs. Her hands were cuffed behind her back. She was trying not to vomit.

◆ ◆

The Fourth of July party, coming just two days after the arrest, was a much more somber affair than typical Dorothy Bradford Society events. Rob thought Katie should have canceled the party altogether since he was sure the membership would be riled up and looking for someone to blame for Kristin Harris's arrest.

"Who else are they going to blame?" he said. "They never liked me to begin with." Some of the fundamentalists in the Society didn't like the idea of Dorothy Bradford being married. They rarely acknowledged Rob, and when they did, they referred to him as William.

Katie decided to keep the guest list small and let Rob invite Mike Van Winkle so he'd have someone to talk to. Van Winkle had collected his fee from the Boland estate and decided to spend some of it on an extended stay on the Cape. After the arrest, knowing that Rob had told Katie about what they'd done, he called her to emphasize that it was his idea to break into the Harris home and that Rob had only tagged along.

Though Katie was saddened by Kristin's arrest, she didn't blame Van Winkle for what he'd done. It was his job, after all, and she knew all too well what it was like to feel compelled to search for answers. As for Rob, she wasn't surprised that he had "tagged along," given his penchant for signing on to other people's adventures, but she still scolded him for taking the risk. Rob tried to deflect her criticism by explaining that he thought they should have kept quiet about the sheath but couldn't because they'd have been accessories after the fact. "Covering up only gets you in more trouble," she said. He asked for her forgiveness, but Katie said there was nothing to forgive. "I'm sad for Kristin because she was a victim, too," she said. "She was a different person then, but that doesn't mean we look the other way. I only hope her parents can afford a good lawyer."

Danny, on the other hand, became uncharacteristically distant and withdrawn. He refused to discuss anything about Kristin or the circumstances of her arrest. He dealt with the loss by running longer training sessions, sometimes twice a day. This, of course, was how Rob had preferred his son spend his time, but he still hated to see him bury his emotions.

"He won't talk about it," Rob said to Katie. "I've never seen him like this."

"He will. He needs time to process his feelings. This is all new to him."

"Dating a murderer?"

"Being in love."

"He was in love?"

Rachel, Lady Agnes, and Martha were at the party, as were

a few society members who were less likely to scowl at Rob. Helen Schantz came with a plate of bite-sized cookies and an explanation of what was in them. Steve Ridgeback wasn't invited and wouldn't have come anyway since he was still laid up with his broken back, which had prevented him, much to his chagrin, from covering the Harris arrest. Elaine Snow was there too, though she treated the party as a celebration of Dorothy Bradford's disposal of Sammy Boland's ghost. She asked Katie if she'd seen the other ghosts since the disposition; she wondered if they might be at the party. Katie shook her head and held up a finger to her lips.

"Dorothy shushed me," Elaine said to Rachel, who was flipping hamburgers on the charcoal grill.

"She doesn't want to talk about that," Rachel said.

"Why not?"

"She prefers not to be thought of as a witch."

"But she is a witch."

"And don't say anything to Danny about Kristin, okay? You can say you're sorry, but don't tell him it was for the best or anything like that."

"It was for the best. I never liked her. She always kind of creeped me out."

"You didn't know her, Elaine."

"It doesn't matter. I won't see her again."

Rob sat by himself and watched Brie pull a hamburger off a folding table alongside the grill. He intended to yell at her, but by the time he could open his mouth, she had already swallowed the thing whole.

"It's too bad the society doesn't still make its own beer," Mike Van Winkle said. "I would have liked to taste it." He had a bottle of beer in his hand and was reading the nondescript label. "Without the LSD, of course."

"Grab a chair," Rob said, glad for the company. He kept his eye on Brie, who still had her snoot at the edge of the table, now trying to lick the hamburger aroma out of the air.

"What did you end up doing with the tabs?"

"I cut them up and stuck them in a bag of coffee grounds," Rob said.

Van Winkle settled in his chair and sighed contentedly, more relaxed now that he was on vacation. "I never asked you what it felt like," he said. "Microdosing."

Rob thought for a moment, remembering the gargoyle scampering down the side of the Provincetown Monument. "I never really knew if what I was seeing was real or not," he said. "But it didn't bother me. Anyway, I didn't know I was on LSD. I just thought it was the beer."

"Well, I brought something for you that might be just as good." Van Winkle pulled a bottle out of the brown paper bag under his arm. Rob thought it was wine at first, but it turned out to be a bottle of bourbon instead—a 20-year-old Pappy Van Winkle.

"What?" Rob said. "So you're a Van Winkle after all." He ran inside to get some glasses—paper cups wouldn't do for something like this—and the two of them sat down and drank.

"Where's Danny?" Van Winkle said.

"He'll be here. I hope."

"Still not talking about it?"

"Nope."

When Danny did arrive, looking timid and a bit unsure of himself, Rachel embraced him, then shoved a plate in his hands. Rob thought he saw a smile. Danny stood by himself for a moment, scanning the faces of the guests. When his eyes settled on Rob and Van Winkle, Rob waved him over, holding the bourbon bottle aloft.

"Come sit," Rob said when Danny approached. "You need to try some of this."

Danny had a hamburger and potato salad on his plate but hadn't eaten any of it. He sat down next to his father, who gave him a glass of the bourbon.

"What is it?" Danny said.

"The best bourbon in the world," Rob said.

Danny took a sip and handed the glass back to his father. "Smooth," he said.

"You can finish it if you want."

He shook his head. "I have to work tomorrow." He poked at the hamburger, then removed the top half of the bun and started eating what was left. Lady Agnes and Martha came over and said hello, mostly to Danny. Danny asked how they were doing, and both of them told him how sad they were about Kristin.

"She's strong," Danny said, the first words Rob had heard him speak about Kristin since the arrest. "She'll pull through. You guys hang in there."

They said that they would and then filtered back into the crowd. Danny finished eating his topless hamburger, then started in on the potato salad. He routinely ate one thing on his plate at a time, something that used to drive Rob crazy since he and Katie never ate that way. Rob took another sip of whiskey and considered whether it might be a good time to tell Danny about his and Van Winkle's role in Kristin's arrest. He was curious about something else, though.

"What did you mean when you said, 'She'll pull through'?" he said.

Danny set his plate on the ground, now empty except for the top half of the hamburger bun. "Can I have another sip of that?" he said.

Rob handed him the glass. "Keep it," he said.

Danny took a sip and once again handed the glass back to

his father. "I think it's probably too good for me," he said.

"It's just bourbon," Van Winkle said.

Brie waltzed over and snapped up the hamburger bun from Danny's plate. Then she started eating the plate.

"Not the plate, Brie," Rob said, pulling it from the dog's mouth. Brie let go and sniffed the ground where the plate had been.

"She wants me to come see her," Danny said, stretching out his legs and folding his hands behind his head.

"Who?" Rob said.

"Kristin."

"What do you mean? Did she make bail?"

"No. She's still in the jail."

"She might have been denied bail," Van Winkle said. "And even if she wasn't, her parents probably don't have that kind of money, even with their house."

Their house, Rob thought, the one he and Van Winkle had invaded—the dolls and cereal bowls being offered by the Harris's as collateral for their daughter's release. "I don't understand," he said. "She called you?"

"This afternoon," Danny said.

He had thought that when Kristin was taken away, her relationship with Danny was taken as well. He wanted to tell Danny to stay away from the girl, but decided on a more tactful approach. "Is that a good idea?" he said. "Going to see her?"

"I'm not sure," he said, pointing and flexing his feet. "What do you think I should do?"

Rob had not been expecting the question. Danny was a pretty decisive person in general and trusted his instincts. Usually, Rob was the one asking for Danny's opinion. He looked at Van Winkle, hoping there might be some legal rationale for staying clear of the girl. Van Winkle cleared his throat.

"You're sure to be questioned by the prosecutor at some point," Van Winkle said. "So will your mom and the rest of the people at the Bradford House. If you see Kristin, you shouldn't talk to her about the case. That's what her attorney will tell her. Does she have an attorney?"

Danny shrugged. Rob could tell from his posture and the tone of his voice that Danny was apathetic about the prospect of visiting Kristin. "What did you tell her?" he said.

"Nothing. I didn't pick up the call. I let it go to voicemail."

"Well, if you didn't want to talk to her on the phone, why would you go see her?"

"So you think I shouldn't go?"

Rob waited a beat and then said, "No," maybe a little too bluntly. It's what he wanted to say, but it sounded cold. He looked down into his glass, or both glasses, the one he was drinking and the one he'd poured for Danny. He offered the glass back to Danny. "I'm sorry," he said.

Danny took the glass. He didn't drink from it, but he didn't give it back either. "For what?" he said.

"I know you still care about her."

Van Winkle, sensing a melodramatic turn, stood up and announced that he was going to mingle. He left the bottle.

Danny watched Van Winkle leave. Sensing his melancholy, Brie lay down on his feet. Danny scratched the dog under her ear and said, "Did Van Winkle say anything to you about what the police found in Kristin's house?"

Rob slumped in his lawn chair, the fabric creaking as it readjusted to his shifting weight. He wasn't going to lie to his son, but he could release the truth in a deliberate fashion, a little at a time, like a slow drip from an IV bag. "A sheath," he said. "With blood stains on it. Boland's blood stains." He paused and suddenly wondered if Danny already knew about the sheath and how it was discovered.

Danny rested his elbows on his knees. Brie was still lying on his feet, and she looked up to see if he was offering food. "She was in the police station for a long time," he said.

Rob nodded. "She was."

'She must have said something that made them suspicious. She was in pretty rough shape when she came out."

"She was in rough shape when she went in."

"She thought Boland's ghost was after her."

Rob swallowed some more of the whiskey. He caught Katie's eye from across the yard. She was watching him, looking sympathetic, and Rob could tell she knew what they were discussing.

"So, the thing is, and what I've been meaning to tell you," Rob said, gaining confidence. "Mike went into Kristin's house before the police did. He was the one who tipped them off."

"He found the sheath?"

Rob fished for the Van Winkle bottle, and while his eyes were diverted, he said, "No, I did."

"You did? You went with him?"

Was that a hint of wonderment Rob detected in his son's voice, like he'd just been told that his father had run a five-minute mile? Danny looked at him, his eyebrows up, his mouth open. Rob knew it couldn't be that easy.

"She was a different person when we found her on the beach," Rob said. "She said some wild things about Sammy. Mike asked her a few questions, and out of the blue, she said that she hadn't killed anyone. But that wasn't one of the questions."

"So you went on a fishing expedition."

"We knocked first. The back door was open." Rob could sense Danny's resentment starting to surface. "Look, I'm sorry for what you're going through, but aren't you better off knowing the truth about Kristin?"

"We don't know the truth. Not yet, anyway. She might have

been defending herself."

"That's for a jury to decide."

"I guess. The whole thing sucks."

"Uh huh."

"I might go see her."

◆ ◆

When the sun dipped below the horizon, everyone went down to the beach to watch the Provincetown fireworks across the bay. They were too far away to elicit any wonderment, and the muted sounds of the explosions were out of synch with the fountains of light bursting over the monument. In any event, someone else started setting off rogue fireworks over Pamet Harbor. They weren't as well choreographed as Provincetown's display, but they were much closer and louder. Brie dug a hole under Rob's beach chair and stuck her head and front paws down there, leaving her back end exposed and her tail tucked between her legs.

Rob had brought the bottle of Pappy's with him. He had thought at first that he would only drink a little and save the rest for special occasions. Van Winkle reminded him that this *was* a special occasion. "Besides, I can always get more."

Katie sat next to Rob, and they shared the bourbon and

watched the fireworks. The evening was cool, and she had put on a sweatshirt with the hood pulled over her head. This reminded Rob of the balled-up sweatshirts he'd found in Kristin's closet. He wondered what would become of those sweatshirts. Would Mrs. Harris fold them up and return them to the closet, keeping them for whenever her daughter returned home? She would be much older then, a different person facing a different world. Could she even return to Truro knowing that every time she went out in public, people would stare and murmur about her being the heroin addict who killed Sammy Boland?

"Things okay between you and Danny?" Katie said.

"Yeah, I think so. He doesn't like how it happened, but he knows it needed to happen."

A whistling shell exploded over the harbor, producing a large, multi-colored floral pattern that crackled and fell. Then came a barrage of sparks, reaching for the star-filled sky. Most of the sparks fell back into the harbor, but one of them arced over the beach and dropped into the bay, though the fire had gone out of it before it hit the water.

"I saw you got rid of the tabs," Katie said. Just knowing they were in the cellar had given her a sense of security—a crutch for her sanity. She felt no discomfort from their absence now.

"You weren't looking for them, were you?"

"I was checking to make sure they were gone."

"No more LSD."

"And no more breaking into people's houses." She leaned her head against Rob's shoulder and noticed that Rachel and Elaine were sitting with Helen Schantz. The ash end of Helen's joint glowed in the darkness. "Is Helen sharing that with them?"

Rob leaned forward. He had a much harder time seeing in the dark than Katie did. It didn't matter. "Helen doesn't pass joints. She'll give you one of your own sooner than she'll let someone else put their mouth on hers."

"I can't imagine Elaine getting stoned."

"She drank Maggie's beer, didn't she?"

"Actually, no. She'd carry around the mug with beer in it, but she'd never drink any. She's always been more of a Puritan than a Pilgrim."

"I can ask Helen for a joint, if you want. She always seems to have a box of them with her."

"A box?"

"You know, like a cigarette box."

"The bourbon is fine, Rob. We don't need anything else."

After the fireworks were over, Brie emerged from under Rob's chair and scampered towards the water, her nose to the ground. She disappeared quickly, her chocolate coat blending into the darkness.

"What's she up to?" Rob said. "Should I go after her?"

"She's fine. She's down by the water."

"You can see her?"

Katie saw everything. Her eyes picked up the tiniest bits of light, some peeking out of the dried seaweed, others spilling out of the feeble waves tripping on the shore. The tide was going out, and a wet blanket of rocks and marine life was left behind—most likely the thing that had drawn Brie down there. Danny jogged after the dog, sharing his father's concern for her intentions. Lady Agnes and Martha followed close behind, Martha trying to match Danny's stride, much as Fat Agnes had, while Lady Agnes, still finding her footing in a male-dominated world, maintained a more leisurely pace. They passed by Mike Van Winkle, who was talking to three of the Bradford members, and then Elaine and Rachel, who were sitting with Helen Schantz and her joint. They might have also passed by two men and three children dancing along the water, not far from where Brie was exploring. Whether they were there or not wasn't important, Katie thought, only that they were at peace.

◆ ◆

The next morning, Katie and Rachel loaded bags of party trash into the back of the SUV, bound for the transfer station. Rob brought a bag down from the main house to add to the load.

The bag contained the coffee-soaked LSD tabs. He brought the box, too, the one with Boland's ashes inside.

"We're not throwing that away," Katie said.

"We need to get rid of it, though."

"Can't Mike take care of it?"

"He doesn't want them either. Nobody does, remember? That's how we got them in the first place."

"Well, we're not throwing Boland's ashes in the trash, Rob."

"I didn't throw them in the trash."

"Leave them," Katie said. "I'll take care of it."

"What if we go into the woods and bury them next to that Ridley guy?"

♦ ♦

The following morning, Rob woke up to the sound of a mourning dove singing in a nearby tree. It was, perhaps, the most peaceful sound he knew on the Cape. He reached over for Katie but found Brie instead, her tail thumping against the mattress. She was smiling and panting, and ready for peeing and eating. Rob was not panting, but he was ready for peeing and eating too.

Katie was on the water, pulling the oars of her rowboat in league with the outgoing tide. She was heading away from the beach, into deeper water, past a family of diver birds hunting for breakfast. When she was far enough out, she stopped and pulled in the oars. The water was still. The wind was gentle. She looked down at the water and thought back to the time when a man with a waterproof camera swam out to the boat and took her picture. The water was rougher then, and Katie was more vulnerable.

"Here we are again, Sammy," she said. She had brought along a pair of scissors and used them now to cut open the top of the plastic bag. She never really knew Sammy Boland. The only time she'd met him was when he took the picture of her, as though she was one of the shore birds he liked to photograph. What could she say about him?

"I'm not sure you deserved to die the way you did," she said. "My guess is that this is where you would want to be…" Interred? Committed? Laid to rest? The words didn't come as easily as when she was dispatching his ghost. But maybe no other words were needed. "Where you would want to be," she said with finality. A flock of black-backed gulls flew over the boat as Katie poured Sammy Boland's ashes into the water. A silvery plume hung over the surface, then settled and dissipated. Katie rinsed the bag in the water, making sure all of Boland was washed out, then folded up the bag and stuffed it in her pocket. When she could no longer make out the shroud of ashes on the water, she took the oars and rowed back to shore.

Acknowledgments

Thanks to Nancy and Chris Plaut and their backwoods tracking skills without which I never would have found Thomas Ridley. To Camden Winkelstein for making time to read a draft of the book while distilling some incredible single malt. To Margaret Manos for her exceptional editing skills. To Maisie for lying on my feet. And most of all to Ellen for supporting and loving me and for picking off the ticks.

About the Author

Paul Ehrenreich grew up in Belmont, Massachusetts. He lives in Bethesda, Maryland and Truro, Massachusetts with his wife and their dog. *Waking Dorothy Bradford* is his second novel.